HIS FORBIDDEN BRIDE

50 LOVING STATES, WEST VIRGINIA

THEODORA TAYLOR

~

Free Book Alert!!!

Want a FREE Theodora Taylor Book?

Join Theodora's mailing list to get a free welcome book along with newsletter-
only exclusive stories, author giveaways, and special sales.

Go to theodorataylor.com for more information

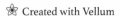 Created with Vellum

INTRODUCTION

A Sexy Southern John Doe
A Wary West Coast Doctor
(with a secret!)
A Secret Identity Romance
With Gasp-Out-Loud Twists

I know everything about him...
Except who he really is.

When a sexy amnesia patient shows up at my hospital, he flips my heart switch on like no one ever has before.

Now I'm happier than I've ever been, and seriously considering a future with someone who doesn't have a past. But when the shocking truth about his real identity finally comes out....

Find out what happens next in this scorching hot Very Bad Fairgoods romance. Perfect for readers who like their alpha heroes sexy, mysterious, and rough as hell.

Keep in Touch with TT
Get a free book when you
sign up for TT's mailing list!
Friend TT
Like TT
Connect with TT on Goodreads
Follow TT on BookBub
Follow TT on Instagram

THE VERY BAD FAIRGOODS
His for Keeps
His Forbidden Bride
His to Own

PROLOGUE

*E*verything in the world stops as I sail through the air. No gulls. No breeze.

The Pacific Ocean goes eerily silent beneath me, as if catching its breath before the drop. Then...SPLASH! My body hits the water with violent force; the anger of the man who threw me in it, powering my descent into its dark, gray depths.

Next comes the sensation of sinking, faster than I normally would without the added weight tied around my legs. Water overwhelms me, rushing into my ears, my screaming mouth, my eyes...I want to close them against the sting of the salt, but I can't.

In those first few moments I lose control of my body. Instead of closing my eyes and gracefully accepting my fate, I thrash and struggle with my eyes open, seizure wide. I fight to get my head back above water, even though I know it's useless. I can't swim with both my hands and legs tied together, not to mention the heavy weight dragging me down. But I also can't think clearly enough to comprehend how little chance I have of ever leaving this ocean alive.

So I thrash and scream, making a bad situation that much worse thanks to my body's instinctive response to drowning. In three minutes or so, brain damage will set in and I'll sink less fitfully towards my coming death. I might even relax a little, the hypoxia placing me in a trance-like state.

I was born and raised in California, but I never tried anything stronger than weed. And I stopped doing that after I got into med school. I wonder for a moment what it will feel like to be blissed out on the heaviest of narcotics: my fast-approaching death. Wonder and thrash. Wonder and scream useless bubbles.

Unfortunately, as far as untimely deaths go, drowning is just about one of the most brutal ways to die. Yes, eventually I'll pass out from hypoxia, but before that happens will come the worst three to four minutes of my short life.

And as I die, all I can do is fight the inevitable and bear witness to my twenty-five years of life as they flash before my eyes.

Beginning with my first memories of my childhood in Compton. My mother's church. Backyard barbecues in January. Dipping churros in vanilla ice cream at the Long Beach street fair. My insane middle school years...Chanel dying in her hospital bed... medical school...and finally my residency in West Virginia.

This is where the slide show of my short life ends all too soon after meeting the same blue-eyed man who, less than a minute ago, looked at me with such hatred... right before he ordered me thrown overboard.

1

———

$\mathcal{I}$ don't think I've ever seen anything more heartbreaking and inspiring than eight of our cancer patients singing, "To Dream the Impossible Dream."

"Yassss!" I tell them after I hit the last chord hard with my guitar pick. "You are going to make our department *so* much money from this YouTube video! Thank you!"

Most of the kids giggle, delighted—in spite of the grim circumstances—at the prospect of the internet fame that will come with being featured in one of my *Chemo Kids Sing Broadway* videos.

But Ronnie Greenwell, the only black kid in the group of kids receiving chemo, raises her free hand. "I have a suggestion, Nitra..."

"No," I answer, not caring that she's in a wheelchair, or the only kid here who's the same color as me. Mostly because she insists on calling me by my old nickname instead of Dr. Anitra like all the other chemo kids.

"But you ain't even heard the question!" she protests, keeping her overly thin arm in the air.

"I don't have to. The answer's always no," I inform her, before returning my attention to lining up my fingers on my guitar. "Okay, everybody, let's do this song one more time, then we're done for the day."

"I'm just saying," Ronnie continues as if I didn't already shut her down. "I think we should switch it up! That girl who sang 'Fight Song' on the internet—"

"Already did it," I remind her. "I'm telling you, Ronnie, Broadway is where it's at. People loved when we did 'Defying Gravity' last month."

Ronnie sucks on her teeth, a suspicious adult in a child's sickly body. "You just saying that because you like that old-ass music. I'm telling you we'd get so many more hits if we..."

Moving her oxygen cable out of the way, Ronnie unexpectedly springs from her seat and launches into a wheezy rendition of "Watch Me Whip."

Apparently her enthusiasm is catching, because the rest of the makeshift choir joins in with her. Most of the kids jerk side to side in their seats, but a few of the stronger ones jump up and start throwing each arm out before waving their left arms over their heads.

I try to put on my best stern look. I mean, I am a doctor after all. Even if my *Chemo Kids Sing Broadway* video series is a tad unorthodox as far as hospital fundraising activities go. But those clips bring in money for our shoestring Pediatric Oncology department, which at this point is barely more than a pipedream with one senior Pediatric resident (me), one attending—who is also responsible for any pediatric cases that come into any other part of the hospital, including the ER—and a couple of oncology nurses to oversee chemo for a kids-only hour in the lounge on Monday and Thursday mornings.

Right now, I can feel the glares of those nurses, who are quite understandably afraid of things like ports getting dislodged while the children dance. And then there are the even fiercer glares of parents, who don't want to deal with tired and cranky kids later on, along with the after-effects of chemo.

But c'mon! "Watch Me Whip" is such a great song. Steadfastly ignoring all the glares from the adults in the room, I get to my feet and dance with the kids. I improvise a few chords on my guitar and drum on its body with my hand to give Ronnie an underlying beat. And for a moment, we forget our roles, and the various cancers the kids are battling, and the maybe/maybe-not life saving chemo as we dance and sing like maniacs.

That is until Ronnie sinks back into her orange and gray recliner, overcome by a fit of coughing, and the exertion it took to not only get out of her chair, but also to sing and dance to the popular Silento song.

I set aside my guitar and rush over to her along with one of the oncology nurses.

"See, this is why we have to do old Broadway songs," I tell her as I check her vitals, and the nurse re-adjusts her oxygen.

Ronnie wheezes and laughs. Like a girl with a rare form of leukemia that so far hasn't responded to any of the treatments her mother's threadbare insurance covers. Like a girl who knows she most likely won't be around much longer, and has to take all the opportunities she can to whip and nae nae, even if it requires everything she has.

Our rehearsals are always a free-floating thing lasting anywhere from fifteen minutes to an hour, depending on the kids' energy levels. Today we made it to forty minutes, and despite Ronnie's episode, I feel good about our progress as I head toward the lounge door with my guitar.

But just as I'm leaving, a voice calls out, "Y'all should've done 'Free Bird!'"

I stop short and look up to find a tall man with the bluest eyes I've ever seen standing to the side of the lounge doorway.

The hospital chemo lounge is on the first floor, and we often get lookie-loos, especially if they're fellow chemo patients—adults scheduled for therapy right after the kids-only hour is up. But lookie-loos don't usually make song requests.

And this guy definitely doesn't look like he's here for chemo. For one thing, he's wearing a full set of UWV/Mercy Hospital sweats, which we certainly wouldn't give to outpatients here for chemo treatment.

Also, he looks...broken.

He's on Lofstrand crutches—the ones with the arm cuffs attached to provide more stability and comfort than the old school axillary crutches—and wearing a full boot on his right leg. So a fracture of some sort, and the doctors want him to keep his weight off of it. Another trauma—not cancer—sign: his longish, honey blond waves have been shaved off on one side, but not in a cool boy band way. An ugly scar snakes around the shaved side of his scalp, parting his new hair growth in crooked two.

Brain surgery, I decide. One of our surgeons clearly opened him up for any number of reasons, but my guess is it was to remove a blood clot or relieve pressure after a blow to the head.

He also has what I've come to refer to as "a hospital Keanu." The kind of unchecked stubble verging on messy beard most male patients get when they've been here too long without a shave. Though unlike the actor I've named this particular look after, this patient's beard is growing in just a shade darker than the golden hair on his head.

But the main reason I'm guessing Free Bird has been in a terrible accident is standing right next to him. Ken, our biggest physical therapist, is leaning on the wall right next to the patient, hands folded at his waist.

As a general rule, Ken doesn't bring anyone but his most depressed patients down here. It's his way of reminding them, "Hey, look, all this PT isn't so bad. At least you're not a child with cancer."

But Free Bird doesn't look as fragile as most of the accident victims Ken brings in to watch us perform during the kids-only chemo. For one thing, he's still in fantastic shape. Tall and wiry, with lean muscles roping both of the forearms encased by the Lofstrand arm cuffs.

For another, he doesn't look at all depressed. In fact, he's staring down at me with his head tilted to the side and a very amused glint in his eyes.

I cut my eyes to Ken and ask, "'Free Bird'? Is this guy serious?"

"Completely," the patient answers before Ken can. "Hey, it's a good song!"

I glare at him and slightly raise the hand holding my guitar. "Hear these words, sir. No classic rock will ever, *ever* be played on this guitar."

A lazy grin spreads across Free Bird's boyishly handsome face. And though he's a patient, and most likely severely injured, I can't help but notice that grin makes him look way more cock-sure than a man wearing a boot and standing on Lofstrand crutches in hospital issue clothing should.

"Well, that is by far the most inhospitable thing I've heard come out of a nurse's mouth," he says, his blue eyes twinkling despite his words.

"I'm a doctor," I answer, pointing to the DR. ANITRA DUNHILL badge on my white coat. My response is a pretty automatic reaction these days. People have been mistaking me for a nurse since I first set foot in this hospital as a medical student. UWV/Mercy isn't exactly a Shonda Rhimes show. I'm the only black female doctor on staff, and only about five percent of the rest of the staff are people of color. So it's a correction I now deliver without much thought.

But the blond man leaning into his Lofstrands continues to lazily grin down at me. "Still mighty inhospitable if you ask me," he says, his light blue eyes lazy and self-assured underneath his hooded gaze.

He's not intimidated by my credentials, I realize, not one iota. And again, even though I'm a pediatric resident, I find myself way more curious about this adult male patient than I should be.

Even so, I must inform him, "Look here, it's one thing to come down here to watch the kids sing. It's quite another to start making such inappropriate suggestions."

"You think 'Free Bird' is inappropriate?" he says, tone disbelieving, even as his eyes keep me trapped in his lazy blue gaze.

"Sir, these children have been through enough already," I whisper dramatically. "Why would I want to expose them to southern mullet rock?"

He squints, his lazy grin finally wavering, if only a little. "Mullet?"

It takes me a moment to realize he's not sure what a mullet is.

"It's a haircut," I quickly explain. "Short on the sides and top, long in the back. It's pretty much the worst thing that's ever happened to hair."

And just like that, the lazy grin is back at full tilt. "Is that right?"

"That is exactly right," I assure him with the conviction of someone who's played guitar since the age of six, but has never once let a mullet rock anthem cross her strings. "And if I were you, I'd reconsider any Lynyrd Skynyrd songs on your playlist."

He makes a considering sound, somewhere between a 'hmphh' and a grunt. Then he says, "Maybe you can visit me on the eighth floor, Doc. Let me know what I should be listening to instead of the songs I've been hearing on the radio. I liked that one you just did with the kids."

On one hand, I'm alarmed by his blatant invitation for me to pay him a visit on the rehab floor. And I'm deeply aware of Ken's curious stare as I continue to talk to his rehab case.

On the other hand, the decent human being in me can't stand the thought of someone being confined to listen to the limited number of stations on the clock radios in the patient rooms.

I don't want to call UWV/Mercy backwoods exactly, but I did come here on a scholarship program intended to bring talent from all over the country to work in one of West Virginia's most rural counties. Located at the very top handle of the state, we're designated to serve the populace who live within the mid-sized city triangle of Wheeling, West Virginia; Pittsburgh, Pennsylvania; and Cleveland, Ohio. Which pretty much means we're in a radio no man's land.

"How about if you give me your email address and I'll send you a Spotify list?" I answer Mr. Tall, Blond, and Broken.

Once again his smile sags. "Only problem with that is I don't have an email address that I know of...or a phone number."

I raise my eyebrows, wondering if he's visiting us from higher up in the nearby Appalachians, where it's not unusual to come across technology-free households. But those folks usually stare openly at me since so few have ever met a real doctor, much less a black lady one.

This guy is staring at me, too. But not like that. The way he studies me with his lazy blues, I have to fight the urge to do a million things that would reveal how self-conscious his attention makes me.

No, I think, as I get a little lost in his gaze. This fellow might have a scraggly beard and an accent that cuts the "g" out of words that end with "ing." But he is definitely not from around here. I've been in West Virginia for seven years, and I've never, ever encountered someone who speaks like he does: deep and melodious. And I've definitely never come across someone who looks at me the way he does.

Like I'm not a complete freak who has no business being here.

"So you don't have email or a phone number," I say consideringly. "How about a name? I can drop a CD mix or something off with Ken. And he can give it to you at your next session."

But Free Bird shakes his head again and the smile drops all the way off his face. "I don't have one of those either."

"What? A CD player?" I ask, not really that surprised. I'm not even sure my laptop has a CD player. And come to think of it, I don't really know how I'd go about burning a mix tape onto a CD with the technology I have on hand...

But then he says, "Afraid I don't exactly have a name at the moment either."

2

*D*octors can be the worst gossips, often using patient files as stories in the break room. But unfortunately UWV/Mercy's only neuro attending, Dr. Raj Pawar, isn't one of those doctors. Stiff and easily irritated, he's known around the hospital as a brilliant cutter with zero bedside manner. And I've consulted with him on enough brain tumor cases to know he's completely uninterested in contributing to patient gossip. In fact, I doubt he'd say hello to me in the hallway, much less give me information on a patient who falls nowhere near my jurisdiction. Which is as it should be.

I've been working my ass off to prove that me getting into this combined med school/residency program wasn't a joke on the University of West Virginia's part. After seven years in the program, I've finally managed to garner the respect of the hospital staff and my peers. So I have no business wondering about the sexy head trauma patient, much less seeking out more information about him.

I know that.

I *know* that.

Yet somehow, I find myself rushing into work two hours early on Wednesday to attend Ken's bi-weekly staff yoga class.

What are you doing? What are you doing?! I shriek at myself through all the up and down dogs I could be doing just as easily at home.

You are an idiot and you need to stop this right now, I tell myself even as I pretend to stay in savasana way longer than I need to, just to allow all the other students to file out before I finally sit up.

"You were really feeling it today, huh?" Ken says with a sympathetic smile as I roll up my mat. "Hard week?"

I nod, because that much is true. Today's the day I have to sit in on a consult with Ronnie and her mother, regarding a new palliative care plan. Which is the nicest way of saying Ronnie's leukemia has progressed to the point that chemo is no longer working, and it's time to start thinking more about her quality of life than trying to sustain it.

Yet another reason I shouldn't be here. But I smile back at Ken and answer, "I don't know why I don't come every Monday and Wednesday." Because I know how much my fellow yogi appreciates any feedback on his sparsely attended classes.

"I keep telling Dushner we should make it an official hospital requirement," Ken complains as we leave the activity room, "But he said no, because then he'd have to attend."

Dushner is the hospital administrator. A number of staff members refer to him as Douche-ner behind his back, which should give you an idea of his charming personality.

"Speaking of Dushner," I say as a way to transition into what I'm really after. "How does he feel about this amnesia case of yours?"

And that's how—a few minutes later—I find myself in Ken's closet-turned-office, leafing through his scant file on the John Doe. I was right about the head injury. After losing a fight with a drunk driver going the wrong way on a back country road, John Doe was knocked off his motorcycle. Now that would have been bad enough. But apparently he hadn't bothered to secure the strap on his helmet, so hello traumatic brain injury.

Fortunately, the drunk driver had been enough of a good Samaritan to call 9-1-1. But the hospital in Wheeling was full and diverting cases that night, so John Doe ended up at our humble patchwork of departments, and just in time, too. He'd had a few hematomas on his brain, which explained the surgery.

And the retrograde amnesia.

But that's where John's case stops making sense.

He'd had no ID on him, and when the police attempted to trace the bike's plates, it led to an abandoned coal mining town in the middle of the state.

"So he's like in a motorcycle gang or something?"

Ken considers my question with a tilt of his head. "Well, that's what the police wondered. And they've been by a few times to question him. But I've seen my share of bikers around here, and he doesn't have the usual tells. No tats, and according to Glenna, his rehabilitation nurse, he was a whole lot prettier when he came in here. Clean-shaven and, well, you've seen those eyes— kind of dreamy, right?"

That they were, though I doubted Ken's "roommate," a nerdy Lockheed Martin aerospace engineer, would appreciate hearing Ken describe his current patient like that. After all, he had absolutely no reason other than love to share a house with Ken, or live in Wheeling, which was halfway between the towns where they both worked. But I kept that observation to myself.

Like me, Ken prefers to keep his private life very private, which was one of the reasons we got along so well.

Ken strokes his chin thoughtfully. "A few of our organ donors have found abandoned motorcycles and fixed them up as projects. Maybe this was a home project gone really, really wrong?"

Organ donors were what most of the staff called motorcycle riders, but in this instance, the term made my heart clench. Looking at John Doe's PT case file, which I knew wouldn't be nearly as grisly as his patient file, I couldn't help but think how close this guy had come to dying.

If the drunk driver hadn't gotten out of his car, or hadn't had enough presence of mind left to call 9-1-1. If Dr. Pawar hadn't been on hand that night to take John Doe straight into surgery. Well, those dreamy blue eyes would most likely be six feet under right now.

But I force myself to stop thinking about that as I observe, "Maybe, but he doesn't exactly sound like he's from around here."

Ken greets my observation with a huge smile. "Oh my! Look at Ms. Nitra, finally learning to tell us West Virginia folk apart from everybody else."

I roll my eyes. My continued inability to distinguish between Pittsburgh, Ohio, and West Virginia accents after living my entire life in California, was a constant source of amusement around the hospital. Right along with the past I was still trying to live down.

"Yeah, yeah, yeah," I say to Ken. "But seriously, he's from the South, right? I mean deeper South than here?"

Ken picks an invisible piece of lint off his t-shirt. "Well...I may or may not have put $10 down on Arkansas in the pool me and some of the nurses got going."

"Seriously? The poor guy's in here with amnesia and you've created a betting pool on him? Real professional," I say, shaking my head as I continue to flip through his file. The file I'm technically not supposed to have access to. Talk about the pot calling the kettle black.

Before Ken can comment, I quickly circle back to the main reason I'm in his makeshift office. "How about fingerprints?"

"The police ran them but nothing came back."

I thought of the family I'd left behind in California and asked, "And no one's stepped forward to claim him? No family or maybe a girlfriend? Kind of finding it hard to believe this guy doesn't have a girlfriend out there somewhere."

"Me, too," Ken answered. "It's a real struggle to keep it professional, especially when he gets all sweaty while he's lifting..." Ken gets a faraway look in his eyes, which I once again doubt his nerdy boyfriend would appreciate. "But so far no one's contacted us. We've called in social services, and they're still working on it. But for now, the guy's a complete mystery, and he's here on nobody's dime since we don't have a social security number on file. So we're already getting pressure from Douche-ner to release him sooner rather than later."

"What?! But he has a traumatic brain injury!" I protest on the John Doe's behalf, and because I've had more than one run in with Douche-ner over his bad habit of focusing on the bottom line rather than on patient needs. I can't even count the number of times he's tried to push me to release the kids with shitty insurance sooner than anyone with a conscience would recommend.

"Actually, John Doe is recovering faster than you'd expect—at least from the physical stuff..."

Ken looks over both shoulders as if we're on some sort of reality show, before leaning in to impart, "But the traumatic brain injury is turning into something else. I'm not exactly a doctor here, but at the last team meeting about John Doe's case, Dr. Pawar and the psych team went on for a while with the social worker. Pawar's saying his head scans are checking out, but then psych's concerned because he's still got amnesia, yet he knows a lot of general stuff, and check this out..."

Ken takes the file and flips through a number of typed documents to a page of handwritten notes from the last meeting of John Doe's team.

"One of the third-year med students decided to run a Neuropsych Evaluation on him for one of her class projects. Look at these scores."

My eyes widen when I see the numbers, some in the three digits. Except for his complete lack of historical and cultural memory, there's nothing on this report to indicate these scores belong to someone with a TBI, rather than, say, someone looking to get into medical school. Or become a rocket scientist.

"So he's close to being a genius even after the TBI?" I murmur. "That's a seriously unexpected result."

"Right?" Ken agrees, nodding. "The team is having a real hard time figuring it out, so now they're calling it Focal Autobiographical Amnesia. I haven't had time to look it up on Wikipedia, but best I can tell, they're saying there might be something more than a hit to the head going on here."

It takes me a moment of mulling over Ken's words and comparing them to what I learned during my fourth year psych rotation to figure out, "They think he's not remembering on purpose?"

"Or that something traumatic happened *before* his accident. He's got a few older fractures according to the x-rays. The kind of ribs and arm stuff you see when Mom doesn't bring her kid in after Dad's had too many and decides to downsize his beating victims..."

Hearing this, my heart pangs for the John Doe. "All the more reason not to release him. I mean, where is he going to go if he doesn't have anybody to help with his recovery?"

Ken nods. "That's the only thing keeping him in here considering he has no insurance to bill. Truth is, we don't have anywhere to send him."

I shake my head in disgust. "So we're just going to kick him out? When?"

Ken thinks about it and shrugs. "Now that he's pretty much healed...I'd say he's here one or two more weeks, tops. Since his injury is no longer looking like a neuro case, Pawar doesn't care too much, and psych's psych—already too overwhelmed to take on any new cases—especially the ones without insurance. Social's looking for a men's shelter who can take him in."

"Okay...okay..." I say, getting it. John Doe has no name so every minute he spends here is costing our already over-stretched regional hospital money.

"But there's got to be some way to help him," I say to Ken. "I mean, we just can't kick him out..."

I gaze down at the linoleum, trying to figure out a solution to this dilemma, only to find Ken smiling when I look back up at him.

"What?" I ask him.

"I haven't seen one of your kind in quite a while. A doctor who cares more about the patient than the patient's condition. Pawar and psych have spent more time tangling over his official diagnosis than worrying that this guy is going to end up in a homeless shelter in a couple of weeks if no one steps up to claim him. But you really care about his well-being, and not just because he's cute, but because underneath that medical degree, you're a decent person."

A small smile whispers across my lips. "Well, I did get into UWV-Med off the wait list."

Ken lifts his eyebrows. "Then maybe they should let more people in off the wait list."

I'm not sure how to respond. I know a few of my fellow program mates, many of whom are now fellow residents, think I was let into the program for not the best reasons. One guy outright asked if this was a joke when I walked into Brain and Behavior on the first day of winter semester and it was announced I'd be taking the place of a med student who'd dropped out.

It doesn't surprise me that same guy is now the senior neuro res here. Anyone who works with doctors knows neurologists have a reputation for not being the most sensitive or socially clued in people. Truth is, he might have been right about the program's intentions when it came to my acceptance. But it doesn't matter why I was accepted. I chose to come here, and that's the only thing that matters to me at the end of the day. Still, I can't help but feel flattered by Ken's approval. It's nice to know at least one person at UWV/Mercy thinks I deserve to be here.

Still, the John Doe upstairs is totally effed. We both know it.

"The best any of us could do for that guy right now is hope he remembers who he is," Ken tells me before I leave his office. "Because at this point, that's the only thing's going to keep him out of a homeless shelter."

3

_S_o yeah, John Doe has a sad story. A really sad story. But you know, shit happens. Believe me, I know that after Chanel's death. Just this week alone, my attending resident had to pass on two heartbreaking preliminary diagnoses to families who could barely afford to take time off of work to talk with us, much less find the money to pay for what could amount to months or years of treatments.

I've had patients a lot worse off than John Doe. Ronnie Greenwell's mother broke down crying, even as her daughter sat there and nodded, when the peds attending and palliative care counselor told them we'd run out of treatment options later that day. And this is only a small hospital in West Virginia. I can imagine the number of difficult conversations I'd be sitting in on at a larger facility.

In fact, I won't have to imagine it for much longer. Because two weeks ago, I received news that I'd defied the odds of my upbringing, and been matched with a Pediatric Hematology-Oncology Fellowship at The Children's Hospital of Seattle.

Which means in two months, I'll be out of this backwater regional hospital, and moving on to a new life in the Emerald City after a short visit with my family in California.

So I really shouldn't be losing much thought or sleep over an amnesia patient. I mean, yeah...it sucks. As close as my family is, just the thought of John being here in this hospital, all alone, without anyone to help or advocate for him, makes me feel pretty bad. But he's still alive. He's not dead or dying, which is way more than some of my past and current patients can say.

I should be doing any number of things during my lunch hour, including searching for apartments in Seattle. Or getting my monthly call home to my family out of the way. Sandy's always complaining about me putting it off until the last second.

So yeah, John Doe's case is none of my business. *He* is none of my business. And this morning, when he came down with Ken to watch the kids again, he settled for standing near the doorway and leaving before rehearsal was done. No more "Free Bird" requests, and absolutely no reason for me to get too wrapped up in a patient completely outside my field of residency.

But instead of calling my dad, instead of looking at cute apartments in a cute city that I can't wait to call home after I'm done with my three-year residency in June, I find myself outside a certain door on the eighth floor.

Don't knock. It's not too late to turn back. Go! Go now! I tell myself, even as I raise a hand and knock on the partially closed door.

"I'm doing something, but come on in if you have to," a gruff voice on the other side calls out. He sounds more authoritative than I would have guessed. Like he's used to being in charge.

Maybe he was a cop, I muse as I slide inside.

The room, not surprisingly, is the smallest one in this wing, with a view of the parking lot rather than the Appalachian foothills. There's barely enough room for a single visitor recliner, and I highly doubt the thing could actually recline with so few inches between it and the bed. The curtains are open, but the room is still dim, thanks to the relentless West Virginia gray, which still hasn't quite given over to spring sunshine. Even worse, his radio is turned on and a classic rock song is playing. I don't know the band, nor can I see them, but I swear I can hear their mullets loud and clear.

After a moment of adjustment, my eyes find John on the bed, his half a head of blond locks hanging down as he finishes writing in what looks like one of the cheap, brown kraft-paper journals the psych counselors are always issuing to our older kids. So they have someplace to put their feelings while they go through treatment.

That would explain his rather reluctant response to my knock.

"Sorry, I'm interrupting. I'll come back later," I say and start to back the very short distance toward the door.

But when he hears my voice, he looks up. And his entire face softens when he sees me standing there.

"Hey, Doc! You finally came to visit me," he says, like my arrival in his room was long overdue. He closes the journal and reaches over to his cabinet night stand to switch off the radio.

Even with the snaked head scar, he is so freaking handsome. So much so that it's kind of hard to look at him without feeling flustered. To distract myself, I reach into my bag and pull out a recyclable sandwich container.

"I...um, brought you a sandwich."

I hand it to him, and he appears delighted, but then baffled when he gets a look at the sandwich itself.

"Where's the meat?" he asks, like that's a way bigger mystery than his identity.

"There isn't any," I answer with a small laugh. "It's hummus, cucumbers, and tomatoes with a drizzle of pomegranate molasses on top."

My explanation doesn't put a dent in his perplexed look. "They make sandwiches without meat?"

"Sure they do," I answer. But then have to admit. "Well, maybe not in West Virginia. Which is why I had to make these for us at home. The hospital cafeteria doesn't have anything but peanut butter and jelly, and I don't love all that sodium…"

He continues to look at the sandwich like it's a completely alien substance from another planet. Then he asks, "You some kind of…" his whole face furrows in concentration, but he can only come up with, "…person who doesn't eat meat?"

"A vegetarian? Yes, I am. I'm a vegan, in fact, which means I don't eat meat or any other animal by-product."

"Vegan…" he repeats. "That's new."

I keep my expression neutral, but inside I'm studying him with sharp interest, trying to figure out if he doesn't know the word because of his amnesia, or because of where he's from. Or maybe I'm just bitter because I went from a huge city with a vegan option on every menu, to a small town where the word vegan elicits snickers or suspicion. Or both.

Nevertheless, he takes a bite of his sandwich. Chews, then nods. "Not bad," he tells me.

"Thanks," I answer.

He takes another bite, chewing even more slowly before he swallows. "The way this sandwich tastes is new."

"New?"

"I got this way of experiencing things. Some things feel old, like going to the bathroom and pancakes and 'Free Bird'. I don't remember ever doing or hearing any of it, but my body remembers it. And some things feel...the only way to describe it is 'new.' This sandwich feels new. And your hair..."

"My hair?" I pat the simple twist out I keep my medium-length hair in now that I no longer have any weave specialists in my "Favorites" contact list—or the time to sit through multi-hour hair appointments.

"Yeah, I ain't never seen nothing like it. It's pretty. Real pretty."

An awkward beat, in which I put considerable effort into not pushing a few of those curls behind my ear, like the nervous high school girl I never ever was. At least not until now.

I clear my throat. "You're probably wondering why I decided to stop by..."

With that seriously forced change of subject, I gingerly sit in the guest chair with my sandwich. "So what kind of exercises are you doing to help regain your memory?"

He frowns over his sandwich. "This a friendly visit or a doctor visit?"

"Kind of both." I take a bite of my sandwich. More interested in covering up how his direct stare make my insides feel all squishy than alleviating my hunger.

"Truth is, Doc, I'm over medical visits. I wasn't looking for one from you," he tells me. Despite his rejection of my intentions, his voice has a warm tone to it, amused and husky with a hint of melody that puts me in mind of a country singer.

Maybe he's a country singer? I think. And his music comment makes me remember the other thing I brought for him.

I reach into my huge "V"irkin bag and bring out the smart-phone I wiped and reactivated last night. "Does this feel old or new?"

He glances at the phone. "Old. Definitely old. My rehab nurse let me mess around on hers a few times."

"Awesome," I say, trying to sound more like a friend than a doctor as I bring out a pair of white earbuds and hand them over to him along with the smart phone. "Then you know how to access the iTunes app. I've already put a few songs on there for you..."

"You did?" he asks, his whole face lighting up.

"I did," I answer, finding his happiness too infectious not to smile back. "And if you want more music, all you have to do is download it. I pre-loaded a gift card on there."

He touches the device reverently, as if it's a bar of gold and not just the first device I randomly grabbed out of the box of old special phones under my bed.

"Thank you," he says. He hits me with that blue gaze again, tugging on me with that killer smile of his. "I can't wait to listen to all the music you like."

My heart skips a beat, and I have to remind myself about all sorts of things. All sorts of things a medical professional shouldn't have to remind herself about during the last weeks of her residency.

You're only here to help, I hiss inwardly as out loud I use my authoritative doctor voice to tell him, "If you hear anything on there that jogs your memory, make sure to let your team know."

"Okay," he agrees easily enough. But then he nods his head toward the seat I abandoned in order to hand him his gift. "You going to finish the rest of that sandwich or what?"

"Actually, no I'm not," I answer. "I'm not that hungry." *Because there's a whole swarm of butterflies where my empty stomach used to be.* "And I have a lot of paperwork to do downstairs. Plus, I have some calls to make..."

I shift from foot to foot and say, "So, yeah...I should get going. I'll, um...see you at rehearsal next Monday. Maybe. I mean, if you come down. Not that you have to—I mean, you're on Lofstrands so I don't expect anything of you. But if you do come down to see the kids, I'll see you then. That's all I meant."

You know, I actually used to be cool. Really, really cool. Before I came to West Virginia. Before this exact moment. I'd even gotten rid of my glasses a few months before coming out here, thanks to Lasik. But I fight the urge to tell him that, and instead gather my things, dumping the rest of the uneaten sandwich into the nearest trash bin as I pull my "V"irkin bag over one arm.

But when I turn to say one last goodbye, I find him watching me with the stillness of a predator. One who lets a beat or two pass before saying, "Cane."

"Excuse me?"

"The boot's coming off and they're giving me a cane tomorrow. No more special crutches."

"That's great news!" I say, clutching and unclutching the rolled handles of my mock-croc handbag. "So I guess I'll see you Monday."

"Yeah, I guess you will," he answers.

I start to head out, so happy my skin is on the deeper side of brown, because if I was the same color as the John Doe, I'd be visibly red all over.

However, his voice stops me just as I'm about to open the door. "But, Doc, just so you know..."

He pauses, obviously waiting for me to turn back around and face him like a civilized human. So I do, even though "level-headed doctor" only feels like a part I'm playing at this point.

And his gaze once again completely and utterly catches mine as he says, "Cute as they are, it ain't the kids I'm coming down there to see."

4

---

*S*o yeah, he said that. He said that to *me*. The pediatric resident with a bad habit of being reduced to an incoherent babbling fool whenever he pins me with those beautiful blue eyes of his.

I spend a lot of time...a serious lot of time...trying to pretend he didn't say it. And by Monday, I think I've finally got a hold of myself.

I ignore his presence at my rehearsal that morning. Treating him like all the other people in the hospital who come to watch the ever-changing makeshift choir of children sing.

And yes, I go to see him again on my lunch hour that day, because I doubled up all of my lunches when I was making my weekly meals Sunday night. But that's only because the hospital food is truly and wretchedly awful. And also because bringing him lunch gives me an excuse to casually work with him on his memory exercises.

In any case, I decide not to think too much about how he looks happy, but not at all surprised, when I knock on his door.

"What are you watching?" I ask when I see the black family full-out yelling at each other on his television.

"Dunno, fell asleep watching the news and this was on when I woke up. I think it's called *Rapper's Wives* or something like that. All I know is they fight a lot and say a lot of bitchy stuff behind each other's backs."

"*Rap Star Wives*," I correct with a wry smile. I grab the remote connected to his bed and switch it off. "And trust me, there are way better shows for somebody with a TBI to watch. That show will rot your brain faster than fast."

"Shows like *Devil Riders*?" he asks. "Cuz a message keeps popping up at the bottom of the screen to say it'll be on next."

"Shows like *Jeopardy*," I answer.

"Do they yell at each other and get into a lot of fights on that show, too?"

I laugh and hand him a bento box with today's lunch.

While eating the tofu and quinoa dish, we talk a little more. He tells me the few things he knows about himself. It's a disturbingly short list that includes "likes Lynyrd Skynyrd" and "knows how to ride a motorcycle" and he was "maybe not surprised" about "them neuro evaluation scores."

He tells me "the head doctor" advised him to watch TV—see what sparked his memory. But he doesn't like it much—that feeling is old. So far he prefers radio. He switched over to the country station this weekend and found he really liked that kind of music. Especially a singer called Colin Fairgood.

"No surprise there," I tell him. "That guy seriously crosses over. I mean, he's even done a song with C-Mello—that guy you were watching on *Rap Star Wives.*"

"Is he on that playlist you gave me?" John asks.

"No," I answer. "But I do actually like his stuff. Especially his second album. Here, let me download it for you…"

He hands me his phone and after I download C-Mello's career making album onto it, I scroll to look at John Doe's "recently played" list. Almost everything on the playlist I gave him is there. "Is any of this old?"

He shakes his head. "No, it's all pretty new."

Maybe not so surprising. There's some Top 40 mixed in, but mostly it's a wide range of pop, rap, and indie songs I've come to love throughout the years. Some of them well-known, some of them not so much.

But I have to ask, "Even Eminem is new to you?"

"That's the 'Lose Yourself' guy, right?"

I nod without adding that nine out of ten of the white boys I knew back in California loved his tracks when I was a kid.

He frowns hard before answering again. "No, you're right, he ain't completely new. But it's kind of hard to explain. I feel like maybe I heard him and didn't like him, but now I do. Does that make sense?"

"It does," I answer, before taking a thoughtful bite of my tofu and quinoa—a dish John had declared "really new" after his first fork full.

But he must like it, because he ends up finishing every bite. *Or maybe he just likes you*, a small, secretly thrilled voice inside my head suggests.

Seriously, I have got to start dating as soon as I hit Seattle this summer. In California there'd been plenty of guys, but out here in West Virginia—not so much. Partly because of my patent inability to trust any man's attraction to me, and partly because it's West Virginia and real hospital life is not a Shonda Rhimes show. Whatever the case, I've obviously been in a drought state for way too long if I'm getting all sorts of secret thrills from the prospect of being liked by someone with a TBI.

"Okay, let's work through a few of these cognitive exercises I brought with me before I have to go back downstairs," I say, bringing my iPad out of my bag.

His lazy gaze flickers from warm and engaged to disappointed. "So you ain't really here just to visit this time either?"

"No, I..." I stop and take the time to put together my thoughts before answering. "Look, I know this has got to be unbelievably hard for you. The accident, the head trauma, and then the amnesia on top of it. I'm not trying to be your doctor. I hope you understand as a third-year peds resident, I'm technically not even qualified to oversee your care. But if you had someone with you—like a family member—your team would suggest they do all sorts of things to keep your mind sharp and help you get to a better place."

I hold up the iPad. "Starting with these cognitive exercises to help you with your memory. So I guess you could say that's what I'm trying to do here. Until you leave the hospital, I'll be your family. At least until your real family gets here."

He shifts on the bed, messes with his now boot-free leg. "My family..." he repeats.

And I get that I'm toeing a dangerous line. That I'm about a few seconds away from stepping all the way over it, but I find myself saying, "Yeah, your family. That's what I'm trying to be for you. At least until you remember yours."

His eyes raise to meet mine, and for once they don't look lazy with amusement. "Alright," he says. "If that's the case, then I'll do whatever you want me to, Doc."

Good Lord, why did he have to put it like that? My body heats as images of him doing things—very bad things that a patient should definitely not be doing with a doctor—flash through my mind. And suddenly the mood in the room doesn't feel very familial at all.

Cheeks flushed, I clear my throat and force myself back to the cognitive treatment plan. "Okay then, let's start with a few math problems..."

Our first informal cognitive rehab session goes pretty well. And by the end of it, I know the IQ test they gave him wasn't a one-off. He has a solid grasp of math, and a much bigger vocabulary than I would have (perhaps unfairly) assumed due to his deep southern accent combined with his generous usage of the word "ain't." He also has great recall, and even managed to draw a map of the eighth floor in his journal for me.

By the time we're through, I can see why he set off a few red flags with psych. Other than his persistent amnesia, he scored way above average on all the informal cognitive tests I gave him. Which means it's most likely not his traumatic brain injury keeping him from remembering things, but something else entirely.

I leave the iPad with him and tell him to keep doing the brain exercises on it. "Especially the word associations," I say as I gather up my "V"irkin. "See what comes up."

"Hey, Doc," he says as I'm about to leave. Then he once more waits until I turn all the way back around to finish his thought. "Thank you," he tells me, his tone and eyes sincere.

"Sure," I answer, feigning like I'm not completely locked onto his gaze with a casual smile and a shrug. "Really, it's nothing. It's a nice change of pace for me after dealing with kids all day."

But he doesn't release me from his gaze. "Yeah, well...it ain't nothing to me," he says. "I want you to know that. Understand it. You're a real nice woman, and that's new to me. So thank you."

"You don't know a lot of nice women?" I ask, stepping forward. Because I'm curious, I tell myself. Not because he's drawing me toward him with a term I don't think 99% of the straight guys I've met would *ever* use to label me. *He thinks I'm nice.*

"No," he answers bluntly. The word falls into the space between us like a confession. "I don't think I do. I mean, everyone on the floor has been real kind. But I don't mean nice like hospital staff. I mean nice like you. I'm pretty sure I don't know anybody else like you. You're new. "

I'm new. And he thinks I'm nice.

I rush out of there with the aortic nerve in my stomach full on pounding. Not sure if I should come back to visit a man who makes me feel like I'm waiting for the results of my Pediatrics Board Certifications to download on my computer screen.

Yet here I am again on Tuesday, walking in with two bowls of three-bean avocado salad, and already afraid of what will happen when I leave at the end of the hour.

But this time when I hand him his reusable container, he says, "Tell me how you got into this whole doctoring business. I've been trying to figure it out on this iPad, but I don't see how you could be a Senior Pediatrics Resident."

My heart freezes. Apparently he's been using the iPad I gave him for more than the brain teaser apps. Did he Google my name? Does he know...?

But then he says, "From what I can figure, you ain't anywhere near thirty, and it says here you have to do four years of college, four years of med school, then a three year residency on top of that. So you *should* be thirty, right? But if I had to guess, I'd guess you're no more than twenty-five."

"You're exactly right. I'll be twenty-six in July," I say with a relieved laugh. Then I peek at him to ask, "And how old do you think you might be?"

He shakes his head. "I dunno. Can't tell from looking at myself in the mirror on account of me being all broken up. Also, I get to feeling older than I look sometimes. Does that make sense?"

I nod, thinking of the months after Chanel's death. How silly every other person my age seemed at my arts college. At least until I met my best friend, Sola, a Guatemalan Dream Act student who actually had real shit on her plate.

"Yes, that makes sense," I tell him. "And as for my age, I came out here from California to attend the University of West Virginia on a special combined Bachelor/Med degree scholarship program for Regional Hospitals. It's unusual because not only did I graduate in four years with a combined degree, I was required to do my residency at this particular hospital as part of a state grant I received to complete my education. So here I am at the age of twenty-five. Does that make sense?"

He half-winces, before admitting, "Kind of. Go back to the part where you came all the way across the country to work here... "

We end up talking for the whole hour as opposed to doing the word association tree I'd planned. He wants to know what I had to do in med school. Why I chose peds—especially pediatric oncology—because "ain't that a little sad for you, Doc?"

Then he listens intently as I explain how many doctors, including myself, feel called to their particular specialties. I don't tell him about Chanel. I still can't talk about her, even after all these years.

But I do tell him how I put in a semester at a performing arts college called ValArts, before I was accepted into UWV's seven-year combined medical degree and residency program. How I'd planned to go into musical theater for a while, until I dropped everything in order to take this once in a lifetime opportunity to get my education half-paid for and be of help in a field close to my heart. How, yes, it can be more than a little sad, but also more than a little triumphant, when things work out for my patients.

His questions are so direct and precise, I have to ask, "Does any of this seem familiar to you? Like maybe it's a profession you're familiar with?"

"No," he answers. Then he thinks about it and says it again, "No."

He still doesn't sound all that sure about his answer, so I ask, "Does becoming a medical professional sound like something you'd want to do? Like maybe something you considered doing before?"

He thinks about it again. "More like something I've gotta do. I don't know how else to explain it."

His gaze goes to the window and he glares at the parking lot below. "This is hard," he mutters.

I can only imagine, and I struggle to come up with some encouraging words. Kid patients are easy in their own way. I'm allowed to both ignore their tears and bribe them with the promise of ice cream.

But I put in my rotations in med school before breaking off into my specialty. So I already know: adults are much harder. I feel frustrated with my uncharacteristic lack of a good comeback.

I'm actually really good with words, I want to tell him in that moment. *But there's something about you. You take my words away.*

But obviously, I can't say that. I'm a doctor who shouldn't be here. And he's a patient struggling with a TBI and what might very well be some type of psychosis.

"You mind getting out of here?" he says, his eyes still on the parking lot. "I'm kind of done visiting right now."

I remind myself of all the things I read while researching his type of amnesia. About how amnesia patients, for understandable reasons, often get agitated. How they can easily become depressed. That TBI does, in fact, stand for Traumatic Brain Injury.

I've been trying, but still can't imagine, what it must be like to wake up one day with no memory whatsoever of who you are. I still can't wrap my head around what it would be like to have to piece my life back together with the small amount of information John has. Or having to sort everything I encounter into "old," "new," and "confusing."

God, this John Doe makes my heart ache. And in the moment right after he asks me to leave, I want to do all sorts of unprofessional things. Like go over to the bed and hug him, crooning everything will be all right, even though I can't possibly know that.

But I remember lying to Chanel in the exact same way, and I clamp my lips shut, refusing to do it again. Also, my lunch hour is already five minutes past over…

"Sure," I say. "See you…later."

I don't say tomorrow, because I'm not brave enough to in the moment.

He doesn't answer. Just continues to stare out of the window.

So I'm forced to leave him stewing in his frustration. Which makes me feel the opposite of my good intentions. Like I've made things worse for him, instead of better. Tuesday started off great, and ended up sort of depressing. As I gather my things and go, I seriously don't know if I'll be back on Wednesday.

But I am. We're both awkward and polite until I hold up the pad Thai I made for us on Sunday and say, "So I know you're good to go on soy. I figured we'd see if you're allergic to peanuts today."

"This is new," he tells me after the first bite, "but I like it."

Then he eats the rest with such gusto, I know he was only being polite when he finished the tofu and quinoa on Monday.

Wednesday is a good day. Comfortable like the food. I ask him if he's scared about having to go to a shelter soon.

He thinks about it and answers, "No."

"Why not?" I ask, because just the thought of it terrifies me.

He shrugs. "I don't think I get scared easily."

"What do you mean?"

Another shrug. "People keep asking me if I'm scared because of all this brain stuff, but I'm just, I dunno, really fucking annoyed. I think maybe I'm like Ken."

"Ken..." I repeat, wondering if I've totally misread which team John plays for.

But then he says, "You know. Real calm."

"So you're saying you're a very calm person?" I ask, muddling my way through his meaning. "And you don't often get upset."

"No, I do get upset," he answers, almost automatically. "But if you're mad, you don't need to let everybody know about it. It's something you handle on your own. Inside yourself."

I blink, since that perspective is the exact opposite of the one I grew up with. "Is that a memory or a conviction?"

"Conviction." Again his answer is automatic, with no tripping over my relatively big word. Then he pins me with that blue stare of his and repeats, "Yeah, it's definitely a conviction."

And I'm struck by a very real feeling that we're not actually talking about Ken or John's convictions or anything else, but are instead focusing on the thick sexual tension crackling like a heat fence between us.

This whole professional medical distance thing isn't going well at all, I think on Wednesday night, as I make pasta linguine and a couple of other dishes to get us through the week.

Thursday we get back to the cognitive exercises. And it's all very professional and on plan, right until he hands me back the phone I gave him towards the end of my lunch hour.

"No, no," I tell him. "That's yours to keep."

"Thanks," he answers. "I appreciate it, I do, Doc. But I want you to put some more music on it. I'm thinking about what I'll need when I'm living at the men's shelter."

"You want me to pick music for you to listen to at the men's shelter? I mean, shouldn't you do that?"

"I don't like the stuff I've been picking out as much as the stuff you've been picking out. When you're not here, I listen to the music you chose and it feels like everything's going to be all right."

Okay, I'm trying. I'm really trying, but how the hell am I supposed to keep my heart out of this when he says things like that?

"You know that's a song, too..." I tell him. Then I sing him a few lines of the Bob Marley classic.

And he says, "You've got a good voice, Doc. I've been noticing that downstairs. That performing arts school probably missed you after you left."

I still have no idea who this John Doe was before he landed at UWV/Mercy, but I swear he must have taken a course in how to make girls blush. "I'll put that Bob Marley song on there for you, too," I all but croak before rushing out of his room, away from all that dangerous sexual tension.

On Thursday night, I take a forty-five minute detour to pick up a pair of Beats headphones at the Wal-Mart in Ohio. *Because they're good headphones*, I tell myself, even as my aortic nerve hums with a vision of John surrounded by the Bob Marley track as he rests in his shelter bed.

And on Friday, the song is still playing on a slow and lazy loop in my head as I get off the elevator onto the eighth floor and round the corner of the hallway that leads to his room—

Only to walk into complete chaos.

"Get away from me! Get the hell away from me!"

In the middle of the group, I can see John. He's swinging the cane he was only recently given at a resident—a fellow third year I easily recognize as the one who asked if me getting into UWV's program was a joke on my first day of med school.

"Somebody get psych down here!" Dr. Pawar yells toward the nurse's station, while a flock of young medical students stand around with their mouths agape.

There are two kinds of doctors in this world. Those who stand there surprised when something outside their expected range of duties happens, and those who spring into action. Dr. Pawar is a spring into action kind of doctor for sure.

And I guess I am too, because I charge through the crowd of white coats to get to John, yelling at him, "It's okay! It's okay!" even though I have no idea what's going on.

My poor John Doe is a mess. His blond hair, which looked strange before with it being half-shaved and all, is even wilder now. And his blue eyes are no longer lazy, but completely incensed. Like he's not just going to hit the med student with his hospital issue cane, but plans to use it to beat him to death.

Yet John weakens when he sees me standing in front of him with both my hands raised.

"Doc, no..." he says, with a pained shake of his head. "You're not here. I don't want you here. I don't want you to see me like this."

His voice cracks on the last sentence, and that breaks my heart even as I keep repeating, "It's okay, John. It's okay."

"That's not my name. Fucking hell!"

He raises a free hand to his forehead, and takes a step toward me. All the med students gathered behind me jump like a volcano just belched. Like they know this patient is going to explode.

Somehow I manage to stay exactly where I am. For him. I read about this. I read about all of this. It's completely normal for amnesia patients to get agitated. But John is tall and burning bright. I can feel the fear of everyone in the hallway, and I'm pretty sure security has already been called to handle the situation.

But my expression stays neutral and completely focused on the man looming in front of me. Not the crazy John Doe, but the man I've gotten to know and like over the past week. *There's nothing but him*, that insane voice in my head says before I can quell it with logical thought.

"I know that's not your name," I assure him in a gentle voice. "We're going to figure out your real name, I promise. But until then, I need you to calm down. You're like Ken, remember?"

I remind him of the conversation we had yesterday, even though I'm thinking now, just like I was thinking then, that he is absolutely, positively, *nothing* like Ken.

However John nods in agreement. Like the crazy words coming out of my mouth make total sense. Then he stands there, as if awaiting my next command.

Maybe he was a soldier, I think as I slowly lower my hands, my body relaxing from the pretense that I could have actually done something to stop him if he decided to charge me or someone else in the room.

"What happened?" I ask the senior neuro resident with a killing look, because I already know this is more his fault than John's.

"I don't know," he answers, defensively. "We came into his room for rounds, and he jumped out of the bed and started yelling at me. Chased me into the hallway."

My eyes go to John, silently asking him to explain this to me.

"He smells like something," John answer, his voice just as confused as I must look. "Something I don't like. No, that's not the word. Want. Something I don't want."

The med students and Pawar all turn to the resident, and I swear you can hear them sniffing the air around him like a pack of bloodhounds in white coats.

"He's been smoking!" a student with a ponytail yells out. "It must have triggered John Doe."

Then, probably remembering how John just said he didn't like being called by that name, Ponytail blushes. "I mean the patient. Maybe he's associating something bad with the smell of cigarettes? I don't blame him. I hate cigarettes." She darts a mildly disgusted look at the resident.

My eyes go to John. "Cigarettes. Old or new?" I ask him.

"Old!" He shakes his head, as if he's trying to get away from something inside of it. "Old! Fuck...old!"

He's getting agitated again. He drops the cane, and slams the balls of his palms into his forehead, doing his brain violence it doesn't need.

"It's okay," I tell him. But it's too late for okays.

He yells "Fuck!" again, and unleashes all of his anger and frustration in one burst. Smashing a fist into the nearby wall like it's done something to him. I can hear the crack of bone against the solid wall, and I gasp out, "John!"

"Don't call me that! Don't fucking call me that!" he yells back, as if I, and not the wall, have physically hurt him.

The elevator dings in the distance and I can hear the thunder of boot clad feet. "No, let me..." I start to say.

But my words are lost in the clamor of bodies shoving past me. Two large orderlies and a security guard. All yelling words at John Doe.

I watch them haul John back into his room and strap him to his bed. Then the needle comes out, and that's it for this episode of Amnesia Horror Story.

"No..." I say. Maybe out loud, maybe only in my head as I watch him collapse into a sleep I know he doesn't want.

5

So John's episode buys him another few days at the hospital. But unfortunately he's moved to another floor where he's put on psychiatric hold. Which means I can't see him because the visiting hours are for family members and spouses only.

I spend the missed lunch hours loading more brain games onto the iPad and downloading more songs onto the iPhone I'd been planning to return to him on that fateful afternoon. C-Mello, some Colin Fairgood tracks, and the very few country songs I know and like. Songs I think might be "old" to him.

Of course, I'm not there to see him when he's released back to the eighth floor the following week. But I swear I just about run to the stairs like a Whitney Houston song as soon as the clock strikes twelve on the first day he's back.

I'm a panting and sweating mess by the time I get to his new room. But I hesitate in front of his door, not sure of what I'll find inside. He was so crazed the last time I saw him, so out of control...the way he'd yelled at me... Who knew if he even wants to see me now or if it will only upset him further?

With a deep breath, I enter the room, braced to be thrown right back out.

Which is why I'm surprised to find him scribbling in his journal with one hand, while the other, now encased in a white cast, rests on his folded leg.

So he did fracture it, I think with a heavy heart just as he looks up.

He stills when he sees me, his blue eyes so intense I find it hard to look at him.

Hard to squeak out, "Hi! I just, um..." I search my mind for a valid reason as to why I'm here, and finally settle for the plain truth. "I was worried about you. And I wanted to make sure you were alright."

A beat passes during which he only stares at me. Then he says, "You came back. I didn't know if you would. I didn't think you'd want anything else to do with me after what happened."

I step forward, almost unconsciously. "No! You had an episode. It was completely understandable. And it wasn't your fault. The only reason I stayed away is because they would only let family visit where you were, and I didn't want to upset you. I almost didn't come here today, because I was afraid it might—"

I stop speaking when he reaches out, his good hand curling around the back of my head, pulling me down toward him with surprising strength. Before I can even register what's happening, his lips have claimed mine.

Wait. What? Who? How? When?

My mind blanks out as his lips draw on mine, drinking me, savoring me. Making it so I can do nothing but stand there as I risk my entire medical career on one very inappropriate moment.

"No!" I whisper, finally finding the strength to protest.

I push away and put as much space between us as possible in the tiny room. "That's not why I came here. I only wanted to make sure you were okay."

Even though I'm several feet away from him, his blue stare is just as relentless as if he's still kissing me, still holding me.

"Yeah, I'm okay," he answers, his voice hoarse with emotion. "Now. You okay?"

His reply has so many shades of wrong hidden within it, I'm afraid to answer.

But eventually I manage to lie, "Yes, I'm fine. Totally fine."

He studies me, blue eyes sharp as an x-ray machine. "I scared you. With the episode and the kiss. I'm sorry about that, Doc."

"No, you didn't," I start to lie again.

But he cuts me off, "Let's not lie to each other, Doc. I don't want lies between us."

"I'm just..."

Finding it really hard to keep myself emotionally disconnected from you.

I settle for, "I'm glad you're okay. I was worried about you."

He tenses, as if my concern hurts him somehow. Then he taps a finger against the journal, "Don't worry about me, Doc," he says. "I don't want you worrying about me."

But how can I not?

I quietly leave the room, and try not to look back.

John doesn't come down to see the kids, and I don't bring him any more lunches.

Three days after his return to the eighth floor, I get a call from Ken. "Social worker found a shelter over near Washington, PA to take him," he tells me. "They're discharging him on Saturday."

Not my business. Not remotely, ethically, or medically any of my business.

But on Saturday, it's me, and not the usual taxi, who pulls up to the curb in front of UWV/Mercy to pick John up as Ken rolls him out of the hospital in a wheelchair.

Yes, me. Clutching the wheel; wondering what the hell I'm doing, and why I've taken on this particular task when I'm supposed to be at home editing the next *Chemo Kids Sing Broadway* video. I watch as John stands up and shakes hands with Ken.

Ken rushes to pull open the back door of my Prius C, but John shakes his head and opens the passenger door.

In one smooth movement, he pushes his cane through the space between our seats before settling into the two-toned seat beside me, with the blue-and-white plastic bag the hospital gives discharge patients for belongings on his lap. The bag is huge, but it doesn't look like there's much inside. Just the imprint of one solitary rectangle I'm pretty sure is his journal.

"Hi," he says to me, after waving good-bye to Ken.

"Hi," I answer, still not quite sure why I'm doing this. "You ready to go?"

A beat, two, three, during which it feels like he's speaking volumes even though only a single word is uttered. "Sure."

"That's new," he says when I push the black button toward the right of the steering wheel to start the car. Then "Are we waiting for something?" when I don't put the car in drive.

"Seatbelt," I answer, nodding toward his untouched strap.

A small frown of disgust mars his face as he pulls the belt across his body. "I don't think I like seatbelts," he says, after he's clicked it into place. "Feels like I'm trapped in a goddamn cage."

"You were riding around on a motorcycle without a secure helmet and you don't like seatbelts," I say as I pull away from the curb. "So what you're trying to tell me is you're either a very dumb bitch or suicidal."

He goes tense and very, very silent in the passenger seat.

And I regret my words almost as soon as I say them.

"I'm sorry," I tell him. "That was unnecessary. I can be catty sometimes."

"You got nothing to be sorry about, Doc," he answers.

Yet I am sorry. For what I said. For the fact that we aren't any closer to finding out who he really is. Also because I don't love the idea of him having another episode like the one in the hospital in a place where there's no trained medical personnel to sedate him.

"So this men's shelter I'm driving you to is run by a church," I tell him, regurgitating what Ken told me on the phone in lieu of stewing in my anxious thoughts of what might happen to him going forward.

It feels like I'm reassuring both him and me when I say, "I looked them up on the internet and they seem like really good people. Really good people. The community is lucky to have them. Ken and I made sure the hospital social worker called ahead to update them on your case. They'll try to help you with some job outreach, but it's going to be tough going because you don't currently have a birth certificate or a social security number. They'll have to figure out how to get you paid..."

I trail off, scaring myself with that line of thought. Of thinking about how John will fare until his memories finally come back.

"Anyway, here's your phone back," I say, reaching into my purse with my free hand and passing it to him. "Please don't hesitate to use it if you need anything. Anything at all. And of course, I'll try to visit whenever I can."

Until then, I might as well have been babbling to myself, because he doesn't say one word until I offer to visit him.

"No. No, Doc, I don't want you visiting me there," he answers with a firm shake of his head.

"Why not?" I ask. "Seriously, it wouldn't be a problem for me to stop in after work. It'd be like having an old fashioned home visit from the doctor. I could check in on you, make sure your healing process is coming along as it should..." *Help you get home when you finally remember who the hell you actually are*, I add to myself silently.

I don't particularly like romance novels, but for whatever reason, I feel desperately invested in John finding his happy ending.

But he doesn't seem at all concerned with the many practical reasons why a visit from me, a medical professional, might be a good thing.

"After work—that would be at night? You want to come visit me at an all-men's shelter at night?" He asks these questions like I'm certifiable.

"Well, not exactly at night, per se," I answer. "I get off at six, so it would be more like early evening...before sunset."

But he just shakes his head, his face stony and unyielding. "No. I don't want you visiting me there, Doc."

"Okay..." I answer, not really knowing how else to respond. After a moment of thought, I come up with, "Then maybe we can have lunch sometime. I bet there's a restaurant we can meet up at."

"Yeah," he agrees, a little of the stone slipping off his face. "Let's meet somewhere. That'd be better. I could see you on the weekend, maybe."

"Yes," I agree with more enthusiasm for the idea than I'm actually feeling. A coffee shop meet-up just doesn't feel like a good enough substitute. But I tell myself it's better than nothing as I follow my navigation app southeast to a small neighborhood just outside Washington, Pennsylvania.

Really, he's lucky. According to the hospital social worker, a lot of these places have waiting lists a mile long—especially for men. John was lucky there was a place to take him within the tri-state area. And Washington is a super cute city. Lots of old tan brick buildings, a quaint little downtown, and it's less than a thirty minute bus ride from Pittsburgh.

I might be able to convince John to let me visit him at night after all, I think as I drive through Washington's classic American downtown.

But the neighborhood we eventually end up in isn't the sort with cute little corner cafes, or even a Starbucks. In fact, the only buildings not abandoned on the seedy street we pull onto is a methadone clinic and a halfway house—which I know after a few years in my rural medicine program often takes the place of rehab centers in smaller cities. There's also a bar, I note, scanning further down the street. Wonderful.

We pull up to the Union Baptist Men's Shelter. It's a squat, red brick building with one solitary steel security door. The door's been painted over several times with various shades of blue, probably to cover up gang tags, and it looks very, very heavy. I'm sure there are people inside, but the door remains firmly shut when we come to a stop at the curb alongside the building. I very much doubt anyone will be coming out to meet us.

But if John is freaking out anywhere near the level I am, it doesn't show. His face stays neutral and he even throws me a lazy smile as he unbuckles his seatbelt and says, "Well, thanks, for everything, Doc—"

He cuts off, slamming backwards into the passenger seat when the car suddenly accelerates forward. Speeding, not just merely rolling, away from the shelter.

"Oh my gosh, I'm sorry!" I say, glancing at his cast-covered arm, then at his leg, which is better, but definitely doesn't need to be subjected to the sudden movement as I drive like a maniac *away* from the men's shelter where I was supposed to drop John off.

Oh my gosh! Oh my gosh! Oh my gosh! I scream in my mind. Out loud I yell, "What am I doing? What am I doing?!?!" as I continue to drive from the shelter with my hands tight on the wheel.

But I don't stop. And John doesn't say a word as I round a corner, my tires making a screeching sound straight out of *The Fast and the Furious.* Fact is, I'm asking my Prius to step way outside its comfort zone as it speeds away from the men's shelter faster than an ambulance.

I can't believe what I'm doing. Can't reconcile it. But when we finally come to a stop sign at the side of a two-lane road between nowhere and nowhere, I check my Waze app to discover I'm over three miles from my intended destination.

I rest my head against the cool steering wheel. Breathing hard. Still not believing what I've done.

I can feel poor John watching me in that quiet way of his as I squeak, "What am I doing? What am I doing? What am I doing?" over and over again.

Which is why I can only laugh when he finally clears his throat and asks, "So Doc, what *are* you doing?"

I shake my head, still resting on the steering wheel. Weary, though my day off has technically only just begun.

"I have no idea."

6

But I guess I must have some clue. Because the next address I insert into Waze is my own. Yes, the place where I live. Even though I'm a doctor, with a medical degree, at the end of a three-year residency, driving around a former hospital patient who, up until a short while ago, I was supposed to drop off at a shelter.

"This is just for a little while," I explain to John as we walk through the door of my one-bedroom apartment. "I'm going to talk with your social worker on Monday. I bet there are lots of housing programs for people with disabilities. Places where you can live until your memory comes back. She probably didn't look into it because you didn't have anyone to advocate for you, but I'll call her. And I bet it only takes a week or two, tops, until we're able to find you somewhere better than that shelter to live."

John doesn't answer, and I'm once again hit with the feeling that I'm providing more reassurance to myself than him—and not doing a particularly great job of it.

No matter how many words I throw at this situation, I don't feel any better about my unorthodox solution to John's current problem. John, for his part, seems more interested in checking out my little second-floor apartment than in listening to anything I have to say about him moving out of it soon. He walks around the living room, taking in everything, before coming to a stop in front of my beige couch. His self-tour doesn't take long. There's just not that much to see, thanks to the space's total absence of pictures or anything else that would indicate someone actually lives there.

Luckily, the apartment had come fully furnished. Otherwise, John would be sleeping on the floor tonight. I haven't added a stick of furniture or ambience to the place since I moved in, and it looks exactly like how I intended it to be when I came to the small college town of North Independence seven years ago. One step up from a hotel rental until I fulfilled my program obligations and could move.

Even so, I cringe at the beige couch. It's perfect for me when I'm nestling in for a weekend of editing *Chemo Kids Sing* clips on my laptop, with the TV running old musicals in the background. But it's only six feet long. His feet will probably hang over the sides.

Which is how I find myself offering, "Hey, why don't you take the bed?" as I cross the room to stand in front of him. "I practically live on the couch anyway."

He tilts his head to look down at me. "You brought me here, Doc. To your home. And you think I'm going to take your bed and let you sleep on the couch?"

"Well, the couch is probably not big enough to accommodate you, and I don't want you sleeping on the floor—especially with your recent injuries."

He holds up his right hand and shakes his head. "Doc, stop. Just stop," he says, like I'm confusing him more than the amnesia. "You brought me here. To your home."

"Yes," I answer. "And I want you to be comfortable here."

He considers my words, then says, "The only place I'm going to be comfortable is in your bed."

"Yes, exactly!" I answer, relieved that he finally gets what I'm saying. "So please don't feel bad about taking it—"

But then he steps closer to me and says, "That don't mean I'm going to let you sleep on the couch, Doc."

It's the word *"let"* that sets off the first alarm bells. I find myself swallowing hard, my brain scrambling to deny, deny, deny what my instincts are telling me he's really trying to say.

"Okay," I say, taking a step backwards. "I think there's been a misunderstanding."

"Maybe on your part." He takes another step forward, and this time, he only leaves enough space between us for his cane. "You understand I ain't a dog, Doc? That you can't just bring me home and foster me."

"Actually, I've never had a dog," I babble.

"And you still don't got one," he informs me, his face somber. "If a dog's what you want, take me back to that men's shelter and go to the pound."

"No," I answer, my brain completely fried by what I've done, and what is happening now because of it. By his sudden nearness, the way he looms over me in the small space between the couch and the coffee table. But somehow I manage to say, "I don't want a dog. First of all, it's against the terms of my lease. Second, I don't really have the time or the lifestyle to keep up with one. Third—"

He kisses me before I can finish with my list.

Not like a dog.

Not like a patient.

But like a man.

A man who knows exactly what he wants.

And is the world supposed to spin when someone kisses you like that? Maybe I need to schedule an MRI. Because I've brought a guy I barely know home with me. And when he kisses me, everything tilts and twists, whipping us around and around each other like we're on a carousel.

But I've been in relationships before, and unlike his, my memory is still fully intact. I know this is not what a kiss is supposed to feel like. I know someone's lips claiming yours shouldn't suddenly unhinge you and make you feel like you're going to fly away.

However, that's exactly how I feel when John kisses me.

And I grab on to him, if only to make the spinning stop. Wrapping my arms around his neck to get my bearings.

But clinging to him only makes the spinning worse. And when John's arms wrap around me as he deepens the kiss, the world spins even faster.

I can't think like this. Can't breathe. All I can do is kiss him back, waiting for it to stop.

And then it does. Not because the kiss ends, but because we collapse on the couch. His cane crashes against my uber-bland, seven-year coffee table. Then his heavy body is on top of mine. Rolling and kissing, rolling and kissing. So much muscle memory as he shoves down his hospital-issue sweatpants.

I can't believe this is happening. But then again, I can. It all feels so inevitable. His lips claiming my mouth...me kissing him back. His hands pulling down everything beneath my waist...me watching as my joggers and underwear go flying over the coffee table. His long body settling on top of mine...

My thoughts cut off when he suddenly pushes into me. Penetrating me deep with one claiming thrust. Not like a first-time lover, but like someone who was always meant to be there.

And the way he looks at me in this moment, like every dream of his has finally come true...

"I knew you'd be ready for me," he tells me. "Knew you wanted this just as bad as me."

With a lazy smile, his hips lift and he pushes in again, his dick dragging against my clit as he does so. He sinks into me even deeper this time, and I moan as my core tightens around his cock, swallowing it whole.

The grip of my sex pulls a matching groan out of him. "Oh God, you fit me, Doc. Can't believe how good it feels here inside you."

I chuff out a laugh and answer with the truth, "Me either."

Then his lean body starts moving between my legs, hard and powerful despite the accident. At first his strokes are slow. As if he's relearning his broken body, learning me.

But he proves to be a quick study, because soon the lazy smile is back on his face. He watches me, eyes hooded with lazy intention as he takes me with deep, penetrating strokes.

I watch him. So curious about him and the one-of-a-kind feelings he's arousing in me. But not for long. A crude orgasm erupts inside me, and all too soon I'm crying out, my sex tugging on his as a wave of unadulterated pleasure courses through my body.

My only solace for coming so quickly is that he is not unaffected.

"Doc..." he groans, kissing me again. His thrusts take on a certain sharpness, becoming way more intense before he explodes inside me with another pained groan.

"Ah fuck, Doc," he says, lowering his head again. His forehead presses into mine as he kisses me. Then he asks, "Is it...is sex always like that for you?"

For a moment, I can't talk. But eventually I find the words to confess, "No, it's never like that. At least it's never been like that until now."

He considers my words. "I don't think it's ever been like that for me either."

"And, um..." This part makes things even more awkward. "We're supposed to use a condom. Condom—is that new or old for you?"

"Old. Real old," he answers like it's a very familiar concept. But he doesn't seem cocky about it, just matter-of-fact.

"Yeah, well, we should have used one. I have an IUD, so we're okay on that front—"

I cut off when I see his confused look and explain, "You know, birth control?"

"Yeah," he says with a nod. "That's old, too. But not this IED."

"IUD," I correct. "It's kind of like permanent birth control that they surgically put inside you, so no kids, but, um...we don't exactly know..."

Unfortunately, I have to be blunt because, hello, amnesia victim! "We don't know if you have any sexual diseases."

"I don't," he answers. "They told me I didn't at the hospital."

"Okay, but still, I'm a doctor and I should've known better. I have no business having unprotected sex." I wince. "Especially with a patient."

He doesn't know me. Not really. But he must sense how close I am to unraveling into a panicked spiral, because he calmly answers, "Doc, I'm not your dog. And I'm not your patient."

Then before I can respond with another "but" he says, "*But* I will promise to put on a glove next time... as long as you promise to let me sleep with you in your bed tonight."

I'm pretty sure I'm going straight to hell for what I just did with John. Or at least straight to the front of the hospital's review board. Maybe both.

I still can't believe it after my shower, even as I replace the Henley and joggers I was wearing earlier with a t-shirt and pair of jeans. Did I seriously bring a John Doe patient home? And then almost immediately spread my legs for him?

I think about hiding in my bedroom for longer than I want to admit, but eventually I make myself return to the main room. There I find him with his clothes back on, bent over my empty fridge.

"Sorry about the no-food situation. I get a regular delivery from the grocery store on Sundays and Wednesdays," I explain to him. "That way, the ingredients are always fresh, and I have to cook or risk them going bad. It's my way of trying to stay healthy. Plus a lot of the stuff I need to cook is special order, so that gives the grocery store time to get it in..."

I trail off. I'm babbling again. And I once more think about how cool and confident I used to be before I burned my old life to the ground in order to move out here without my parents' support or approval.

"What do you do on Saturdays, then, Doc?" he asks, his eyes twinkling with amusement.

"Well, I tell myself I'll go out to eat. Like drive into Pittsburgh where they have vegan restaurants. But usually I just end up ordering enough Chinese food to get me through the weekend."

"All right. I guess I'm about to find out if Chinese food is old or new."

So we eat Chinese food—it's new, but John likes it. And then we end up back in the living room, most of the day suddenly gone.

He doesn't even blink when I explain I don't have so much as an antenna on the early aughts-era TV in my living room, just a huge collection of DVDs that I feed into its built-in disc drive. Old musicals I'd been watching over and over again as opposed to the current fare of reality shows and nighttime dramas.

"Though I am planning to finally give *Grey's Anatomy* another go when I move to Seattle," I tell him as I push the DVD into the TV's disc drive. "It's so unrealistic, but you know, when in Rome..."

He responds with a quizzical look.

"*Grey's Anatomy* or Seattle or Rome?" I ask, feeling like I already know that look all too well.

"Seattle," he answers. "When?"

I clamp my lips not wanting to divulge more about that part of my life than I need to. But in the end, I tell him the truth.

"In about five weeks I'll be leaving for a visit to California, you know long enough to get my car shipped out. Then I'll be driving to Seattle to start my fellowship. But you don't have to worry about that. I'm paid through the summer on this apartment; it's a year-to-year lease. You can stay here until August, even after I've moved out."

But he continues to frown at me from his position on the couch. "That ain't what I'm worried about, Doc."

A chill goes down my back, because even though we've done something intimate, what we've done was also very, very stupid. As are the feelings rolling around in my chest right now. Feelings that weren't there before. Like regrets about leaving West Virginia. And sorrow about not having met him sooner.

"Anyway," I say, changing the subject with no grace whatsoever. "I think you're going to like this film, *Tommy*. Lots of seventies rock. Plus Tina Turner and the Who, back before they were co-opted by every single show and thing."

Also, it's a total sexual tension killer, I add to myself silently as I place myself as far from him as possible on the couch.

I'm right about him liking the movie, and wrong about it killing the sexual tension. The credits roll and by the time I've turned off the TV, he's standing above me. Cane in one hand, the other held out to me.

No discussion. He leads me to the bedroom with his hand clasped firmly around mine.

"I'm going to take a shower," he says when we get to my bedroom.

"Hold on..."

I go to the kitchen and come back with a plastic bag from last week's delivery. He watches me tie it over his cast, his blues eyes twinkling with lazy amusement.

But I pretend not to notice as I secure the knot and say, "There's a little closet with towels in it, but it's right behind the door, which means you have to actually close the door all the way to get to it."

"Thanks, Doc," he says. Then he presses a kiss onto my forehead and disappears into the bathroom.

It should feel like a reprieve. But it really, really doesn't.

In fact, it feels like I'll never let go of the breath I'm holding as I rush over to the dresser and pull out the warmest, most body covering-est pajamas I own.

The one thing I know is I don't want to be standing around like an awkward fool when he returns. So I get into bed. Pull my good-enough-for-seven-years comforter over my legs, and the hardcover novel off my nightstand. I pretend I'm reading a Karin Slaughter thriller as opposed to thinking.

Thinking about how crazy I am for sleeping with a patient. One who has amnesia. Thinking about what I'll say when he comes out of the bathroom.

And having no answers for any of it.

But when the door opens, all pretenses of reading come to a dead stop. Before he'd gone into the bathroom to take his shower, I'd tied a plastic bag over his cast and told him where to find a towel, expecting him to use both. And he had. But while the plastic bag is still wrapped around his forearm, the towel is draped casually around his neck. More of an afterthought than anything else.

And as hard as I try not to respond to the sight of him naked, I feel my entire body heat as he approaches my side of the bed.

I'm a doctor, but I haven't worked with adult patients in nearly a year. And John doesn't look like any patient I've ever encountered, naked or otherwise. His body is hard and solid, packed with powerful muscles. Gym or hard labor, I have no idea.

Or maybe prison, my rational brain points out. I think of all the rap videos I'd seen growing up. The ones with hard-bodied singers crowing about how much time they'd done in jail.

But he doesn't have any tattoos, I notice. And I've never met an ex-con without at least a few tats. This guy doesn't look like an ex-con. More like a muscular system model who just crawled out of one of my old anatomy text books.

His muscles move like cords beneath his skin as he walks over, his heavy cock swinging lewd and uncaring between his legs.

"Tried my damnedest to get this off by myself," he says when he stops in front of the bed. "But I couldn't do it."

Only when he holds up the cast with the plastic bag wrapped around it do I get what he's talking about. But by then it's already too late. My mouth is watering in ways it definitely shouldn't at just the thought of...

Thanking God for the ability most doctors develop to control shaking hands, I untie the plastic bag's knot and toss it into the nearest waste basket, without a thought toward recycling.

"You okay?" he asks. Probably because I've yet to look at him.

"I'm..." *fine, fine, fine* my rational mind screams at me. But when I open my mouth, the truth falls out. "Thinking."

He tenses, his lazy gaze becoming sharper and less amused. "Thinking about what?"

I squeeze my lips into my mouth, biting them a little before I confess, "About what we did this morning. About how I was crazy to do that with you. I was trying to help, but I've only made things worse. A lot worse."

He considers my words, and I brace myself for an extremely awkward conversation about stepping back and reconsidering our actions.

But then he asks, "Where're those condoms?"

"What?" I ask, not quite understanding.

"I made you a promise about using condoms the next time. So where are they? I assume you got some, being a medical professional and all."

He's teasing me. I can see how amused he is by the way his eyes crinkle slightly at the corners, and I don't quite know how to respond.

I swallow. "Um, yes, I do have condoms in my nightstand drawer, but—"

"This one right here?" He's already bending over and pulling the drawer open.

Before I can answer, he's got a blue square package in his hand. He tears it open and then, to my wide-eyed horror, starts putting it on.

I should look away, but I can't find enough modesty to do so. I openly stare as he rolls the thin rubber sheath up his swollen shaft, using the fingers on his casted hand to pinch the tip. His eyes once again find mine when he's done, and my body swells under his gaze, nipples hardening against the inside of my top; the space between my legs becoming heavy and damp.

"I..." My voice comes out all squeak and I try again, "I thought we were having a conversation."

"You're having a conversation, Doc. I'm ending it. Now turn over. Get on your hands and knees."

"Are you serious?"

Before the question's fully out of my mouth, his hands are on me. Cast bumping different parts of my body as he pulls my long-sleeved pajama top up and over my head.

His eyes darken at the sight of my breasts, now fully exposed.

"Wait—" I start to say, crossing my arms over them. Only to be interrupted again when he easily places me on my stomach.

The doctor in me wants to warn him about putting too much strain on his fractured arm. And the woman in me is screaming, shocked to find herself face forward on the bed less than a minute after having introduced a very awkward point of conversation.

My conflicting responses all add up to one outraged, "What the hell are you doing?!" when he crawls over my back.

"Teaching you a lesson about thinking too much," he answers matter-of-factly before roughly pulling down my pajama pants. I gasp. Once, and then again when he lowers his body down on mine.

It's a strange position. A *very* strange position. I'm flat on my stomach and he covers me like a blanket. But when he shoves my legs further apart with his muscular thighs and settles his heavy cock into the back of my pussy, my body responds like it's just been hit with a defibrillator. I buck, then buzz from every nerve ending as I helplessly squirm beneath him.

"No, don't..."

"Is that a real no?" he asks, dark and low in my ear. "I want to make you feel good, Doc. But if you don't want that from me, tell me right now and I'll get off you."

It is a real no...at least it should be. But my body is buzzing so hard now. The ribbed duvet cover of the bed playing havoc against my exposed clit. I can't stop myself from squirming, from lifting my hips off the bed, only to find his cock. Then settling back down, only to have the blanket rub against my engorged clit all over again.

I have never in my life been put in such a position...or been so turned on by it.

He takes my silence for acquiescence, or perhaps my squirming which, on the face of it, could easily be taken for what it actually is. Wanting. I'm now so helpless with desire, I'm going against everything I believe and know. So desperate to have him fill me, that neither my mind nor my body knows what to do.

I gasp when he pushes into me, giving me all of him in one hard stroke. I'm so wet, it's easy for him to get all the way in, even in this position. Above me, I hear a deep, approving growl tumble out of him.

Right before his voice turns mean.

"You wanted to have a conversation," he practically snarls into my ear. "Let's have a conversation. How about we talk about how lost I was feeling before I met you? So fucking confused and weak. Then I saw you. Beautiful as hell. Teaching dying kids to sing. How about we have a conversation about you showing up in my room with that sandwich and that music?"

He thrusts into me again and again, his voice hard and nasty. "If you really want to talk so bad, let's talk about you telling me you're my family now. Let's talk about you bringing me into your home so I could give you what you deserve. Everything you deserve for being such a beautiful angel to me."

I cry out, his words and his rolling thrusts devastating me, melting me, despite, or maybe even because of, his cruel tone.

"You want to talk to me about protocols and professional standards and a bunch of other stuff I don't give a shit about. Not when it comes to this, Doc. Not when it comes to us."

Us. "Yes!" I cry out to a question only my soul dares to ask.

But he mistakes my "yes" as something else. His thrusts become stronger, more intense until he says, "Fuck talking. I already got all the answers I need."

With that, he forces his cock into me one more time. The orgasm that washes over me very nearly breaks my mind. I scream as pleasure rushes through me, obliterating every thought I have of who I am, what I should or shouldn't be doing, and why I should never have allowed this to happen in the first place.

Above me, I can feel John coming. He talked a lot while he was fucking me out of having a logical conversation. But now he's gone quiet, his forehead pressed into the back of my neck as his body quakes with his final release. For what feels like eons on end, we come; squeezed together in a rictus of intense pleasure.

"Okay, Doc, okay..." he says when we're finally done.

He rolls off and eases himself out of the bed.

"I can..." I start to offer.

"I got it," he answers, removing the condom and tossing it into the small wastebasket next to the nightstand.

His leg hasn't escaped unscathed, I notice, as I watch him grab the cane he left hanging on the bathroom door. John's limp is a little bit more pronounced as he walks back to the bed. But despite having been in a sexual relationship with him for less than twelve hours, I already know how he'll respond if I express any remorse or sympathy whatsoever.

So I decide to focus on getting back under the covers. I burrow beneath and turn on my side with my back to him so I don't have to watch what he's doing. Or feel guilty. And confused.

The bed depresses when he gets in, and I reach over to the lamp on my nightstand to turn off the lights.

Then I lie there in the dark, trying not to think too hard about what all this means. For my career. For my sanity.

But when I'm not worrying, new thoughts pop up about what just happened. His hot, sweet words melting my heart even as his hard, unrelenting sex completely dominated my body. Seriously, who is this guy? And where the hell did he come from?

"Doc, you still awake?" he asks on the other side of the bed.

"Yes," I admit quietly.

"I need to tell you something."

I turn over on the pillow, not sure my thoroughly used body can tolerate another "conversation" and prepare to protest. But I find him lying there on his back, heavy cast slung over his eyes.

"You think I'm too messed up in the head to be serious," he says from beneath the cast. "But serious is exactly what I am."

My heart tightens and beats hard in that confused way it does whenever I'm around him.

As if echoing my erratic heartbeat, he says, "I got a lot of confusion in my life right now. But you and me—that's the one thing I'm 100% clear on. Stop questioning this, Doc. You gotta believe me when I say you're the best thing that ever happened to me. Because that's what you are."

I don't answer him. Of course, I don't answer him. How could any sane person respond to that?

What I need to do is go to sleep. I'll feel more rational in the morning. That's what I tell myself. But long after he falls asleep, breathing steadily beside me, my heart remains restless and awake in the dark. Beating with an emotion I'm afraid to name.

8

*E*ventually sleep does come. And the doubts stay away while I'm off in dreamland, but they come right back the next morning as soon as I wake up, wrapped in John's arms, my muscles aching, and every soft part of my body—from my breasts to the skin between my thighs—tender.

Easing out of his arms, I get up and stumble into the kitchen, attempting to go through my normal morning routine as if there isn't one hell of a first act surprise waiting for me back in my bedroom.

Switching my mind to the Left Coast, I check my current special phone which I keep in the catch-all drawer. There's a missed called from Dad, followed by several pissed off texts from Sandy.

"Sorry!" I text Dad. *"Can't talk this morning. Work emergency. Will talk with you same time in four weeks. Okay? Thanks! Sorry! But thanks!!!"*

I know Dad won't find that answer remotely satisfying, and I pre-emptively turn the phone all the way off, lest he and Sandy start inundating me with calls I really don't want to take with a certain amnesia victim in the house.

So instead of talking with my dad, I make John and myself the most gourmet of breakfasts: Kashi Cinnamon Harvest cereal with almond milk.

Okay, not exactly the breakfast of champions. But it's what I grew up eating back in Compton, and also one of the few things I have left to eat in the house until the grocery delivery comes this afternoon.

I don't expect John to be all that impressed when I walk back into the room with the tray of hastily prepared food. But I also don't expect to find him sitting on top of the bed in a pair of boxer briefs, strumming out a song on my guitar.

After a few bars, I recognize the melody.

"That's 'Ghosts,' a Colin Fairgood song," I say, setting the tray down on the never before used nightstand on his side of the bed.

"You know it?" he asks, looking up at me.

"Yeah, pretty much everybody does. It was his first super huge crossover hit." I bring out my iPhone and after a few swipes and touches, Colin Fairgood's voice fills the room.

John tilts his head to the side. "Yeah, that's the song. It's 'old' to me. I like it."

"Country isn't my favorite," I admit to John. "But I like it, too. And hey, look at you playing a guitar!"

I take my guitar back and press the bowl of Kashi into his hands. "Maybe you're some sort of musician," I say as I set the guitar back on its stand in the far corner of the room. "I mean, if you've got country songs down like that."

But he shakes his head. "I don't think so. I saw your guitar sitting over there and I got this feeling if I played it, I'd be more relaxed."

"You're feeling anxious?" I ask, studying him sharply and remembering what happened when that neuro jerk accidentally triggered him.

But then he throws me a lazy smile and says, "Not now that you're back."

I look away. "You really shouldn't say things like that."

"Why not?" he asks. "It's the truth."

"Because..." I shake my head, unable to explain all of it to him. About boys and girls and the games we play, so no one will be accused of liking the other too much. "It's just not what most guys do..."

"So, I'm different," he says after considering my words for a quiet moment. "Tell me, Doc. How am I different from the other guys you know?"

"Well, you're a lot more direct. I mean, you say whatever's on your mind, and you don't seem to care how it makes you look. Most guys hold their cards a lot closer to their chests than you do. Does that make sense?"

"Hmm," he says after a long while.

It's my turn to ask, "What?"

"I'm listening to what you're saying, Doc, but I'm also thinking, 'she's talking about other guys. And I don't like that.'"

Again, I'm not quite sure what to do in the face of his stark truth, so I treat it like a medical mystery. Keep my voice neutral as I answer, "Yes, I noticed you're kind of dominant."

"Dominant," he repeats.

"Controlling. Like you expect to be in charge. The way you had sex with me last night—it was like you were putting me in my place. Establishing who was in control."

He doesn't answer, but when I dare to look up from my cereal bowl, a new presence has joined our conversation. His cock has hardened into a long, thick line under his thin boxer briefs.

"So that turns you on?" I ask, swallowing to contain my breathlessness at the sight of him. "Dominating me?"

He holds my gaze, blue eyes shrewd, like he's thinking really hard about his answer to my question. But in the end, he nods. "Yeah, it does. When we're together like that, I want you under me. That's all I know."

Again I have to swallow.

And he crooks his head, studying my reaction from his superior height. "That scare you?"

I try my best to explain without confusing him even more. "It doesn't *not* scare me. I had a friend who had a controlling boyfriend. He got worse and worse and then, when she tried to break up with him, he hit her."

"I'd never hit you," he answers so automatic, it could be easily mistaken for fact. "I don't hit women. That's a conviction. I know I'd never do anything to hurt you, Doc."

I look at him, and he looks at me. Neither of us really knowing his true self for sure...

Eventually I decide, "Okay, I believe you. Maybe that's just your thing in bed. Wanting your partner beneath you. Hey, I'm from California. That means I've pretty much seen and respect it all. Namaste."

It's a gentle joke, meant to diffuse. But his gaze continues to hold mine. And though we're just sitting there with bowls of Kashi Cinnamon Harvest in our laps, it feels like he's fucking me again; going hard and then slow on top of me.

"Anyway..." I say, deciding it's time to get out of this bed. "I was thinking maybe we should do some yoga after I wash the dishes."

I stand, take both empty bowls, and set them on the tray between us.

He doesn't say anything, but I can feel his hesitation to go along with my yoga suggestion in his perfect stillness. And I get the sense he's considering putting me underneath him again. Trying to decide whether or not to take back control of this morning.

But in the end, he throws me a lazy smile and says, "Yeah, Doc, let's do some yoga."

"I'm not going to lie, I kind of hate West Virginia. But I love living this close to nature," I tell him as we walk on the footpath behind my apartment building toward the nature reserve—the only thing North Independence is known for other than the University of West Virginia.

"This new?" I ask him, after we make it to the main dirt walking trail.

"Old," he answers with a shake of his head. He wraps his hand around mine, enveloping it as if walking with me like this is a must, despite his cane. As natural as the sun's steady rise above us. Then he smiles over at me and asks, "You don't have nature in California?"

"We definitely do," I answer. "But I grew up mostly in a place called Compton until we moved when I was twelve, and let's just say my family isn't exactly into nature walks."

He scans the path we're hiking up, taking in the brush, trees, and dirt as far as you can see. "I don't think I used to go on a lot of walks either. But I like being outside," he says. "This feeling I got right now is old. I feel more free out here than indoors."

"Me too," I answer. "But don't get used to it. We're having a warm week, but spring in West Virginia is super funky. Next week it could be all rain. Or snow. Then in the summer, you'll have to deal with the mosquitoes."

He goes quiet, and I wonder if he's familiar with mosquitoes. But then he asks, "Why Seattle?"

I shrug. "Why not Seattle? It's a beautiful city. And they have a wonderful children's hospital. I'm lucky they want me to serve there." More than lucky, I think to myself, especially considering my past.

But John doesn't know about my past, and he says, "You said you love your family. That you miss them. Then why aren't you going back to California to live near them?"

I shake my head, a chill going up my spine at the mere thought of returning home. "It's a long story. A *really* long story," I answer. "I just can't go back there."

"You can't go back to California, but you hate it here in West Virginia," he says.

"Well, hate's a strong word," I say

"But that's what you said."

"I said I *kind* of hate it."

"Because you don't like to use strong words."

I glance over at him, kind of getting—no, *really* getting that he's been listening to every word that comes out my mouth.

"No, I'm fine with strong words. But West Virginia and me have a complicated relationship. On the one hand, I never would have been able to become a Pediatric Specialist if not for this state's program. On the other hand, it's West Virginia."

He shakes his head. "What does that mean?"

I sigh, not really wanting to get into a conversation about race and ignorance right before we're supposed to zen out with some yoga. And his innocent question makes me wonder anew about him.

In his old life did he ever date a black girl? Maybe he prefers them. That would explain why he was so instantly attracted to me, and why he's such a Colin Fairgood fan. I think of all my girlfriends who suddenly decided they loved country music when the handsome singer showed up to the Grammys with an African-American fiancée on his arm.

"It's different from California," I answer vaguely. Then I gratefully change the subject when I see the patch of green grass where I like to do my morning practice in warm weather. "So here's my favorite place for outdoor yoga..."

After we set down our mats, I lead us through a routine that's half mine, and half of what Ken included in John's discharge papers. But I never quite find my center. John is better at yoga than I'd expect a man with his injuries to be, and it's hard not to watch him instead of focusing on my breath and form.

"Is yoga old?" I ask him as we walk back down the path.

"No, it's new, but I like it," he answers. "The strength training stuff is old though. I like that, too. Like moving my body, even when it's hard."

Trying not to think about my prison theory from the day before, I consider his situation. Without insurance, the hospital wouldn't be too keen on him coming back to use their rehab facilities. Poor Ken was forced to release him with little more than his discharge paperwork. But it's not like he can join a gym without ID...and even if he could, there isn't one nearby other than the facility at the university.

"I'll pick up some weights on the way home from work tomorrow," I decide out loud.

But he shakes his head, his hand squeezing the cane tight. "I don't want you buying any more stuff for me, Doc. You're already doing enough."

"But you should be doing resistance training at the very least—it's in your paperwork," I point out. "Plus, I've been meaning to get some weights anyway."

I don't mention that I haven't bothered up to this point because my temporary housing in Seattle also includes a gym. Instead I insist, "Seriously, it's no big deal."

He doesn't answer, but his jaw ticks in a way that makes me suspect this situation—having a woman buy him things—is most definitely "new."

We walk back to my apartment, and I can tell the yoga and brief hike took it out of him. As soon as we get inside, he heads to the couch and puts both legs up on the ottoman I placed for him beside the coffee table. And by the time I return from the bathroom, he's dozing, chest rising slowly up and down.

He looks so peaceful that I don't bother waking him. Instead I eat a sunbutter and banana sandwich, my version of a mid-morning snack. I make him one, too, but he's still sleeping when I finish. I hesitate, not wanting to wake him, even though there's food waiting.

Also, there's something so inviting about him sleeping on my couch. The position isn't great for his back or leg, my inner-doctor notes, even as my inner-girl convinces me to set the plate with his sandwich on the table and sit down beside him.

But then the awkwardness comes back. Real life is so much harder than I thought it'd be when I left California. Figuring out what to do with my body and words between all the specific stuff—like doctoring and editing videos and playing guitar and half-watching old musicals—that's hard. Knowing what to do with myself when I am in the same room as John—even harder. *What would a real life person do in this situation?* I wonder to myself.

I gingerly lean back and rest my head on his shoulder. Only to let out a little gasp when he immediately moves to accommodate me in his sleep, shifting so his arm is around my waist, his cast rests on my thigh, and my head has no choice but to lie on his chest.

I might not have known what to do with myself, but he seems to know exactly what to do with me. He presses a kiss onto the top of my head before settling back into a deep sleep. And either his tiredness is contagious, or I must be pretty wiped out, too, because I wake up a few hours later, dazed and confused.

There's a hand inside the waist band of my yoga pants, and a voice in my ear, "Wake up, Doc."

The sandwich I left on the table is gone, I notice, as two fingers push into my already swollen pussy. Eliciting a groan as he captures my mouth with his. His kiss tastes exactly like the sandwich I ate earlier, but I quickly become hungry for something else as his hand moves between my legs.

That is until he pulls out his fingers and cuts off the kiss.

I mewl, confused and disappointed. But then he pushes my t-shirt and sports bra up before shoving me back on the couch. My pants come off next, and I have to fight hard not to feel self-conscious when he spreads me open on the couch in the late afternoon sun, taking in my naked sex and half-exposed breasts with hungry need.

He moves my hands, one at a time, onto my breasts.

"I'm going to make you feel good, Doc, and I want you to keep your hands right there. Don't drop them, no matter how excited you get. If you need something to do with those hands of yours, rub on them pretty breasts for me. That's a good way to keep from getting punished."

His suggestion is so bald, so lewd, and without hesitation or self-consciousness. Yet my nipples pebble behind my hands, begging me to fondle them exactly as he's told me to.

"Condom," I say breathlessly, before he forgets, before I forget. Again.

But he doesn't move off the couch, just repositions himself. And the next thing I know, his head is between my legs, his tongue dominating my slit almost as slow and unrelenting as his cock did the night before. His nose presses against my clit, teasing me, erasing my pride and embarrassment. Soon I'm desperate, rubbing and squeezing my own breasts as his tongue works me below. Fighting to keep my hands on my chest and not grab his head.

The orgasm, when it comes, feels like a reprieve. A welcome release from holding myself back as it washes over me.

"You did good, Doc," he says with his lazy smile as he crawls over me and covers my body with his. "A little too good. I'm kind of wishing you'd done bad."

Before I can ask why, he hits me with another soul-stripping kiss, pushing my head into the back of the couch as his lips once more claim mine. I greet his kiss with an aching moan, helplessly aroused by the feel of him between my legs below. His sweatpants are doing little to cover the fact of the long, hard cock underneath. And perhaps unintentionally (a very small perhaps) his erection is teasing me, pushing into my still engorged clit, reminding me of how good it was last night with him. How good it could be again if one of us goes back into the bedroom to get a condom.

I break off the kiss to offer, "I can get a condom. I really don't mind."

But he only smiles—no, smile isn't quite the right word. More like bares his teeth. The expression he wears isn't nice enough to be labeled a smile. And the heat in his eyes practically burns me alive as he says, "I'll let you know when it's time for me to be inside you again, Doc. But right now, c'mere."

He rears backwards and pushes down his sweatpants, just far enough that his cock springs out, long and heavily veined. "I've been dreaming of seeing your beautiful lips take this," he tells me as he leisurely guides his cock into my mouth.

I receive him docilely, more curious than ashamed. His scent is impossibly virile: sweat and man and something earthy and wild I can't quite put my finger on.

I swallow him in, controlling my gag reflex in order to take him deeper and deeper. I want to please him more than I've ever wanted to please any other lover I've ever had. And it feels like a true achievement when his back suddenly caves, and a pained groan erupts from his chest before he grabs my head and releases a jet of cum into my mouth. I drink him in, my mind buzzing with his pleasure and my own, because I'm the one who did this to him. Caved his back, made him relinquish some of his tight-fisted control.

When he's done, he drags me up his body in a sort of kneeling hug. "Fuck that was good, but c'mere. I want your mouth, Doc."

As with everything, he doesn't wait for my permission, just grabs me up in another kiss, his cast thumping into the small of my back as his mouth moves over mine, lazy and hard.

Soon I'm squirming against him. And maybe I've lost my mind, because I want him inside me again. So bad, I can feel my sex milking the air, begging to be filled.

So bad, it feels like I'm being reprimanded, when he sets me away from him and says, "How about something to eat, Doc? That sandwich was good, but it's getting late and I'm starving."

9

He's not the only one starving, I think bitterly a little while later when we're both in the kitchen.

Then I immediately reprimand myself. Because he's broken, and I'm the medical professional in the wrong. *Sex wasn't your original intention*, I remind myself as I place the vegan lasagna in the oven. Meanwhile, my lunches and dinners until my next cooking day on Wednesday are simmering on all four of the stove's burners. A seeming reflection of my mood, and I can feel his blue gaze following me as I move around the stove, checking and stirring the various dishes.

I try not to be irritated. It's not his fault that having him watch me cook has my body all riled up. But tell that to my striatum; the section of my brain that controls sexual desire is completely out of control. And I'm glad I chose black yoga pants this morning, because I am dripping. So wet, I'm sure there'd be a visible damp patch at my crotch if they were any other color. So wet, I can smell myself, smell how much I want him inside me again.

"This is new," he tells me when everything is either simmering in a pot or baking in the oven.

"Cooking?" I ask, looking over my shoulder at him.

Big mistake. He looks so sexy leaned up against the counter. My pussy clenches, sending a yearning ache straight through me.

He nods. "I don't think I cook. Ever."

And my stomach knots, wondering if he has someone who cooks for him. Someone he'll remember any day now.

His expression darkens. "I like how smart you are, Doc. But sometimes I don't like it."

"Sometimes like when?" I ask.

"Like right now, when you get to thinking too much," he answers. "C'mere."

I go to him, helpless as a marionette, and my body sizzles like coconut oil meeting heat when he pulls me into him for a long, hard kiss.

"You like kissing me as much as I like kissing you?" he asks me.

I nod, too turned on to tell him anything but the truth. "Probably more," I say.

He chuffs. "Definitely not more, Doc. It ain't possible for you to like me more than I like you."

I'm not sure about that. After all, he's in my home, and unlike him, I don't have a traumatic brain injury to use as an excuse for my way-too-soon feelings.

"You're going to have to show me some of those no-meat recipes," he says, resting his cast against the small of my back. "I want to feed you when you come home to me tomorrow."

I have no idea how to handle that statement, so I concentrate on the feeding part. "That's seriously not an issue. I usually just eat leftovers. I mean, there's not going to be enough for leftovers this week, because I didn't know I'd be cooking for two. But I'll stop by the grocery store on the way home. Maybe you can text me a list?"

He stares down at me, his good hand stroking the side of my face like he's thinking of bringing me in for another kiss.

One of the many timers I set goes off on the microwave, interrupting the moment and releasing me from his spell.

But only for a little while. We eat the mushroom lasagna for an early dinner, and neither of us so much as suggests watching a musical before bed.

"No pajamas," he tells me before disappearing into the bathroom.

I napped earlier so I'm not tired. I'm something else that my medical vocabulary doesn't cover. As soon as I strip out of my yoga gear, my core presents with fever. Hotter than I've ever felt it, damp all over and slick at the slit at the thought of what will happen when he returns from the bathroom.

I think about, but don't end up, putting on a set of pajamas this time. Instead I climb into bed, welcoming the feel of the cool sheets on my hot body.

But as turned on as I am, I can't stop thinking about the fact that I have to go to work tomorrow. Look all those doctors and parents of patients in their faces as I pretend to be someone I'm not. Someone with ethics, someone who's not letting sex overrule her better judgment...

"I swear, Doc, I could hear you thinking all the way in the bathroom."

The bed dips and I'm pulled backwards into strong arms. He employs the arm with the cast like a sort of weight, using the heaviness to anchor me against his chest while his free hand settles on top of my fevered pussy.

"What did I tell you?" he asks, voice low and mean as he plays with me.

"No thinking," I answer, drunkenly pushing myself into his hand, though I've had nothing to drink at all.

"Hand me a condom, Doc."

I fumble the nightstand drawer open. Find what he asked for, and hand it to him over my shoulder. He removes his hand from my pussy, and I can feel him putting it on behind me.

With one hand.

I'm giving my body to someone so familiar with sex that even when he loses his memory of everything else, he can still put on a condom single handedly. *Seriously, what the hell are you doing, Anitra?* my rational brain demands.

But the more sensible part of me shuts right up when he roughly pushes into me from behind. "Remember that talk we had about me being possessive?" he asks after a few lazy strokes.

How could I forget? I want to say, *You mean the one that kind of scared the shit out of me and made me doubt my sanity for doing any of this with you?* But I just whimper into my cool pillow, unable to form words.

He must take that as yes, because he continues, "I'm trying to give you some breathing room here, Doc. Give you time to catch up to where I'm at on this. But I can hear you thinking. And I don't want you to go to work tomorrow without a full understanding of what's going on here. The minute you walked me through that door, you became mine. That means you belong to me. You understand that?"

I clamp my lips closed, because I'm afraid of what will come out of my mouth. But my hips don't stop moving. Even his outrageous words can't keep me from pushing back on his dick. So needy, so desperate, so thirsty...

"Let me know you hear me on this, Doc," he says behind me. His teeth graze but don't quite bite my ear. "Give me some reason to believe I don't have to keep you here...don't have to worry about you not coming home to me because you've been thinking too much. Tell me the truth, Doc; do I need to make you take off work tomorrow so I can fuck you all day until you're too tired to think any more of them thoughts?"

I shake my head. I'm so close, almost there. I think I'd promise him twice what I owe in medical school debt to take me the rest of the way.

But instead of giving me what I want, he pulls out. And then I feel something that I only keep in my medicine cabinet for hook-up emergencies.

Lube. I tense. Lube, which he's now smearing onto my no-go zone.

"Relax, Doc, relax," he croons when I start to struggle against the cast. "It's only going to be this once. But I can't leave any part of you untaken. You understand that, right? I can't send you to work not knowing who you belong to."

He doesn't do his usual rough push in this time. Instead, he plays with my pussy, moving his fingers in deep. "You think I don't know how much you want me to take your pussy? You think I ain't been going out of my mind with the smell of you all day?"

And just like that, I go from struggling to melting. From protesting to helpless. His tox report came back clean, but he's the drug, I think. And I find myself once again becoming aroused, even as his erection circles into the slit of my ass. He's a drug, and he's killing all my willpower.

"You don't think you know me, but you do," he tells me. "You're going to give me what I want, because you know I'd never do anything to hurt you, Doc. You know at the end of it, I'm going to make you feel good."

I grab on to his words. "But I don't think it will feel good. No guy's ever..."

"Yeah, I got that. And that makes me want it even more. Fuckin' all of you, Doc. I ain't settling for nothing less."

He continues to plunge his fingers into me, kneading the top of my pussy until a druggy arousal takes over my core.

"But I want you inside me," I tell him. "In my pussy. Please..."

A dark laugh erupts behind me. "Oh, you'll be getting me back in your pussy. Probably about two or three more times before this night is through, but first we got some loyalty to prove."

This is stupid. So stupid, I have to tell him. "This is stupid. You're being stupid. I don't have anything to prove to you."

"Humor me, Doc," he whispers in my ear. "Please..."

His rough please is what finally makes me stop fighting him. I find myself curving forward, spreading my buttocks a little wider. Giving him the invitation to get it over with, so we can get back to the other stuff.

In the next moment, I feel my ass being split apart by his cock, pushing in, inch by inch.

As big as he is, it's not painful. Not at all. He takes it slow, pushing in a little at a time. Giving me a second or two between each push to get used to having him there.

Then I can feel his balls on my butt cheeks.

"Okay, Doc..." he whispers.

His hand finds it's way between my legs and he starts moving again, this time with deliberate care. And it's...not nearly as bad as I thought it would be. In fact, the only pain I feel is one of bittersweet need as I get closer and closer.

I finally understand what my best friend Sola meant when I worried about the Russian fiancé who followed her abusive ex.

"There's a difference between dominant and domineering," she'd told me when we'd flown back to California to attend the funeral of one of our favorite ValArts teachers and met for dinner beforehand.

Ivan Rustanov was so large, so commanding. I couldn't help but worry. But Sola assured me he was nothing like her ex, and I could see how happy she was with him. So I'd chosen to believe her, stood up at her wedding less than a few months later, still not quite understanding, but somehow accepting in my heart that Ivan Rustanov was a good fit for her.

But now I get it. I know exactly how it feels to give yourself to someone with more trust than you could ever imagine you possessed.

John's thrusts speed up, and he whispers all sorts of dirty words in my ear. Telling me I'm really his now. That I belong to him. That I'm so fucking beautiful, and I've saved him.

The orgasm hits me, unexpected and brutal, ripping through me and tearing me completely apart. I'm incoherent and babbling by the time it's done, and so far gone that I don't realize he's coming until he pulls out of me.

I've just come from my first ass fucking. And surprisingly, it's still not enough. I lie there, battling tears even as my pussy clenches and unclenches, once again milking air it's so desperate to be filled. The bed rises up again and the next thing I hear, other than my hitched breaths, is the sound of water running in the bathroom.

Then he's there on my side of the bed, filling up my blurry vision, opening the nightstand drawer again.

"Move over, Doc," he tells me.

I do, trying to get a hold of myself, as he sits on the bed with his back against the wall. I'm a Pediatric Oncology Specialist at the end of her residency. I'd thought I'd pretty much trained myself out of crying.

But not with him. He unravels me. Completely dismantles me. Scares the everlasting shit out of me.

And he's putting on another condom.

"C'mere," he says, voice somewhere between a command and a sigh. "Climb on."

I sniffle. "I thought you didn't like women on top."

"I don't," he answers with a hitched smile. "But I'm pretty sure I'll like it with you."

You'd think my being close to tears would have diffused everything in the achieving erection department, but on the contrary, his half-flag becomes full-on Viagra when I climb on top of him.

"Your leg... I don't want to hurt you," I start.

"Not your patient, Doc," he reminds me. Voice mean until it gentles to say, "It'll be all right. Trust me."

I do trust him. It feels like this entire weekend has been one long trust exercise, culminating in this act which he told me earlier he never allowed.

I sink down on top of him, pussy soaking wet and slovenly grateful to finally be getting what it's been wanting all day.

He curls a hand around the side of my face and asks, "You still like kissing me?"

No words. No words for how this man makes me feel. I can only silently nod.

"Kiss me, then. Let me know I didn't break you worse than I did me. No traumatic brain injuries."

I'm shaken, I realize, but not broken. I lean forward, hips rolling into his, and this time it feels like I'm the one doing all the dominating as I fuck him the way I've been wanting to all day.

I can tell he's holding himself back with me. His hands fall to my hips, but he let's me enjoy the ride as I kiss him.

I want to go like this all night, but I come faster than a teenage boy in this position, moaning and going wild in his lap.

At first he watches me come with that lazy blue stare, but then he inhales sharply, his head jerking to the side as if he's been hit with something unexpected and foreign. "Oh, fuck, Doc, I think I'm going to..."

No more holding back now. His cast knocks against my hip as he pulls me into him. Again and again. Until he explodes into the condom, pitching forward against me with a yell.

And now I'm the one lazily watching him as he looks around with the wild disbelief of an ER admit who's just been resuscitated with a defibrillator.

Then he looks up at me, gaze awed and humbled as he says, "Damn, Doc, I really didn't think I could come that way."

I give him an ironic smile. "Think about all the stuff you were missing with those other girls."

But instead of laughing, his face clouds over. "Why did you say that?" he asks. "Why you bringing other girls into this, Doc?"

I shift, uncomfortable on his lap now. "Because there must have been other girls," I answer, my tone frank. "Maybe even one who's looking for you right now, one you'll eventually remember—"

"No, Doc, there's only you," he says. "I'm brain damaged and confused. But you..." He pats his heart with his good hand. "You fill up my chest, and I know there ain't anybody else but you in here."

I swallow. Wanting to believe him. Upset because I'm even thinking about taking the word of a man who can't so much as remember his name.

"Okay," I say. Voice small. Agreeing with him just to get out of a conversation about disagreeing.

It's been a long day and I barely have the energy to climb out of bed and go to the bathroom to wash away all the things he's done to me.

He lets me clean up. But he says, "No pajamas," his voice sharp, when I return and start to head to the dresser drawer.

I simply reverse direction and climb into the bed without a word of protest. Trusting him to keep me warm. Trusting him more than any woman has any business trusting a man she barely knows. A man who barely knows himself.

No, he definitely doesn't have to keep me home from work tomorrow. He's already fucked me out of thinking too much. But still...

I go to bed wondering how bad or possibly good it will be when he finally remembers who he really is.

10

MASON

SHITTY LITTLE STATE. Shitty little warehouse packed with SFK's guns. Shitty MC's standing around while Mason "questions" their prospect.

Mason's becoming more pissed off by the second that D's put him in this position. Somebody's going to pay. Mason doesn't know who, but somebody's definitely going to pay.

Maybe it'll be the guy hanging in chains in front of him, while the rest of his motorcycle club, including the prez, watches.

"Where is he?" Mason demands, stabbing his bowie knife through the prospect's shoulder. A family heirloom, passed down from a grandpa who would definitely approve of the way Mason was using it now.

The biker screams, but none of his fellow MCs step forward to help him. They know better. Know who Mason's family is, and what they'll do if any of these West Virginia fuckers so much as raises a finger to help this guy.

New Rebels, his ass. Mason wouldn't be at all surprised if a few of these pussies peed themselves watching his bowie go into the prospect's shoulder, then come back out with the sickening squelch of skin and muscle losing against steel.

In fact, the Rebel's prez looks like he's going to lose his dinner as he snivels, "I swear on my mother, man! I don't know where he is. This prospect and the old sarge did the deal with him and he left with the money. We ain't heard from him or seen him since. I swear!"

The old sergeant at arms, the New Rebel Mason questioned last month. Meanwhile, the prospect hanging from the chains starts full on sobbing.

Oh for fucking...

Mason studies the prez, then the prospect. Decides. They're telling the truth. They don't know anything.

Which means D. is either dead or hiding. Mason has not one ounce of Native American blood in him, but he senses it's the latter. Which only makes shit worse. Hiding is way worse than dead in Mason's opinion. One earned a little bit of Mason's respect. The other earned his bullet.

If D. is hiding from him, ignoring all Mason's calls to his burner phone...

Mason's hand clenches and unclenches around the bowie's wooden handle, and he suddenly decides to put it back in his waist holster. Not because he has to, but because D's been missing near three months now, and these New Rebels fuckers have no clue where he went.

These baby motorcycle clubs that keep springing up all over the country make him sick. Bunch of wannabe bad-asses who'd let anybody in, and when push really came to shove, you got a lot of them crying like pussies instead of taking a beating like a man.

Mason puts the knife away.

Then he pulls out something else his grandpa gave him before he died. A Beretta .92 compact. Now the prospect really starts sobbing. And screaming. And begging the other Rebels to help him. But not for long. Mason shuts him up with a bullet straight through his forehead.

A hell of a lot nicer and cleaner than what he'd done to their sergeant at arms the month before, letting the guy bleed out with his bowie in his gut for not knowing what Mason wanted him to know. But a few of the New Rebels actually jump back like this bullet is so much worse, just because the sound of the shot hurt their sensitive little ears. Like they're trying to figure out whether to run or stand their ground.

Before they have time to decide, Mason holds up a picture of the man he's looking for: a man who is the opposite of Mason, without any of his hulking darkness. No, this guy is clean-cut, blond, blue-eyed, and too clever for his own good. Mason suspected that about him from the start, and now it's pretty much been confirmed.

"Listen up!" he yells at the shitty group of men daring to call themselves a motorcycle gang. The men who ordered SFK guns, but have no idea where D went with the money they supposedly paid for those guns.

"We been through this two times already!" Pointing to the prospect now sagging good and dead against his chains, Mason yells, "You fuckers know who I'm looking for, and what I do each and every time I come here and you don't have anything new to tell me. I'm going home, but I'll be back in another four weeks..."

Now Mason's eyes connect with the large swastika on the New Rebels President's jacket. "And I swear *to fucking Hitler*, next time I ain't settling for no prospect. I'll take another one of your board members. Maybe even your president."

Nobody answers, but nobody has to. They know his reputation. Know he means every word he says. They'll either figure out where D. got off to by the time he comes back, or be fully disbanded.

Either way, Mason has no plans to stop looking until he's found D. dead or alive, along with the SFK's one hundred grand.

11

*N*o more thinking. A month passes faster than I ever imagined it could.

John and I settle into a routine fairly quickly. He's not my patient, but he lets me guide him through yoga every morning. His jaw clenches when an Amazon delivery with six sets of sweats, a 12-pack of boxer briefs, a bunch of weights, resistance bands, and a small all-in-one gym arrives. But I often come home to find the workout mix I made him blasting rap on his Beats headphones, while he lifts more weight than recommended.

Cooking is new, but he's taken over my kitchen, making recipes we both like and adding meat at the end to his plate. He's not the first meat-eater I've been with, but he is the most respectful. Never mixing it in the same pans or making recipes with chicken broth, or any of the other million things that can come between couples on opposite sides of the vegan line.

Which makes the fact that he's dominated me every single night that much more curious. John is a man made up of contradictions. Tender and mean. Serving and dominant. Proud and humble. 100% clear on his now and a total blank on his then. I don't know what to make of him, and I wonder if he knows himself.

Or if his mystery frustrates him as much as it does me.

Everything about us feels so fragile, but our co-habitation is shockingly strong.

Weekday mornings, I go to work while he goes outside, no matter the weather. I'm still not quite sure what he's doing out there, but I often imagine him taking long, meditative walks to the "Walking" playlist I made for him. Communing with nature like Walt Whitman, before he comes home to listen to a lot of gangsta rap while working out on the sad little home gym we set up in my living room.

"Doctor Dunhill? Doctor Dunhill?"

A voice rips me away from my thoughts and back to the real world. The one not filled with the crazy sexy mystery that is my John Doe.

I look up from Ronnie Greenwell's chart to find one of the peds nurses at the door of the office I'm allowed to use when my attending is making rounds. "Veronica Greenwell's mother is here. She's asking to talk to you."

I start. "Do you mean Dr. Higgson? She's doing rounds, but if Caren has more questions..."

"No, she's already met with Dr. Higgson, but now she's asking to speak with you directly."

I look back at Ronnie's chart, then close it before standing.

"Okay," I say softly. Not wanting to speak with Ronnie's mother. Deeply aware I'm a three-year fellowship away from becoming an official Pediatric Oncologist. But knowing I can't turn down her request.

"Okay," I agree again. Then I get to my feet and take a deep breath.

THE HOUSE SMELLS amazing when I walk into the apartment that night; the very opposite of a hospital. As usual, John's finishing up his workout in the corner, so instead of bothering him, I go straight to the kitchen and find a curry simmering on the stovetop.

"Indian food?" I ask a few minutes later when he joins me in the kitchen; Meek Mill's "Ima Boss" bleeding out of the the black-and-gray Beats around his neck. "Is that new?"

"Yeah, Indian food is new," he tells me, pressing a kiss into my temple. "But the recipe sounded good and you had all the ingredients."

"Thanks to Amazon," I grumble, thinking of the first time I discovered that unlike L.A., most grocery stores in West Virginia don't carry garam masala.

"Speaking of that...you got a package delivered. But it ain't from Amazon."

My eyes go to the rather large box waiting for me like a specter on the coffee table. I sigh, wishing it had come any day but today.

"You want to talk about it?" he asks.

"My day or the box?" I answer with a tired smile.

"Either," he answers back, hooking the cast behind my back, and caressing my face with the side of his knuckles.

"Not really," I admit. Because it's the truth. Because I don't feel like recounting my day or my past to him tonight.

He studies me for a moment, shrewd eyes gauging. But in the end, he presses another kiss to my temple and says, "All right, I'm gonna go take a shower before dinner."

As soon as he's gone, I go over to the box. I don't even bother to read the return label. It's from Sandy. Of course it is. Inside I find the usual: a Hermés Birkin, which I will never actually wear on my person; a new special phone with a post-it reading "same number" attached; a couple of shoe boxes, most likely filled with the kind of heels a real doctor wouldn't wear outside a TV show.

After a few minutes of fishing things out, I throw everything but the new special phone back in the box and go through the monthly routine. Print out the label from my laptop. Tape it to the box with the same industrial-sized roll of packing tape I've been using for years. But this month, instead of putting the package by the door, I take it all the way downstairs and throw it into the trunk of my car.

"How many times do I have to ask you to stop sending me these boxes?" I text Sandy after I close the trunk.

"Eight more days," is all she texts back.

When I get back to the apartment, John's already out of the shower, and he's got our plates set up on the same coffee table where the box Sandy sent me used to be. I can feel his curious gaze on me as I go over to the small wine rack sitting on the kitchen counter. Since it's Friday, and I don't have to work the next day, I pick out a white to go along with this week's beer.

We've established that beer is "old" to John. So I've been trying a variety of beers from Pabst to Bud to see if anything sparks a memory.

But so far, the only thing we've really established is that John likes beer and doesn't "understand" wine.

He squints at the Stella Artois I set in front of him, takes a swig, and says, "That's new. But I don't like it as much as the Yuengling from last week."

"Okay," I say, trying but failing to keep the irritation out of my tone as I take a sip of my wine.

He continues to watch me instead of eating. And after a moment, he says, "Got something to say, Doc?"

"No," I answer, picking up my plate. "You're just...I don't know, frustrating sometimes."

Another long silence, and I'm deeply aware I'm the only one eating during it. Finally he says, "I'm frustrating you?"

No, he's actually the best thing that's happened to me in a long time. The best part of a shitty day. But of course I don't say that. Of course, I let the old Nitra take a hold of me and snap, "You just don't seem to be putting any effort into finding out who you really are. Hell, I think you've searched harder for vegan recipes than clues about your past this last month."

A dark look flashes across his face. And in an instant, I'm brought back to the episode on the eighth floor. When it looked like he would kill our neuro res because of something he triggered in John's past.

But he doesn't say anything. Just sits there, as if waiting for me to go on.

So I take another sip of wine, washing down the food before I say, "I mean, let's face it. You're a very good-looking guy. The chances of you not have a girlfriend are like zero to—"

"I could say the same about you, Doc. I'm still trying to figure out how a pretty gal like yourself ain't already taken."

The lazy smile's back, and now it's my turn to study him. To wonder what he's really thinking about this line of conversation.

"You know what? I'm tired and I've had a really long day. Do you mind if we just watch a movie or something instead of talking?"

A beat. Then, "Sure, Doc. Whatever you want."

What I want is to not talk for a while. Or think. So I get up and pop *Sweeney Todd* into the player, and we finish our dinner, letting Johnny Depp and Helena Bonham-Carter do all the talking and singing. I clear our plates when we're done eating, and only come back to the living room because it's easier than having a conversation about going to bed early.

I settle onto the other half of the couch and keep trying not to think. Maybe it works. The next thing I know, John is waking me with a tender kiss pressed to the side of my head.

I'm no longer on the other side of the couch, and my head is in his lap. A familiar position at this point, because I've been falling asleep during our nightly musical wind down a lot this week.

Fatigue. That's a sign of depression, I think to myself. And I have to wonder if all of this: the sleepiness, the unorthodox relationship, the sudden sadness about leaving West Virginia, are latent signs of a grief I'd thought I was dealing with by upending my life to go to med school. My past and my present have been colliding a lot this week and apparently it's exhausting me.

"C'mon, Doc," he says, interrupting my thoughts about Chanel. "Let's go to bed."

When we get to the bedroom, I go straight to my long unused pajama drawer.

"You looking to get punished tonight, Doc?" he asks my back as I strip out of my scrubs and bra.

I don't answer, just reach for the t-shirt I pulled out. But before I can put it on, he's behind me, hard erection pressed into my back. Reminding me of how fast he can move now that he's no longer using his cane.

"How do you think this is going to end, Doc?" he asks, voice low and mean.

"I don't know, *John*," I answer, purposefully stressing the name I've been forbidden to use. "With me sleeping on the couch because I'm too tired and bitchy to do this with you right now?"

"You tired, Doc?" A hand finds my breast, stroking it, bringing it to life. "You don't feel too tired to me. And as for the bitchiness, I got some ideas about how to handle that."

His hand drops from my breast and slips inside my underwear, fingers working me. I bite my lips, determined not to respond, determined to stay angry for reasons I can't quite explain. But his touch is magic, and soon I feel my tightly held tension slipping away, my resistance weakening as my body becomes softer and softer.

"You had a bad day, Doc?" he asks, voice thick in my ear. "You need me to do the doctoring tonight? Make you feel better?"

I nod. Silently, helplessly, having no idea that's what I needed until he said the words out loud.

"Okay, here's what we're going to do," he informs me. "I'm going to put you under me. Punish you for this pajama move you just tried to pull. Then we're going to talk about whatever the hell is bothering you, because I just now decided we ain't going to be one of those couples who go to bed mad."

Oh God, his touch is melting me. Making even the hardest parts of my heart feel softer. But there must be a little bit of bitchy Nitra left inside, because I answer. "We're not a couple. I'm leaving next week. We're just—"

I cut off when I'm suddenly spun around and all but shoved toward the bed.

The next thing I know, my back's hitting the mattress and he's on top of me. Using his weight to hold me down.

His erection pushes against me as he reaches across to the night-stand, and even though I'm still wearing panties, I can feel him inside my slit. Hard as stone.

Same as his expression as he rears back, holding my gaze while he puts on the condom.

Same as his voice when he pulls aside my panties and roughly pushes himself into me.

"Say that again," he growls, voice guttural with unchecked anger.

It's an unfair command. Because as soon as I open my mouth to point out all our truths: that we're not an official couple, that I'll be leaving soon, that neither of us really knows who the other is —he devours my words with an angry kiss.

I end up moaning against his lips as he slams my arms above my head and holds them there with his good hand, grinding into me with coarse strokes. So good. So good. I cry out, reveling in the way his lean hips feel between my legs. Loving how he makes me forget. About Chanel. About Ronnie.

None of that matters as he fucks me into the bed.

He's so rough in his take down, dominating me completely in just a few moves, but I soon realize this isn't the punishment.

No, the punishment is when he pulls out, then eases back into me. But this time, he doesn't move. Just kisses me. Lazy as a Sunday morning, even though it's Friday night.

"What are you doing?" I demand, nipping at his lips. "C'mon. C'mon!"

But he doesn't come on. Not until my entire body cools down, but still doesn't completely forget the fire he started to build up inside me.

"If we're not going to—" I begin in a huff.

Only to have him start moving inside me again.

So good. So good. Until he stops. Again.

"What the..." I try to squirm under him, try to initiate the movement he's refusing me. But it's no use. He's too heavy.

So we lie there. Until I once again begin to cool down. Only to have him once again start lazily fucking me. Hard enough to feel pleasurable, but not so hard I actually come.

When he stops the third time, I scream out in frustration, tugging on my hands, "Just let me up, if you're not going to—!"

"Oh, I'm going to, Doc," he says, slamming my hands right back down on the bed. "I just need an update on our relationship status before I do."

I bare my teeth at him. "I don't even have a Facebook page."

My angry protest only seems to amuse him even more. "Then humor me, Doc. Answer these questions for me. What would you do if the both of us walked out of this apartment together? Would you claim me as your man? Let people know you were my lady?"

"Claim who?" I all but spit back in his face, hating him in that moment for forcing this conversation after the second longest day of my life. "You don't have a name, or a social security number, or anything else that proves any of this is real. Most the time I don't call you anything, because there is literally nothing to call you."

He goes still above me, his face colder than I've ever seen it. "You think this ain't real, Doc? You think we ain't something just because I don't have a name?"

He jerks into me, punctuating his next question with a dragging thrust. "Well, what is this you're feeling between your legs? Who's nameless dick are you about to come all over because you can't help yourself? Can't keep yourself from feeling for me the same shit I'm feeling for you? How many times I got to make you come before you admit no matter where you go, you fucking belong to me. How long's that going take? How long?"

This time he doesn't stop. This time the orgasm he's been holding back from me rushes through me. Lighting up and then blowing out my entire nervous system, as the pent up pleasure finally has its release.

He gives me what I want. Which is why I really don't understand what comes next. Me screaming filthy words as the orgasm threatens to shut down my central nervous system. Me babbling apologies for how I acted, for the insensitive things I said.

Then me moving beneath him. Begging him, "Please come, baby. I want to feel you. Please..."

His forehead rests down on mine. "No, Doc," he says, continuing to hold back. "I love you so fucking much. I don't want to come in you if you don't feel the same. I can't. I can't..."

His words get loss in an aching groan. And I can tell holding back like this is hurting him. That he's in pain. Because of me.

I don't owe him my heart. Or my love. I'm leaving in less than a week. The truth is, it would be wiser to draw back, to try to wean ourselves off each other so it doesn't hurt so bad when I get on the plane to California.

I think all of that. But out loud I say, "Baby, you know I love you. I'm a doctor and you were a patient, but you're here with me in my bed. Obviously, I love you. It's making me crazy!"

My words do what my body and pleas couldn't. He comes hard above me, his whole body involuntarily shuddering as I murmur, "I'm sorry. So sorry for confusing you even more with the way I acted tonight. I love you. Love you so much, baby."

12

*S*o. Much. Drama.

The complete opposite of anything I wanted when I came out here. But I don't take the words back. And I can't bring myself to regret them. Even when he rises up and climbs out of bed, giving the bad thoughts ample opportunity to rush in and tell me how crazy I've become over a guy I just met.

But the warmth of my confession stays with me as I listen to the sound of him going into the bathroom to clean up. And the truth of my words is still glowing inside me when he returns and gets back into bed, spooning me into his arms, and resting his heavy cast against my naked breasts.

"I'm going to take that off for you before I leave," I tell him, fingering the cast. "I just need to run into Meirton tomorrow and get some kind of oscillating tool at the hardware store."

"Meirton... can I come with you?"

"Into Meirton? Sure, I guess," I say. "You want to get out of the house?"

"I need to stop by the police station. They still have my backpack from the accident. I've been meaning to go there for a while, but..."

"The bus doesn't stop here, so you needed a ride." Belatedly I remember Meirton is where his accident took place. Where he lost his past.

"Why didn't you ask me to take you earlier?" I demand.

"Because I didn't feel like leeching off of you even more than I already am, but if you're going there already..."

Being super-careful about his cast, even though it's about to come off, I turn around in his arms.

"Hey, baby, you're not leeching off me! You're just getting better. And you've done me the service of healing here rather than someplace else. Please don't ever put it that way again. Plus, all the cooking you've been doing? So worth the price of rent, which by the way is like pennies compared to what I'll be paying in Seattle."

I can't see him in the dark, but I can sense his agitation in the way he pulls me closer, like he's afraid of losing me even though I'm right here.

"I like doing for you, Doc," he says. "Taking care of you. Making sure you're fed and fucked everyday. But I want to do more for you. Provide for you."

I huff out a laugh. "Baby, I'm a doctor! I don't need providing for."

"I don't know about that. I saw your student loan bill on the counter the other day."

I grimace. "Yeah, well, that bill is kind of intense. But trust me, I'll be all right financially. I don't want you worrying about my stuff. I'm the only one allowed to worry in this relationship, got that?"

It's a joke, but he doesn't laugh like he usually would. We sit there in the dark, and this time it's me who can practically hear him thinking.

I'm not surprised he hasn't fallen asleep when he eventually speaks up a few minutes later. "I've got a plan brewing in my head to follow you to Seattle. You know that, right, Doc?"

No, I didn't, but I guess maybe I did, because eventually I nod and say, "Yeah."

"And when I find my way back to you, I don't want it to be like this. You making money. Me not bringing anything in. I want us to be together, make a life together. I want you to forget I was ever anybody's patient."

His hope, stated so sincerely, makes my heart ache. And though I wish I could let him dream, doctors simply aren't that fanciful.

"Look, I understand where you're coming from. I do. I know how it feels to want something it doesn't necessarily feel like you can have. I'm in West Virginia now because I got rejected from every other combined program I applied to. And I'm super lucky The Children's Hospital of Seattle happened to be looking for a media savvy fellow this year. But your case..."

I struggle for a way to break it to him gently. "The thing is, you can't do much without a proper form of ID. If you want to get a job, you're going to have to go through a pretty intense process. There's not much precedence out there for someone without an identity trying to apply for all the stuff people need to be employed, get health insurance, and open a bank account. In most amnesia cases, the patient has a family, or at least some form of ID to connect to a name. Cases like yours are in a legal gray area. You'll have to pick out a new name. And we'd need to get you a lawyer, someone to advocate for you so you can file for your new name. It'll be like you have to become a brand new person."

"That's fine with me," he answers, voice gritty with determination. "Whatever it takes to be with you, I'll do it."

His words are like him. So sweet. So loving. So completely insane.

"Hold on," I have to say. "You're not okay with me calling you John, but you're like 'Sure!' when I say you'll need a new name and identity in order to come work and live in Seattle with me?"

"Now you're upset about me wanting to be with you?" he asks me in the dark, his voice tight with irritation.

"I'm not upset. I'm just...confused about why you're willing to take on a whole new life when you haven't done much to recover the life you already have. I love you, but I'm also a practical person. So I'm honestly wondering if you shouldn't start seeing somebody before you make any final decisions about moving out to Seattle."

"Somebody," he repeats.

"Yes, somebody like a neuropsychologist."

John's arms stiffen around me. "I already saw a head doctor in the hospital. It didn't help too much."

"I'm not talking about a psychotherapist. I mean the kind of specialist we don't have at UWV/Mercy. A neuropsychologist could assist you with your thinking skills, assess your recent behavior, and help you emotionally process what you're going through."

John's arms were stiff before, but now they drop all the way down. "You're using a lot of fancy words to say you think I need to go see somebody because the way I feel about you is crazy."

"No, the way *I* feel about *you* is crazy!" I shoot back. "I have no excuse. But you have a TBI, and that means—"

"I'm not crazy. I love you. Why can't you accept that? Why can't you just let me love you?" he demands, his voice so even, he might as well be yelling for all the angry emotion I can tell he's holding back.

"Because my specialty is cancer. And I've seen what happens when people deny what's really going on. When they don't take the time to process it. And I can't tell you how many parents— even the ones with excellent insurance—refuse to let their child see a therapist and end up letting them die without any real sense or understanding of what's happening to them..." I don't realize I'm crying until I can't speak anymore.

"Doc? Doc?" he says, sounding alarmed.

A light switches on and the dark is replaced by John's worried face.

"What's going on?" he asks, frowning as he uses his good hand to wipe the tears off my face.

I shake my head. "Nothing...it's stupid."

"Fuck that, Doc. I said we were talking after I put you under me. And you ain't under me no more. So talk."

I don't want to talk about it. Any of it. But then suddenly, that's all I'm doing. Talking. "Ronnie Greenwell died last night. I came into the hospital to do rounds with my attending, and they were like, 'Sorry, she went into a coma and stopped breathing." And my attending told her mom what happened. But her mom wanted to talk to me because I'm black, and she wanted to hear it from a black doctor. And I tried to explain it to her, but she just kept saying, 'You said she could go home. You said she could go home.' Which wasn't what we'd said. The only hospice with an open bed is in Pittsburgh, and we'd said she could go home until we found Ronnie something closer to where her mother works in Ohio. I tried to explain this, but Ronnie's mom didn't understand, and I couldn't make her understand. And Ronnie's not Chanel, but it was hard, because they had the same kind of cancer. And I used to be like Ronnie's mother. I used to not understand what happened to Chanel either, but now I do. I understand exactly what happens when you can't find a bone marrow match because your kid's African-American, and the chemo stops working, and there's nothing you can do other than make someone who really shouldn't be dying comfortable while they die. And usually knowing why it's happening makes it better. But today it didn't make it better. Her mom kept scream-ing, 'I want to take her home! I want to take my baby home!' At one point, all I could do was hold her and tell her, 'She's already home. I'm sorry, but Ronnie's already gone home.' Falling back on my mom's religious platitudes instead of this degree I upended my life for. But I had to tell her that sometimes medi-cine just doesn't work. Sometimes it's completely useless. Just like my degree!"

"Ah, Doc…" He presses a kiss into the top of my head. "You lost one patient, but you're saving lives, too. Your degree ain't useless. Now who is Chanel?" he asks softly.

"My little sister," I whisper, finally discussing the thing I never talk about. *Never fucking again*, I'd sworn to Sandy when she tried to make me. "She died of ALL—acute lymphocytic leukemia—the year before I left for college. She's actually the reason I applied to five-year med schools—why I dropped out of ValArts. But Ronnie reminded me of her. Not a lot. Just enough that I guess I'm feeling it a little more than I should right now."

"A child died," he says, knuckling my cheek. "I don't care what you signed up for, Doc. You got the right to be sad about it. I'm sorry that little girl died. She deserved better than that. So did your little sis."

My face crumples with the truth of his words. "Yes, yes...they both did."

He holds me while I cry for all the lives cut too short by this disease. For all the brave little girls who will never grow up to become the strong women I know they would have been, could have been.

He lets me cry my heart out, rubbing my back with his cast. And only when I'm done does he speak again. "Alright...I understand why tonight went the way it did. But next time something like this happens, remember, that's not us. You got something weighing on your heart, you tell me as soon as you walk in the door. Even when you're in Seattle, I want you to call me first thing when anything gets to bothering you. Okay?"

"Okay," I answer, voice small.

"You promise? I want us to be one of those couples who know how to talk to each other."

"I promise," I agree with a watery laugh. Then I ask, "Couples who talk to each other. Is that old or new?"

"New," he answers, voice a little hollow. "Definitely new. But I want us to be new."

Is it weird that I understand exactly what he's trying to say? That I've felt like a completely new person ever since he came into my life? That I want us to stay new, too, even though I know he'll eventually find out about my past?

He reaches over and turns off the light, but still keeps me cradled against his chest in the dark. And it's when he's holding me like this with no sexual intent whatsoever that I truly understand how deep I'm in with this man. How truly and sincerely I meant every word I said in the heat of our passion.

God, what am I going to do a few days from now when it's time to get on the plane to California? I can't take him with me. But how am I going to leave him behind?

13

*L*ike a scream from the past, my dad calls the next day right at our mercilessly negotiated hour.

"You get my email?" he asks in lieu of a hello when I answer the new special phone.

"Yes, Dad, I got Mom's email."

My dad won't so much as touch a computer or even deal with the email app on his smart phone. My mom, Cassie, handles all of that for him. But Dad always insists on referring to it like he sent it himself.

He must realize I'm in no mood for his bullshit this morning, because he concedes, "Mommy said she sent you the ticket yesterday morning and you still ain't said nothing. You know it wasn't cheap."

"Whatever, Dad. It's a one-way ticket. Stop being a cheap, bitch," I answer in my snottiest tone. But then my voice softens as I admit, "One of my kids died yesterday and it really took a lot out of me."

Dad pauses on the other end of the line. My sister, my job—and especially little kids dying at my job just like my sister did—are all on the list of things we aren't ever supposed to discuss.

But Dad recovers in his typical fashion. "That's why you don't need to be messing around with them sick kids in the first place. You out there watching Chanel die over and over again. How you doing anybody any fucking good with that shit?"

"Okay, Dad," I say with a sigh, steering us back to the main topic. "So it's the first day Mom's been out of town. You know the first day's always the worst. Curt will be back in a couple of months, and I'll be there by the end of the week, so you can disparage my job all you want then."

"Fuck you and Curt, always throwing them big words around. Trying to psychoanalyze me and shit. Your mama's lucky I don't run up in some other ho while she out of town. You know how many bitches round here looking to upgrade me?"

"Yes, you're very handsome, Dad, and you've still got it going on. You should totally cheat on Mom just to prove that. And eat more red meat while you're at it. Oh and maybe start drinking too much on top of all the weed you smoke."

"Fuck you, bitch! I was missing you before I heard your voice. But you think this is why I had kids, so you could call me and come at me like this? Fuck all you ungrateful bitches!"

"First of all, you called me. Second of all, just how many hos do you plan to acquire for this thought experiment of yours? One? Two? You think three would be enough to get Mom to leave you?" I ask, knowing this question will set him off even worse.

My dad cusses me out for a full minute before abruptly hanging up, because he's got better things to do than fuck around on the phone with an ungrateful little shit like me.

So yes, a typical phone conversation with my dad, who only sprinkles regular words into his steady cuss stream as flavoring. And who after twenty-nine years of marriage, still has the nerve to miss the hell out of my mom whenever she leaves, but pretends she and him aren't like the most solid couple on earth —especially by California standards. He's the type who'll send a "not cheap" ticket to West Virginia, so his daughter can fly home to accompany him to the one event my mother can't attend with him this year, but refuses to put a dime toward my medical career because he truly believes the whole thing is ridiculous and morbid.

Now that I think about it, I shouldn't be surprised that the first time I fell hard for somebody, he ends up being made up of a million contradictions. Seriously, look at how I was raised!

Speaking of whom...John pads into the kitchen in nothing but his black sweatpants and presses a sleepy kiss into my temple before saying, "Hey, Doc. You sleep good?"

"Really good," I answer, pocketing the special phone in my knee-length kimono and continuing with my original task of making us breakfast. All that's left is to pour the almond milk, but I find myself feeling like this offering isn't good enough.

I mean, it's fine for a busy, single doctor. But not so much for a woman on the verge of leaving behind the man she...my heart gives a little shiver just thinking about it...loves. The first man she's *ever* loved in this way.

When I sit down at the coffee table with him and our bowls of cereal, I find myself saying, "I bet I can do better than this for breakfast tomorrow. Maybe I'll see if I can pick up some frozen blueberries when we're in Meirton, and some applesauce. I could make us Blueberry Oatmeal Waffles..."

John shakes his head and continues eating. Fist over spoon with his elbow up. "I'm good with cereal, Doc. You don't have to go and do anything fancy for me. Who were you talking to earlier?"

I crook my head, confused.

"On the phone. I heard you talking to someone when I woke up."

"Oh, that was my dad," I answer. Strange, less than an hour has passed but that phone call already feels like it happened long ago. Like it came from a galaxy far, far away on a different time continuum. "He just wanted to make sure I got my plane ticket for my California visit."

"To visit your family back in California," he says in a way that makes me think he's my family in West Virginia, even though that's not probably not what he meant.

I nod. "Dad's getting kind of antsy. Both my brother and my mother are out of town, and he's one of those guys who doesn't do well on his own. It's kind of a long story."

One I don't remotely feel like explaining.

"So you done any thinking about it yet?"

"About what?"

"Introducing me to your family."

I go completely still.

"And I've scared you again."

"No, no..." I insist. "But, see, my family is a lot. I mean, we're really close, but we're not like normal families. We're kind of crazy. Well a lot crazy. *A lot*—a lot. I know you don't think your feelings will change, but I really feel like it would be better if we um...wait."

"Until my memory returns?"

"Or until we've known each other a lot longer than six weeks," I counter.

I grab our dishes and carry them to the sink before he can take the conversation any further, though. Then I rinse off the dishes, doing my best to ignore all the, "What happens when...?" floating around our relationship.

What happens when I leave West Virginia for good? What happens when he gets his memory back?

I rinse out our bowls, but end up lingering at the sink long after I've switched off the water. Why does the simplest relationship that's ever happened to me have to become so complicated as soon as I leave this state?

But I'm not allowed to linger with my thoughts for too long. He comes up behind me, wraps his arms around my waist, and rests his chin on my shoulder. His hospital beard has become a full-on beard now.

"Wanna get a razor while we're in Meirton?" I ask him, stroking the fuzz with one hand. Changing the subject.

His answer: "Whatever you want me to do, I'll do, Doc. You know I'll do anything you want. But if it's up to me, I'd just as soon keep it."

I chuff at his unusual brand of acquiescence. My possessor. My thrall.

"No, do what you want," I answer. "If you want to keep it, keep it."

We stand there together, looking out the window towards the nature preserve where we'd be doing yoga if it wasn't Saturday. Our agreed upon day off from exercise, work, and pretty much anything else that doesn't involve us spending time together.

Had I only been kidding myself about how deep I was getting into this thing with him over the past month? It seriously feels now like we've been a couple from the start. My whole life I've only gone into relationships after putting in a lot of practical thought. Our connection, what we said to each other last night in and out of the heat of the moment; I'm not sure how to process any of it this morning.

"I'm not trying to scare you, Doc," he says, voice sober, as if he's read my thoughts.

I sink further back into his embrace. Grateful for him. Confused by him.

"I know," I answer. "This is just so..." I seize upon the word in a flash of inspiration, "*New*. It's all new to me, too. I mean, my best friend Sola kind of fell fast for her husband. But she was a drama major, and I'm a doctor. I never thought I could feel like this for anyone."

I'm making some valid points here, but I can feel him grinning against the side of my neck.

"Why are you smiling? How is this funny?"

"You thinking about becoming my wife someday, Doc?"

"No, I'm just saying..."

But he cuts me off, turning me inside his arms and silencing me with a tender kiss to my forehead. "You have permission to think those thoughts," he says, knuckling my face as he looks down at me. "Them are the kind of thoughts I like."

"I'm not—"

But he kisses me again until I forget to protest. Until I forget to think. Until I forget how doomed our love may very well be. At least for a little while.

14

$\mathcal{M}$eirton isn't exactly a city, or even a small town. It's more a collection of brick buildings and maybe a hundred or so houses gathered around one main street. However, it's big enough to have a local police station, and most importantly, a hardware store.

After dropping John off at the station, I find what I need at the family-owned store. But by the time I check out, I'm already thinking twice about my plan to meet John at the town's only diner for lunch.

The hardware store cashier isn't mean, but he does seem awfully confused by a black woman coming into his store to buy an oscillating saw.

"You shopping for Father's Day?" he asks me, voice suspicious.

Then he looks even more confused when I tell him I'm a doctor over at UWV/Mercy and need the tool to cut off my boyfriend's cast.

He frowns me all the way out the door, and I'm relieved to pass the time until I'm supposed to meet John at a cozy little independent bookstore next to the shop.

Sipping on green tea, I buy a Karin Slaughter novel I haven't read yet, and it feels a little like serendipity when I spot a baby name book on my way to the cash register.

The lady behind the cash register perks up when she sees the titles of my two books. "Oh, so you're expecting a baby! I should have known. You have that glow about you."

"No," I answer with a laugh, though she's strangely not the only person who's accused me of glowing. A few days ago, my attending straight up asked if I was seeing somebody. I'd demurred and shifted to the topic of the research I'd be doing in Seattle in the hopes that would put her off her question.

"It's for a friend," I tell the cashier for the same reason. To avoid any more questions. To avoid labeling John before I leave him behind.

"Oh, well then! Congratulations to her," the cashier says. "Strange, I usually have such a good instinct about these things. Knew my sister was having a boy before she even opened her mouth to tell me she was pregnant. My mama swears I'm psychic."

I don't have the heart to break down all the scientific evidence against the existence of psychic powers. Or to tell her the glow is due to the fact that I've spent the last four weeks getting sexed beyond my wildest dreams by the sweetest, hottest, most understanding man I've ever known.

No wonder I'm grinning from ear to ear when I enter the diner where we agreed to meet. The place looks like it hasn't been renovated since it's founding back in the sixties, when Meirton was a major coal town. And yes, as a matter of due course, tinny mullet rock is playing on the speakers overhead.

But the waitress behind the counter greets me with a happy, "Hey, hon! Sit anywhere you want."

So though it's doubtful I'll find much of a vegan selection in a place like this, I feel comfortable enough to find an empty booth next to the window. But then I frown when I glance at my watch. It's ten minutes past the time we agreed to meet and John's still not here.

"How's it going?" I text him.

"Good. Almost done. I'll be there in a few."

"What can I get you, hon?" asks the same waitress who greeted me, coming up to the table with an order pad. She looks like she'd be perfectly cast in the role of a weathered, small-town waitress with frosted blond hair.

I order John the meatiest thing on the menu and tell her I'll be eating the salad that comes with it, so please bring them both out at the same time. Then I pick up my phone to check my brother and mom's Twitter feeds.

My mother is having "an inspiring time" on her sermon tour across America. And apparently Curt just killed it as BuhBouncye, a taller and plumper version of the Queen B, in a Montreal nightclub last night. Looking over his feed, my heart lets go of a little pang because I didn't even know he was working on a new character. Strange, I'd come to West Virginia to get away from my family, and I'd chosen Seattle because it was close, but not too close to them. But now even that compromise doesn't feel like enough. Because the closer I move back to them, the farther I'll be moving away from John.

"Hey, Doc," John drops into the booth seat across from me.

"Hi!" I quickly switch the phone off and smile at the backpack he's carrying. "Mission accomplished?"

He nods, but looks tense. "Yeah. The police had a few more questions for me before they'd give me back my bag, though. Sorry I'm late."

"A few questions must have been a lot," I observe, glancing at my watch. "I dropped you off over an hour ago."

"They got a menu?" he asks, looking around.

I'm about to tell him I already ordered when our conversation is interrupted by the arrival of the waitress with our food... and the unholy sound of several motorcycle engines.

Both John and I turn to look out the diner's plate glass window just in time to view something I've only ever seen on TV. A white motorcycle gang, in what I can't help but refer to as "full costume" after growing up in L.A. and my one semester at performing arts college. They look straight out of central casting with flat black helmets, patched up denim vests, and a ton of tattoos. A few of them even have face tats.

Maybe I'm just imagining things, but every single one of them seems to be staring at us as they cruise by on their bikes. Not Harleys, I can see from here. And the lack of brand identification let's me know they are in fact a real motorcycle gang, and not actors hired to look like one.

I watch them pull up to a dive bar a bit further down the street. And my heart pinches a little less tightly when they start removing their helmets and filing into the club. Many of them are shouting so loudly, I can hear them from where I'm sitting through the plate glass.

"The New Rebels," the waitress who brought us our food says, drawing our attention back to her. "They're based a few towns over, but sometimes they come over here to drink at that bar down the street. Damn nuisance if you ask me. Just hope they don't come in here looking for food."

As if called forward by her wish not to have them in her establishment, two of the bikers make their way back up the street and crash through the diner door. Stomping in their big boots toward a small table right across from us.

"That section isn't open," the waitress says, not bothering to cloak her irritation.

"It is now, sweet tits," the bigger of the two men answers. He points at John's plate. "I'll take the same as him."

"Me too," his companion says. He's skinny with a paunch. Probably in his late twenties, I think to myself, but with the dark, under eye circles and patchy skin of a man twice his age. Twenty going on forty because of what I can only assume are a number of shitty lifestyle choices.

The waitress huffs away, but I have a feeling she'll be a lot faster with their order than she was with ours. At least, I hope so.

A chill runs down my back when they both turn in their seats and openly stare at us. My earlier sense, about this maybe not being the best town for an interracial lunch outing, comes back strong. And I peek over at John to see how he's handling their aggressive double stare.

John doesn't look remotely intimidated. In fact, he returns their hard stares with one of his own. "Can I help you?" he asks, flat and mean.

The bigger biker has the word "PRESIDENT" patched across the right side of his denim vest, and I've watched enough episodes of *Devil Riders* to know that most likely means he's the leader of the gang that pulled up to the bar. He looks from John to me. Back to him, then back to me again.

"Heard you were at the police station earlier, friend," he says to John while continuing to squint hard at me.

Cold dread seizes my chest. This is bad, and only going to get worse if we stay here. I throw a twenty down on the table and scoot out of the booth.

"C'mon let's go," I tell John.

"We're not done eating yet," John answers, his eyes never leaving the bikers.

"I know, but I'm not feeling well and I'd really like to go. Right now. Please," I whisper.

"You don't feel well, Doc?" John asks, worry replacing the hard edge in his tone.

I nod, happy to lie if it means avoiding what I know will be a confrontation. A really bad one.

"Okay," he says, as if my welfare matters more than anything else in his world. "C'mon, let's go."

But before we can move forward, the biker president stands up. "Would you look at that?" he observes to the skinny biker with a snicker. "His nigger bitch is scared of us. What'd we ever do to her?"

And just like that, John's quiet deference to my supposed sickness disappears. In an instant he's launching himself at the biker president with the reflexes of a crazed and dangerous animal.

"John, no!" I scream.

But he's already throwing a punch before I'm done begging him not to. His fist slices across the biker president's face so hard, blood spews from his meaty nose.

So hard, the man falls right at the other biker's feet.

The skinny biker's mouth drops open at the sight of his leader groaning on the floor. But then his face goes nasty and hard... right before he pulls a very big gun from beneath his jacket.

My heart screeches to a stop, even as behind me, chaos erupts. The mullet rock playing overhead is completely drowned out by a soundtrack of patrons yelling, "He's got a gun!!!!" and running toward the door.

I don't run. Though I grew up in Compton with strict instructions about what to do when guns were whipped out, I find myself unable to take any kind of cover, unable to leave John with these violent thugs. I'm too afraid for him on several different levels, starting with his head injury and ending with potentially fatal gun shot wound.

"Shoot him!" the fallen biker yells from the floor. "Show 'im what happens when a nigger-fucker messes with The New Rebels!"

"John, don't!" I shout when he takes a step toward the huge biker, good fist curled tight. "Please don't, baby..."

This time, John actually seems to hear me. He raises both hands in the universal sign of surrender. "Okay, okay…" he starts to say. "I don't want any more trouble—"

—only to whip his good hand out, faster than a snake. He snatches the gun out of the younger biker's hand. At the same time, he places a sneaker-clad foot on the neck of the biker he knocked to the ground. Effectively holding one biker down while holding the other at gun point.

Yet his voice sounds calm as a summer day when he says, "Now, I think you two owe my lady an apology."

"I'd fucking let you put a bullet in me before I ever say sorry to a nig—" the biker president starts to choke out.

But he's interrupted by the skinny biker's frantic, "I'm sorry! I'm sorry, ma'am. Please don't kill me, sir. Oh God, please don't kill me! I wasn't really going to use it. I swear!"

John accepts the biker's apology with a squint of his glittering blue eyes. Then he transfers the gun from the small biker to the big one. "How about you, Bubba? What you want to do here? Apologize or die?"

To his racist credit, the biker president actually seems to consider sticking to his fucked up morals for a few seconds. But I guess a gun is a helluva persuader, because he finally mumbles, "Sorry," not quite looking at me or the gun.

I try to answer them, open my mouth to diffuse the situation as best I can before the police arrive. But I don't feel right. The restaurant is hot and the world is spinning.

"Doc? Doc?" John's voice says, farther away in the distance than it should be.

That's the last thing I hear before I'm stumbling down, down...

THE NEXT THING I KNOW, I'm being shaken awake.

I open my eyes and find myself flat on my back with my legs being held in the air by the diner's waitress. Meanwhile, a para-medic I've met a few times at UWV/Mercy is shaking me awake, yelling, "Dr. Dunhill! Dr. Dunhill! Wake up, doctor. Come on back to us."

I blink, woozy and confused. "Monty?" I ask.

"Good, she's coming to." To the waitress, Monty says, "You can drop her legs now."

"Where's your uniform?" I ask when I'm free to sit all the way up.

Monty grins, glancing down at his simple short sleeve button-up and jeans ensemble.

"I was pulling up to have a bite to eat with the wife and kids when that ruckus broke out. I started hustling Shannon and the kids back to the car and then a waitress came out yelling they needed a doctor inside. So I locked the family in the car and responded to the call."

He throws a wry look at the crowd gathered behind him. Strange. All the patrons who went running as soon as a gun was drawn now seem to be back in triple fold. I can only thank the good God this isn't L.A., where the first instinct of every person in the place would have been to pull out a camera phone and roll tape.

But then I notice someone is missing from the crowd. "Where's John?" I ask, scanning the surrounding faces, none of which belong to him.

The paramedic grimaces. "I was afraid he might be telling the truth when that John Doe told the police he was here with you. They hauled him away, along with those two bikers."

"It wasn't his fault!" I start to explain. Then feeling silly, I let Monty help me all the way to my feet before explaining, "He took the gun off the biker. Oh my God, I have to go get him! Where exactly is he?"

"They took them to the jailhouse," the waitress answers. "But they didn't take any statements, so you know they won't be keeping them there long. Least not the bikers. Pretty sure they got that whole department on their meth payroll."

"Man, did he put up an unholy fuss when they took him out of there!" Monty tells me with a shake of his head. "The two bikers went without a word, but that John Doe was yelling about how he couldn't leave you here. It took three officers to get him in the car!"

"Don't call him that. He hates being called that," I snap, unable to keep the rather unprofessional peevishness out of my voice. Hey, I've already been caught out on a date with one of the hospital's former patients, why not exacerbate it with unnecessarily bitchy commands?

I grab my Virkin from a patron who was nice enough to hold it for me while I was resuscitated by an off-duty paramedic. Then I dart back to the table where I find John's backpack exactly where he left it, stuffed up against the window.

"Thank you," I call out to Monty and the waitress, but not necessarily to the huge crowd gathered around them.

"Dr. Dunhill, I'm off-duty so I don't have to report this to work," Monty says as I head toward the door. "But I should ask you a few questions before you leave—"

The diner's glass door closes, the bells ringing over Monty's due diligence. He's right. I just fainted and I should let him, at the very least, check me out. But I can't think about myself in that moment; my thoughts are only for poor John as I rush back to the same police station where I dropped him off earlier.

15

---

*T*here are a lot of great ways to spend a Saturday afternoon. Waiting around for hours for the police to release your amnesiac boyfriend from jail is not one of them.

The waitress is right about the police not pressing charges. Both bikers come out less than an hour after my arrival. Luckily the waiting area is toward the back of the station, and the men don't notice me tucked in the corner as they stride out through the station's front doors. They're both glowering, and the president's nose is swollen in a way I'd definitely insist on examining if he were anyone other than the racist asshole who landed John in jail.

The guy at reception tells me they won't be pressing charges. However, they keep John in there for hours, ignoring all my questions about due process in the meantime. Only after I threaten to call a lawyer do they finally release him.

I expect John to look as miserable as I feel when he comes through the door that separates the station from the cells in back, but all he looks is frantic.

"Doc!" he yells, running across the station to me. "Thank fuck. Are you okay?"

I nod and he gathers me tight in his arms, knuckling my cheek and kissing my temple like he hasn't seen me in a century. "You sure? When you fainted, I just about lost it. And they wouldn't let me stay with you. I've been going out of my mind. Thank God you're all right."

He holds me close with no self-consciousness at all. But I can feel the frost of all the eyes staring at us. Judging. Wondering.

"Let's just go home, okay?" I whisper.

This time I get no argument whatsoever. In fact, he takes me by the hand and leads me out of the station without so much as a backwards glance over his shoulder.

As all about me as he was in the station, he's on high alert as soon as we're back outside. We've been here so long, it's pitch black out and the night has grown frigidly cold, letting me know winter hasn't completely let West Virginia go. It's probably 80 degrees in California today, with a low of "*maybe* you'll need a cardigan."

But now I'm shivering in the zip-up fleece I wore for what I thought would be a simple errand run and lunch. John isn't wearing anything but a zip up hoodie, but he takes it off and puts it over my shoulders, even as he continues scanning the distance.

I want to tell him to keep the sweatshirt, that I'll be fine, but something about his demeanor tells me to keep quiet. That he wouldn't welcome a distraction right now.

So I let him lead the way and don't even argue when he deposits me in the passenger seat of my car and walks around to the driver's side. I'd had the sense he was barely tolerating my driving when we headed into Meirton, and my suspicions are confirmed by the way he easily depresses the start button, even though the first time I'd driven him home from the hospital he'd said, "That's new."

But he must have been paying attention, because he pushes down the brake and puts the car into drive without a hitch. We're smoothly on the road back to my place in a matter of minutes, no navigation system required.

So he knows how to drive, too, I think to myself. *And fight. And easily disarm a man with a gun.*

My cop theory is becoming more and more prominent. Maybe even FBI. But that definitely wouldn't explain why his fingerprints aren't in the system.

I make a mental note to call my best friend, Sola, as soon as I can. I haven't been exactly thrilled to tell anyone I'm embroiled in a relationship and living with a guy I've known less than two months. But today has made me realize just how far I'm in over my head.

And while I don't want to call her Russian husband, Ivan, and his family of "legitimate businessmen" shady, he did make a point of giving me his card before their wedding.

"Sola considers you family, *da*? So if ever there comes a time you are needing something or you are in any kind of trouble, you will call me."

Back then, after defying my family to get my medical degree while living three thousand miles away from them on my own, I inwardly bristled at the idea of needing anyone other than myself to solve a problem.

But I'd taken his card. And not only that, I've been carrying it around with me in my wallet ever since. Almost like I knew I'd need it someday.

And on the silent drive home, I consider making the call I never thought I'd make. Because if anyone has the resources to get to the bottom of John's mystery, it's Ivan and his powerful Russian family.

"Stay here," John says as soon as we pull into one of the parking spaces beneath my second-floor apartment.

He gets out and takes his time coming around to my side of the car. And I don't think it's a southern gentleman thing. Instead, I get the feeling he's doing an even deeper scan of the distance beyond my apartment building than he did when we left the police station.

He does eventually open the door for me, but he doesn't relax until we're inside my apartment.

"Nobody followed us," he says. "That's good."

I open my mouth, but before I can get words out, he says, "Hold on, Doc. I know you got questions. But give me that backpack. I got something to show you that I think might answer a few of them."

The backpack...I'd almost forgotten I still had it. But there it was, strung over my shoulder, right along with my Virkin.

I hand it to him silently, and he takes it, but hesitates before opening it, his intense gaze softening a little as he says, "No lies. That's what I asked you for and that's what I know you want from me. I was trying to figure out how to tell you about this at the restaurant, but them bikers showed up..."

Then he unzips the backpack and holds it wide for me to see what's inside.

My eyes saucer even wider when I see what it is. Money. So many stacks of bills and nothing else but money nestled in a simple black backpack.

I stare at the bounty, trying but failing to process what I'm looking at. And when I finally give up and look to him for answers, his face is grimmer than I've ever seen it.

"There's more than a hundred thousand dollars in there, according to the police. That's why they kept me so long for questioning, even after they questioned me twice at the hospital. They finally let me go. But them bikers showing up at the diner is a little too coincidental, if you ask me. I'm thinking they were tipped off. I told them a few times I had to go meet you at the diner. Maybe one of those officers questioning me told those bikers exactly where I was going and what I had on me. They probably had it all planned out. The big one would distract me, while the little one stole the backpack, but that wasn't exactly how it worked out."

I lower my eyes back down to stare at the money. Everything he says makes complete sense, except, "Why were you carrying around this much money before your accident? And in a backpack of all places?"

He shakes his head, looking as mystified as I am. "I don't know," he answers. Telling me the stark truth, just like he always has since the moment we met.

But right now, even the frank truth isn't enough to allay my fears.

"You should let me drive you to work and back on Monday," he mumbles. "I didn't give the police your address, and I don't think those guys were a real threat, but I want to keep you safe, Doc."

I have no idea what to say to that. What to say to any of this.

"Who are you?" The words tumble out of my mouth, choked and angry. I don't realize I'm so close to hyperventilating until I'm barely able to squeeze out, "Who the hell are you?"

He immediately drops the backpack, so much money ditched like a trash bag on the floor so he can snatch me up in his arms. Hold me, comfort me, until the wave of panic begins to subside.

"I'm sorry, Doc," he says when I finally start breathing normally again. "I know this is scary. And I'm sorry I scared you back at that diner. But I figured them guys out from the door. They weren't old. I didn't know either of them. But something about them felt... familiar. Like I knew what they were about, knew they'd be nothing but trouble. I was trying to keep you safe, but I made you faint instead. You don't know how sorry I am about that. There ain't enough apologies in the world."

I can only shake my head into his chest, both comforted and confused by his heartfelt apology. "You moved so fast. Are you, like, a cop? Or some kind of special forces? Like Jason Bourne or something?"

"I don't know," he whispers into my hair. "And I can't explain it. He pulled that gun, and it was like I went on autopilot."

"But the things you said to him." My stomach flips over, threatening to eject my breakfast and lunch at the thought of it. I don't want to say it, but I find myself whispering into his chest, "I think you really would have killed that guy if he hadn't apologized. The look in your eyes..."

"Look at me now, Doc." He takes my face, cupping it between his cast and his hand so I have to look into his eyes, which I find shining with emotion. "All I know is I was sure they were there for the backpack and they might hurt you to get it. Then I just...I can't explain it. If I could, believe me I would, if only to take that look off your face. But you look at me now, Doc. You believe me when I say I would have done anything to them to keep you safe, but I would *never* hurt you. Not in a million years. And that money..." His eyes dart to the backpack on the floor.

"That ain't my money, it's *yours*. Do whatever you want with it. Pay back your student loans, give it to the hospital, put it in the bank—I don't care. It's yours. I'm yours. Everything I have is yours. If you don't believe anything else out of my mouth, believe that. Please believe that."

It's so crazy. But I do believe him. And I'm just about to say so, when instead of words, my earlier meals come spilling out as I throw up all over the man I unequivocally love.

 ASON

M ASON'S not surprised when the president of the New Rebels calls him two days short of the month deadline he gave those failed abortions.

Ironically, he calls during a board meeting about next steps now that it's been four months since D. disappeared with the money. The burner Mason bought in West Virginia goes off just as he's thinking of saying out loud that none of this makes any sense.

SFK has used D. for bigger sells than this one. $100K just wasn't enough to stay in hiding for as long as he'd have to stay in hiding to avoid SFK's wrath. Either D. was a lot more stupid than he'd ever let on, or something else was at play here. That was exactly what Mason was thinking about saying when the West Virginia burner started beeping in his jacket pocket.

"All phones are supposed to be left outside on the table," Mason's father, the club's vice president, says with a hard look at his son.

"Not this one," Mason answers, unafraid in a way only a sergeant at arms of an infamous MC can be.

Mason ignores the disapproving stares from the other board members, flips open the burner, and says, "Yeah," as he walks out of the meeting room. He's prepared to hear some serious begging from the New Rebels prez. Begging he plans to ignore.

But instead of begging, the prez says, "I think we found your guy. I wasn't sure at first for a bunch of reasons. But he has the black backpack the old sarge said he gave him, and he took me and one of my guys down so quick, I'm sure it had to be him."

Mason stops in his tracks, all plans to kill this fake motherfucker completely forgotten. "Where did you see him? When? Tell me everything you know right fucking now."

17

*T*he hours after I throw up all over John are mostly a blur. But there a few moments that I'll remember forever—perfect and clear.

His lack of upset that I'd vomited on him for one. He simply whipped me up into his arms and carried me to the bathroom.

I remember him putting my twisted curls in an ouchless ponytail holder and telling me he'd be right back. Him leaving the room, then coming back in his boxer briefs, his soiled clothes deposited somewhere unseen.

"Tell me what you need, Doc," I remember him saying as he pressed a glass of water into my hand.

I remember how good the water tasted in my foul mouth. How I immediately felt better after the first sip.

I remember the sight of him bent down next to me, blue eyes filled with remorse.

"Not your fault," I tell him. "It's probably a..."

These are the moments I remember most: trailing off because my inner-doctor is throwing down a big red flag in the back of my mind.

She's saying that other than fainting, I've felt fine all day. Healthy and happy. Usually you see a stomach flu coming before you throw up. Also, I have no fever or any other indicator of a viral infection. In fact, I can't keep myself from eyeing John's now naked torso, regretting that I'll definitely have to sleep on the couch, which means none of the amazing sex we've been having every single night since he moved in four weeks ago.

I freeze. Not because of the medical implications of being so sex-crazy that I'm actually resenting a stomach flu for keeping me out of John's arms tonight, but because of the "every single night" part.

How is that possible? My period has always been like clockwork, and my last one ended a couple of days before John moved in.

Now my stomach is rolling for a different reason. Or maybe for the same reason it's been upset all along. What happened in Meirton. How it was so weird for someone who'd grown up in Compton, with a man who regularly bragged about his body count, to faint like that. Even weirder for someone who'd put herself through med school and managed several ER rotations without fainting once.

Then I think of that old Facebook meme, "See I knew I wasn't a weak-ass bitch!"

But I don't chuckle. I can't chuckle.

And I ask John to bring me my phone.

More blurring after that. Phone calls. A ride to the hospital, where I'm assured the on-call OB will be waiting for me with an ultrasound machine.

The sac, clear as day on the monitor screen. Then the decision that has to be made.

So much happening all at once. But all I can really remember is the look on John's face when I come out to the tiny waiting area that's usually reserved for non-spouses waiting to hear about the arrival of their newest family members.

I remember him standing up as soon as I step foot into the room, as if he's been staring at the door and waiting this whole time.

I remember thinking I've got another letter of apology to write to Shonda Rhimes now, because is there dramatic music playing in the background of my head at this moment? Yes, there is.

Until there isn't.

Until somehow John's closed the gap and I'm back in his arms.

Until everything goes quiet. And there's only words. The only words I remember from the blur that was Saturday night.

"What's going on? You all right, Doc?"

"I don't know…the ultrasound…it said I'm pregnant."

The expression on his face going from worried to stunned. I remember that.

Then me babbling on for a while about how it was uncommon to get pregnant on an IUD, but not impossible. One of the first things we learn in medical school. Even if a drug has a huge success rate, every doctor has to go in knowing there's no guarantee any given patient won't be in the remaining small percentage of people it doesn't work for. Someone has to be one of the less than eight out of every thousand women who get pregnant while using an IUD.

John's only answer to this explanation is to shake his head and say, "You were on birth control, but you're pregnant. You're pregnant with my baby?"

"Yes," I remember answering, still in a daze. "But...but...I had them take it out."

The way he freezes after I say that. The look of absolute horror on his face. I'm so confused until I realize, "Oh...no...I had them take the device out. So it wouldn't hurt the baby. I'm still..." I have to stop and catch my breath before finishing the sentence, "I'm still pregnant."

Then I wait to see what he'll say next.

18

"*I*'m coming home!" my brother hollers on the other side of phone. "I'm coming home right now!!!"

"No, Curt!" I insist on a whisper in the bathroom of our Las Vegas hotel room.

"So you call a sister up, tell her you pregnant, and you about to break the news to Daddy tomorrow, but no, you don't want Cee-Cee to come home. Bitch, you is out your monkey-ass mind if you think that is even a request I'm capable of granting!"

"Curt, please don't make me regret calling you instead of Sola," I whisper into the phone.

"Why you whispering?" Curt demands. Then before I can answer, "I wish you would call that Guatemalan bitch first. I wish I could flash forward in that alternative timeline just to see how far up your ass my heel would be if you called all the way over to fucking Russia before you called me in Chicago."

"Seriously, Curt, please talk to me like a regular human being. I really need my brother right now. Not Cee-Cee..."

He must hear the real desperation in my tone because his voice drops a dramatic octave, and the next voice I hear is the one of the man who told me he would always be my brother, right before he left for a tour to perform as Glammette Jackson in his first headliner drag show.

"Okay, Nitra, I'm here for you, baby girl. I'm listening," he says, just as C-Mello's heavily gangsterized version of "We Are Family" starts playing in the background of our call.

"Isn't that your cue?"

"Them bitches can wait. Talk to me."

"It's nothing. I just need your blessing."

"My blessing for what?"

I bite my lip and look down at the thin wedding band on my hand, thinking back to earlier in the day.

"Is it okay if I use some of your money to buy something?" John asked as we crossed into the Eastside Las Vegas city limits.

"It's not my money, it's yours," I repeated for like the umpteenth time on our multi-day trip across America.

"So that's a yes?"

"It's a 'do whatever you want with it,'" I answered, unable to keep the irritation out of my voice. Seriously, the closer we got to California, the bitchier I felt.

The prospect of having to introduce John to Dad. And even worse, having to confess everything about my past. My stomach was rolling for reasons that had nothing to do with my first trimester.

"Woods," John said, tearing me away from my thoughts.

"What?" I asked, coming back to the boiling hot Las Vegas afternoon. We planned to stop here for the night after four days on the road. A long trip by anyone's standards, but not nearly long enough as far as I was concerned. There were less than twenty-four hours between now and when John discovered who I really was.

"You said I needed to pick out a new name, and I like being out in the woods. So I decided that's going to be my new name."

"Woods," I repeated with a little smile. "I like that."

He grinned over at me. "For real, Doc? You could see yourself being with a man named Woods for the rest of your life?"

"Sure," I answered, my mood much lighter because he smiled at me. "At least until you remember your real name."

The smile faded then. And I was struck once more by how little concern he seemed to have about his focal amnesia.

"Woods," I started to say, a soft introduction to a heavy song. "That's something we're going to have to deal with when we get to Seattle. Remember what I said last week about seeing somebody?"

He nodded. "Yeah, I do, Doc. And I'll do it. I'll do anything you want me to do. You know that, right?"

This love of his...like ten different red flags from my psych classes go off in my brain, even as my heart melts.

"I know," I answered, giving him the simplest reply I can, because everything in our lives will be so much more complicated after he meets my dad. And Sandy. Oh God, Sandy...

The only thing that kept me from having a low grade panic attack at just the thought of how tomorrow will go down is the man across from me declaring, "All right, my name's Woods from now on. That's settled. On to the next topic. You know you've got to become my wife before the baby's born, right? This ain't something we're going to have to discuss tonight in bed, is it?"

Discuss tonight. His version of a threat...and of settling seemingly every argument.

But then he sobered and said, "Seriously, Doc. I want this settled before I meet your daddy. Say you'll marry me."

My breath hitched as I realized this is it. He's asking me to marry him. For real. Like, this is a real life proposal happening right now as we drive through Las Vegas.

"Technically, you're not allowed to drive this car," I answered on my choked breath. "Much less marry me without any kind of ID."

"So if I had some ID you'd marry me?" he asked.

"If you had some ID, you'd remember who you are and then maybe you wouldn't want to marry me. Especially if you already have someone waiting for you back home," I answered.

He lifted my knuckles to his lips. "There ain't nobody but you, Doc."

I shook my head. Looked north, even though my mind is casting south. In the direction of wherever he got his accent from, and the possible real girlfriend who has no clue where he is.

As if reading my mind, he said, "You keep wondering if I have a girl out there, scared I forgot somebody important. But you're new to me, Doc. And these feelings I got for you, they're new, too. It ain't just that I can't remember, it's that I can't fucking imagine feeling about somebody else the way I feel about you. So stop feeling guilty about a woman who don't exist. There's only you, Doc. I know in my soul there ain't nobody else."

His words sped up my heart. How could they not? But...

"Getting a new ID won't be easy. Remember our conversation about the lawyer? And even with a lawyer, Seattle's going to want you to at least do due diligence. Your patient file is pretty inconclusive as far as your mental health is concerned."

He sifted through my words and came back with, "You're trying to say you think I'm crazy. Crazy for feeling the way I do about you. Crazy for wanting to marry you."

"No, I'm not saying that," I answered, though obviously I'd been thinking it. "What I am saying is TBIs change people, and we should get you more tests when we get to Seattle since they did such a half-ass job back in West Virginia because you weren't covered by..."

I stopped, suddenly realizing, "Yes, we should get married! That's exactly what we should do. As soon as we can get you a new social security number. That way you'll have excellent health insurance and access to the best doctors."

"Doc, I only got about four months of real memories, but I'm going to tell you right now: that is the least romantic marriage proposal acceptance there ever was."

"Sorry," I said, seeing why he might feel that way. "But I'm a doctor. Hospital shows notwithstanding, a lot of us can be, um, weirdly analytical. To us, solving the problem is often more romantic than planning the wedding."

He considered me for a long hard moment, then let me off with a lazy grin. "That's all right. I'll take it."

Then he made a sharp right.

"Where are we going," I asked as Waze busily recalculated the route on his smartphone screen.

"You'll see," he answered as he made another sharp right into a strip mall parking lot.

He quickly found a spot, and when I looked up, there was a jewelry store looming over our little car, our little relationship, so big it blocked out the sun.

~

AND A FEW HOURS LATER, I'm on the phone with my brother, asking for his blessing while looking down at my brand new wedding band.

"Here's my promise to you, Dr. Anitra Dunhill," Woods said, as he slipped the simple silver band I picked out onto my finger, right there in front of the sales person standing behind the glass counter.

Then he turned to the seller who'd rung up our humble purchase, all while peering at me in a suspicious manner.

"Know what? I'll take this same one in a men's size for me too."

Woods may very well be crazy. He insisted on wearing his own wedding ring, even after I told him most men don't wear a ring before they're officially married. At least, not unless they're Irish.

"Then I guess I must be Irish," Woods answered as we made our way to the cheap hotel room I'd booked for us on Priceline. "Because that's exactly what I'm going to do. I don't want any confusion about my intentions when I meet your daddy..."

"That is fucked up romantic, sis," my brother declares on the other end of the line, after I finish telling him the story. "And you say he good in bed, too? I don't care if he crazy. You got big brother's blessing, and a 'go head with your bad self, Miss Nitra!'"

A host of annoyed deep voices sound in the background, and I can hear the crowd chanting angrily.

"Thank you, Curt. You better get to your show," I say.

"Either that or go troll the local ERs for an amnesia victim. You got me wondering now. Though I am sad I won't be there when you introduce him to Daddy."

I groan at the mention of the meeting. "Please don't call him and tell him about this," I say, knowing how those two love to gossip. "I really don't want to give him time to formulate a reaction to the news."

"Yeah, you probably right about that. Sandy said she made sure there weren't no more real guns in the house when we moved, but you never know with him."

"Okay, bye Cee-Cee..." I say with a real chill going down my back. "Love you."

"Mwah, love you too, Nee-Nee. Now let me stuff this dick back into my hot pants and go wave these fake titties!"

I laugh, amused as always by my brother's refusal to take anything in life that isn't death seriously. "Break both them legs," I tell him, before getting off the phone, already knowing he will.

Then I go back out to the hotel room. To the real life scenario that's even crazier than anything my brother could possibly come up with for his show.

I find Woods already in bed. In typical fashion, he's found an old movie for us to watch.

"*West Side Story*," I say, recognizing it with a fond grin.

"Is that what it's called?" he answers, holding out his now cast-free arm so I can get in bed with him.

"Who were you talking to in the bathroom?" he asks after I curl up beside him.

So he'd heard. Or guessed.

"My brother," I answer.

"You tell him about us?"

"Yeah, everything."

"And what'd he say?"

"Basically, go'on girl. But he's a drag queen so, you know, his response to this is going to be different from most."

"A drag queen..."

"A man who dresses and performs as a woman. He also dates other men, but never when he's dressed as a woman. It's kind of complicated, but he's one of the best friends I have in the world, other than Sola," I explain. And then I wait. For him to say something bad about my brother. For him to give me an excuse to stop being crazy about him.

But after a moment he says, "I do recall seeing somebody like that on one of them reality shows when I was in the hospital. I remember thinking, that it was definitely new."

"New good? Or new bad?"

"He's your brother and you love him, so he's got to be new good, unless something he's doing is hurting you in some way," he answers, as if feelings of sexual orientation are a simple matter of family loyalty.

Maybe on a base level they are to him. But I have to admit, "You're taking this way better than my mother did. She's an evangelical pastor. Is that concept old or new?"

"Old," he answers after a moment of thought. And strangely, this is when he chooses to tense up. Then he says, "We got a long drive tomorrow. Mind if we just watch the movie?"

No, I don't. But there's one more thing I've got to deal with before we get to L.A.

"Ah, John—I mean Woods. How would you feel about me introducing you as my husband tomorrow? It will, ah..." I struggle to come up with a good excuse, and end up settling for, "...be easier if everyone thinks we're already married."

Now he drops all pretense of watching the movie to look down at me with a pleased smile. "Doc, I already consider you becoming my wife a matter of bullshit paperwork. I'd be honored to be introduced to your daddy with my true intentions in mind."

I have to shake my head at his easy acceptance of my request. "You're like a southern gentleman on steroids."

"I don't know what that means."

"It means I love you, Woods," I say out loud, while inside I can only hope he'll still love me when I tell him the truth tomorrow.

But tonight, I decide not to think about tomorrow yet. I curl up inside the shelter of his arm and play with his Irish-but-not-really wedding ring before falling asleep while Tony sings about instantly falling in love with a girl he just met. One named Maria.

As INTIMATE AS sex was with John before, it's somehow even more intimate with Woods that night.

He wakes me from my doze with a gentle press of his lips to my forehead.

"Did you like the movie?" I ask, my voice husky with sleep.

"Yeah, Doc, I liked it. I liked it a whole lot," he answers, his voice husky with something else.

He undresses me slowly. Easing everything off my body with deliberate care. Then he palms one breast as he lowers his head to the other, suckling so tenderly, it feels like more of a promise than a kiss.

Everything he does to me feels like a promise that night. The way he lowers me back onto the bed before slinging one leg over his shoulder, and worships my pussy with his mouth until I'm coming so hard, I find myself crying out his new name.

I'm still coming, my pussy trembling, when he braces himself above me and fills me with his bare cock. Even after a week, we're still deeply aware of all the new sensations. Deeply aware of what this means to the both of us to be together this way.

Tonight his claiming goes even slower than usual. Deep, dragging strokes that give me plenty of time to accept who is the one in control, and who is the one being treasured in this relationship.

Woods, I've noticed over the last few weeks, is a bit of a talker when it comes to sex. But tonight he takes me quietly with the lights of Vegas shining into our room, brighter than the moon. Tonight he tells me everything both he and I are feeling without uttering a word.

And it feels like the most inevitable thing in the world when we break the quiet together, his cum coating my sex as the orgasm crests over us both. Two perfectly matched stars in a universe of love.

19

*I*s it any wonder I'm so relaxed on the drive to L.A.? No more throwing up. Just a lot of shared smiles and hands clasped over the center console as we make the relatively short journey out of Las Vegas to L.A. and then crawl through the heavy traffic of Downtown, before we're finally able to get off the highway at Forest Lawn Drive, and then into more congestion on Barham.

"Welcome to L.A.," I half apologize.

"How did you live here full time?" Woods mutters, eyeing the congested road in front of us grumpily. This street is wider than some West Virginia highways, but completely stuffed with cars. Like anyone dealing with L.A. traffic for the first time, or even for the hundredth, I can tell he doesn't love all the stop-and-go we've encountered since getting into town.

Definitely not the time to tell him, I decide, thinking how unfair it would be to drop my bomb while he's trying to navigate the lunch time chaos of the Barham pass.

However, Woods frowns when Waze finally tells him to turn left off of Barham into a much quieter scene. Roads that become narrower the higher you go, lined on each side with expensive cars. Audis, Teslas, Range Rovers, Maseratis, Porsches, Maybachs, and just about every other car with a six-figure price tag currently on the road.

Woods squints at the Waze app on his phone, which he hasn't really trusted since we left West Virginia.

"Are you sure we're going to the right place?" he asks as my Prius makes the long climb toward the address I keyed into his phone. "This isn't exactly how I imagined Compton would look from your descriptions and the pictures I saw on the internet."

"Um...actually Compton is where I used to live until I was, like, twelve. It's a lot further south. Then we moved here. Right now we're in the Hollywood Hills."

Woods's brow pulls low as the houses get bigger and bigger. "So you were struggling to make ends meet back in West Virginia, but your family lives here? In one of these big houses?" he repeats. "Are they, uh... live-in servants or something like that?"

I grimace. "No, it's a long story. But I guess you could say my dad didn't support my decision to move to West Virginia and become a doctor. Really didn't support it, in fact. And Mom is old-school. Like one of those women who believes whatever the man says, goes. So I ended up having to do it on my own dime."

He digests this information and opens his mouth to ask another question. But then the nav system interrupts with a command to turn right onto to the small access road leading to our house. And then he's left without words, because he's too busy ogling the white stucco mansion sitting just beyond a double gate with two microphones sculpted into its iron bars.

We stop at the gate, because according to Waze, we've reached our final destination.

Woods stops the car, letting it settle into a silent electric idle as he continues to stare at the house in front of us.

"*This* why you didn't want to bring me home to meet your family at first?" he asks me. "You're ashamed of me, because I don't have nothing to my name but a backpack full of money and your daddy's got all of this? Is that why we're pretending to be married already, because you know they ain't going to accept me as the father of your baby unless they think we're already hitched?"

Woods's tone is so sincere, his expression so hurt, his questions so valid given how little I've told him of my past. Which is probably why I come off as a straight up bitch when I burst out laughing.

"No, no! That's not it at all," I answer. "If anything, my dad's going to love you. Like love you way too much, and then immediately try to use you."

Woods just shakes his head at me. "Call me dumb, Doc, but I'm not even close to understanding any of the words coming out of your mouth."

"I know," I answer, sobering. Then I take a deep breath because this is it. No more stalling. I need to come clean with him about everything.

"Before we go in, there's something I have to tell you," I say, peeping up at him. "Actually, it's a big something about my family..."

But just as I'm about to spill the beans and share everything I didn't tell him back in West Virginia, the microphone gates part and my larger-than-life father comes out dressed in boxer shorts, a white tank top, and a velvet robe.

Of course he's holding his smart phone—the exact same make and model as my latest special phone—at chest-level. And he makes sure we're fully lined up in the shot before yelling, "What the hell, Nitra! You got married to some random white nigga in Vegas and you didn't tell me?!?!"

20

*O*h, eff the internet. I'd been living so long in a place where every other person and their child does not have a smart phone, I'd forgotten how everywhere it could be at all times here in Los Angeles.

As romantic as yesterday was, I now curse our impromptu trip to the jewelry store. I *knew* that sales clerk was up to no good the way he was eyeing me. Yet, I'm incapable of feeling violated. Not after how I grew up.

Right now, I only feel worried. Mostly about Woods, who's already out of the car and getting between me and my father like a Southern wall.

"Excuse me, sir, I'm not sure who you are, but I cannot and will not allow you talk to my wife that way."

Dad looks over John's shoulder at me, popping his eyes and, because he's my dad, asking out loud what most folks would only think, "Nitra, is this nigga serious?"

Then he lowers the phone to whisper-ask me, "Did you not explain things to him?"

"I was about to," I answer, coming to stand beside Woods. "But then you came out here, dropping n-bombs in your underpants."

I snatch the phone out of his hand, making sure to turn it all the way off before I put it in my back pocket.

"Hey!" My dad starts to yell.

But I cut him off with my introduction. "Woods, this is my dad. Curtis Dunhill, but you know him better as C-Mello."

Woods comes out of his protective stance to blink down at me. "C-Mello?" he repeats, probably thinking of all the hardcore lyrics from the songs I'd included on his workout mix. "C-Mello is your *dad*?"

"No, *Curtis* is my dad. C-Mello is the role he plays..."

"Fuck that! Tell this nigga I will go back in my house and get a gun to put a cap in his ass if he doesn't stand down right now and let me get this hug in."

"A role he plays, like, all the time," I finish wearily as I step forward to present myself for one of Dad's signature bear hugs.

Dad grabs me up in his arms like I'm still a kid, and kisses me on top of the head.

"Good to see you, Nee-Nee. Hair and make-up will be here in about an hour or two. And the rest of the crew's going to meet us at the VMH awards." But in a flash Dad goes from informative back to hurt. "You seriously didn't tell him nothing about us?" he asks me.

"I didn't know how to," I admit, casting my eyes downward and to the side, pretty much as far away from Woods as I can.

But then I force myself to look back up at him, if only to say, "I wasn't planning on letting him ambush you like this. I was going to tell you before we went in."

Now Dad is looking at Woods sideways, like I've brought home a green alien. "Okay, since you took my phone, I'm just going to straight up ask: where did you find this boy? He been living up under a rock or something?"

"He's got a rare form of retrograde amnesia," I admit to Dad. "So even if he'd heard of us, he wouldn't remember it."

Now Dad's eyes really bug. "No shit!?!?"

"No shit," I grudgingly confirm, really not loving how much delight he's taking in Woods' ongoing medical condition.

"Hot damn!" Dad says, rubbing his hands together. "Wait till Sandy gets a load of this nigga! She going to lose her fucking mind."

But Woods is shaking his head, obviously having a hard time processing this. "So your father is a rapper, and your mother is a pastor, and your brother dresses up as women for his career. You guys sound a lot like that reality show I was watching in the hospital..."

Dad nearly loses his shit then. "Nitra! You have got to be fucking kidding me with this!" he yells.

"He has amnesia Dad. Amnesia!" I shout back, full bitch. "I seriously couldn't figure out how to tell him, okay?!"

But then I force my voice back down to a much more pleasant register, turning back to Woods to say, "Funny, you should mention that..."

As if on cue, a 90s era Hummer comes tearing around the corner.

"Ooh, Nitra, you going to get it!!!" my dad sing-songs, pointing at me like a kid in the schoolyard as the oversized car screeches to a halt in front of the gate.

At my dad's words, Woods once again goes into his protective stance, fists bunched, ready to meet whoever comes out of the car head on.

That is until the door flies open to admit a five-foot tall, middle-aged woman screeching, "You've got some freaking nerve, kid. First West Virginia, and now this? Did you really get married without telling me first? And if so, tell me you've got something on tape other than that shitty security camera footage!" She glares at Woods. "And he's cute, kid, but if you found him on a competing network, I swear to you, I will lose it. I will kill you and your entire family and tell VMH exactly why I did it at the contract negotiations."

Woods goes from defensive to confused. Really confused. "I'm guessing this isn't your mother, the pastor," he says to me.

"Worse," the little woman answers. "I'm her mother fucking executive producer. But the real question is, who are you?"

"So, Woods..." I say in the quiet that follows. "I'd like you to meet Sandy, the executive producer of *Rap Star Wives*, which, ah...just so happens to be the reality show my family sort of headlines."

21

"I've got a joke," the twelve-year-old version of me tells everyone gathered around the dining room table at her unusual parents' swanky new Malibu mansion. "Why did the chicken have a gun?"

"Why, baby?" my mother's honey-warm voice asks as she sets a beautifully roasted chicken down in the middle of the table.

"To defend itself against the cruel humans who were trying to eat it," twelve-year-old me answers.

Beside me, my sixteen-year-old brother, kitted out in waist-length dookie braids and a full face of heavy make-up, falls out laughing.

But my father and mother stare at me stonily as my six-year-old sister, Chanel, asks, "What does 'cruel' mean?"

"It means somebody at this table need to get her ass whooped," my dad answers, glaring at me.

"Curtis..." my mom starts.

"Or a pistol whipping. See how many chicken jokes she be making then."

In the screening room of the same mansion, Sandy pauses on that image to crow to Woods, "This scene's got over ten million YouTube views!"

"And then look what she does next. Look at it..." my father, who's sitting beside Sandy in the front row of red velvet stadium chairs, adds.

On screen, twelve-year-old me pulls a microphone out of nowhere and drops it on top of her empty plate.

Dad falls out laughing. "Oh, no she didn't! *No she didn't!* See, that right there is why we're the first family of *Rap Star Wives*! Why we'll *always* be the first family." Dad gives Sandy a pointed look as I sink even further down into my seat.

I'm sure there are worse ways to confess to your pretend husband that you grew up on a reality show called *Rap Star Wives*. And that your family "visits" are, in fact, a contractual obligation to make four appearances on said reality show every year. But seriously, I can't think of any.

Luckily, I have the show's long time executive producer and America's most embarrassing father—*Entertainment Weekly* voted him number one in a list that included Gary Busey and Charlie Sheen a few years back—to explain things to Woods that I just can't.

For the next hour-and-a-half, Sandy and Dad narrate a literal highlight reel of my life, which, yes, the show just happens to keep on hand. They start with my introduction to America as the bitchy vegan middle daughter of rapper C-Mello and his wife, Cassandrea, an evangelical pastor. The show, as first conceived by Sandy, a graduate of Columbia University's prestigious journalism school, was meant to be controversial. An incisive and somewhat feminist look at the real lives of rap star wives.

Our family had been the main focus of the original show, thanks to Compton rapper C-Mello's refusal to tone down his language or violent lyrics, despite having a wife in the ministry. Also, because of his and my mother's complete acceptance of their cross-dressing son, Curtis Jr.

After securing funding from Video Music Hits, a then-flagging music video channel looking to make the jump into unscripted programming, Sandy had gone into the first season of *Rap Star Wives* hoping for a Peabody. However, what was supposed to be a six-episode character study, ended up garnering huge ratings and attention for the music network airing our little "docudrama," thanks mostly in part to our strange family dynamic.

Eventually *Rap Star Wives* became a franchise. Many of the other rap wives would come and go on the show, but C-Mello and his family remained the anchor of *Rap Star Wives*. My mother went from Cassie Dunhill, the pastor at a little Compton storefront church, to Cassandrea Mello, a "spiritual advisor" who regularly sold out stadiums in cross-country tours. And my brother moved up from cross-dressing to becoming Cee-Cee Mello, one of the most well-known drag queens in America.

In Season 1—which is nowhere on my reel—we're exactly what we say we are, a loving family living in Compton. By Season 3 however, we've got a house in the Hollywood Hills, and I'm dropping my now iconic "dinner plate mic."

On screen, Woods watches with squinted eyes as I go from a know-it-all twelve-year-old vegan, to a super spoiled teenager constantly stirring up catty drama amongst her crew of carefully curated friends, to a heartbroken eighteen-year-old crying over her little sister's dead body and screaming at the cameras to get out.

"Just fucking get out of here!"

At this point we're in Season 1 of my spin-off show, *Rap Star Wives: College Mic Drop*, in which me and three of the other kids who grew up on *Rap Star Wives* (barely) attend various colleges around California.

The next highlight is of me rolling my bag up a set of concrete stairs and collapsing in the middle because there isn't anyone around to carry my bags for me. This is typical Nitra Mello behavior. Not only am I the snottiest vegan ever, but I'm known to fly into ridiculous rages when not shown proper respect by servants, friends, and ex-boyfriends alike. I also expect L.A.-level service every single place I go. Even if it's a college dorm.

At least that was how the show portrayed it. But in reality, I collapsed and began crying for much different reasons. Because my little sister had died of a disease that didn't give a fuck what popular reality show she was on six months prior to my first day at ValArts. Because the end of her life had been a ratings bonanza for both the original *Rap Star Wives* and my new show. Because here I was, pretending to haul my own luggage up the stairs, when obviously, *obviously*, there were like a million burly crew guys within a few feet of me who could have helped me do it.

Because I didn't have any real friends.

Because I had never had a real relationship.

Because for the first time, I was realizing how silly and fake my entire life had become.

For that and a million other reasons, I ugly cried on those stairs.

And though the next few scenes go on to show quite a few ill-advised adventures with hard-partying "friends," the only true friend I have is the one who never appeared on any episode of the show: Sola, who until a few years ago, was technically an illegal immigrant and therefore considered a legal liability and never filmed as a result.

The last highlight in my reel is of me coming home to tell my parents that not only was I dropping out of ValArts, I was moving across country to a place where the cameras couldn't follow me to become a doctor.

On camera, my parents do a good job of acting like themselves. My dad tells me my decision makes no goddamn sense because it ain't going to bring Chanel back. While my mom goes into full pastor mode, saying we should pray over it. This is our lives as lived on TV, so of course they don't show the truly ugly stuff.

Dad yelling at me about ratings. Sandy, who no longer gives two shits what the Peabody folks think of her, threatening to sue me to the moon and back if I leave a half season into my new contract. Technically, America hates my spoiled, vegan ass—especially the parents who had to deal with an onslaught of children dropping toy mics on their empty plates whenever they didn't want to eat what was being served for dinner. But the truth is, the ability to engender rabid hate is one of the true qualities of a reality star. So I'm easily the most popular character on the college spin-off show.

In real life, the producers knew the college spin-off wouldn't survive without people tuning in to hate-watch my overly bitchy vegan dramatics. In real life, one of the reasons I couldn't afford medical school without substantial loans was because I had to spend so much money on lawyers to get out of the reality jail they wanted to keep me in.

But on screen, my mom prays and cries over the fact that her baby is moving over three-thousand miles away. And no one mentions the months of litigation and screaming fights, or the fact that by the time this scene is filmed, I've already completed a semester of my combined program. Or that this episode is a part of a new seven-year "compromise contract" that requires me to film at least four episodes of *Rap Star Wives* a year.

Sandy watches my last highlight with a shake of her perfectly frosted head, "A born reality star, our Nitra. Too bad she decided to completely ass-fuck the franchise seven years ago."

Dad shakes his head right along with Sandy. "Ratings took a real dip after she left," he tells Woods. "And now the network's talking about not renewing the Mellos contracts for next season, since Nitra won't be coming back. Don't think any of us ever going to forgive Nitra for leaving."

"But maybe if she makes a big enough splash this weekend, that will be enough to convince the network to let the rest of you stay," Sandy points out to Dad, though obviously, so ridiculously obviously, her comments are directed toward me.

But I don't care about their latest guilt trip. Only about Woods who's watching the credits roll in our dark screening room. His face unreadable.

I miss him already. His hand on top of mine. Our closeness. It feels like it's all slipping through my fingers with each bitchy highlight of my on-screen life.

Shame and concern wash over me, making me want to talk this out with him and run away at the same time.

But in the end, hair and make-up makes the decision for me.

"NITRA!!!!" Frannie and Carlos, my freelance hair and make-up team, yell from the doorway of the screening room.

The next thing I know, I'm being pelted with questions. "Is it true. Did you really get married, girl? Is that him? Where'd you find a hottie like that in West Virginia?" Frannie and Carlos demand, never giving me more than a millisecond to answer their questions

"Take her upstairs," Sandy tells them irritably. "I've got to get him cleared and into hair and make-up, too."

"But—" I start.

"We've only got a few hours to get you camera ready and rewrite the scenario for the Vemmies tonight. Do *not* fuck with me on this, Nitra. This is your last episode, and we've got our lawyers on standby…"

She's right. I am too close to finally meeting my contractual obligation to risk having her go back to the deal table now.

"We'll talk later, I promise," I tell Woods as I'm dragged away by Frannie and Carlos. "Until then, don't sign anything!"

"Why would you tell him that?" Sandy yells after me.

And the last thing I hear her saying to him is, "She shouldn't have told you that…"

22

───────

*S*andy's right about how long it takes to get me looking like a reality star as opposed to a sensible doctor working in an understaffed hospital. By the time they're done, Frannie and Carlos declare themselves true geniuses when they turn me around to face the vanity mirror over the dresser in my room.

But I can only shake my head at the woman in the mirror. Nitra Mello stares back at me now, a black-and-honey blonde lace-front wig cascading in waves over my shoulders where my kinky twist out used to be. The doctor who can barely bother with lip gloss has been replaced by a heavily contoured goddess with the lushest fake eyelashes money can buy. In place of her scrubs, there's now a bright yellow floor-length Versace evening gown with a plunging neckline that gives way just as the skirt of the gown does.

This is who I really am. Who I still am as far as most of the world is concerned. Seriously, at this point I've been playing the part of Nitra Mello for longer than I ever played the part of Anitra Dunhill.

Usually it takes no more than this mirror transformation to turn me into her again. Just looking at myself dressed up like Nitra Mello makes cruel and cutting words magically appear in my head.

But today my mind stutters, and it feels like I'm staring at a complete stranger as I mumble a quiet, "Thank you," as opposed to a more Nitra-appropriate, "Yeah, I guess you bitches didn't fuck up your job this time. Congrats."

"You're welcome," Fran answers carefully for the both of them, probably wondering what the hell is going on. Nitra Mello hasn't so much as said please a day in her life, much less thank you to anyone providing her with a service.

I can feel their eyes on me as I leave my suite and head back downstairs in stilettos to find Woods. Only to be waylaid by Sandy in the hallway.

"Great, you're out of hair and make-up. Let's talk about you making your boyfriend, or husband, or whatever he is to you, get on board with this new scenario. Every time I try to run anything past him, he says he doesn't have any answers for me until he's talked to you. And I've got producers on stand-by with Terrell's people to figure out how we're going to play this."

"Where is he?" I ask, wanting to pinch the bridge of my nose but restraining myself because the last thing I need is to go through another hour of contouring with Fran and Carlos.

Sandy sullenly points a blood red stiletto nail downstairs and I rush in, ignoring the call of "T-minus ninety minutes to show time!" that she lobs after me like an army general sending her soldier to war.

～

Explain this! Fix this! That's all I'm thinking as I walk into our large receiving room to finally talk with Woods. However I stop short when I see him standing at the piano, near the wall of floor-to-ceiling picture windows.

My parents paid quite a few million for the spectacular view of the Sunset Strip that the receiving room's wall of picture windows overlooks. But in that moment, I can easily say Woods is way more gorgeous than the multi-million-dollar view.

Apparently he did agree to one thing Sandy asked. He's now wearing an on-trend tuxedo with the collar open for that extra bit of music award show cool. His formerly half-shaved head has been evened out on both sides for a more classic cut that hides his scar. The beard is also gone, revealing an even squarer jaw than I'd suspected beneath his hospital turned why-the-hell-not beard. The truth is, he looks like one of the stars who will be receiving awards tonight.

Better than Colin Fairgood even, I think, my mind going to the only other blond I've ever found remotely attractive before falling into this relationship with Woods.

But this man isn't my John Doe. Even as I easily see why Sandy would order the beard, which wasn't low enough to be cool or big enough to be hipster, completely removed...my heart cries out.

I don't make a sound when I come into the room, but he turns around as if he senses me there. And my distress must be written on my face because he says, "You don't like the new look?"

"No, it's not that," I assure him. "You look wonderful. So handsome..."

I trail off, because how do you explain to the man you love that you're sad he no longer looks like the man you love? Woods didn't just clean up. He's drop-dead gorgeous, and sexy as hell. Plus, he now has that All-American white boy thing going for him, which puts him in deep contrast to my last "boyfriend," a young rapper named Terrell on C-Mello's imprint label.

Even if we'd held auditions, we couldn't have cast him any better. This Woods now looks exactly like someone Nitra Mello would deign to date. This Woods looks like he belongs in the receiving room of a Hollywood mansion. In fact, if I didn't know better, I would have assumed he, and not my father, owned this place. And though it's no fault of his that I dragged him into my world, the full erasure of the John Doe I fell in love with makes me kind of sad.

"Hi," I say. I feel like a stranger, introducing herself to someone who's never met her before, but who knows every single thing about her. In other words, I introduce myself to him the way I introduce myself to just about everyone who's ever seen my show.

"Hi," he answers back, looking down at me with squinted eyes. Like I really am a stranger now.

An awkward second ticks between us.

"Is this why you fought being with me so hard?" he asks, raising both tuxedoed arms to indicate the opulent bedroom with its spectacular view of the Sunset Strip below a darkening sky. "Because you're rich and I ain't? You thought I was after your money?"

Somewhere in the distance, I can hear Sandy cursing because he's saying the perfect lines in one of the show's favorite filming sites, but he hasn't signed a release yet.

I lower my voice to tell him, "No! I didn't think you were after my money! I technically don't have any money. Most of my royalties and residual checks go toward paying back my student loans, and my mom and dad's financial advisors locked all but fifteen percent of the money I earned before I turned eighteen into a trust I won't have access to until this July. So no, that's not why I was hesitant to get involved with you. And it's definitely not why I waited to tell you."

He shakes his head as if my denial has only confused him more. "Then why?"

"Because I didn't want you to know this part of me," I answer, too on edge to be anything but brutally frank. "I liked the way you saw me when we met. The way you called me Doc, as if my profession defined me more than this stupid reality show did... does. I didn't want you to look at me like most other people look at me. Thinking they know me, even though none of this is real."

Damn pregnancy hormones. I've played a hard bitch on TV for more than half my life, but I once again find myself overcome with real life emotion. I hold my head back so the tears won't fall. Won't ruin the hair and make-up that makes me Nitra Mello, and therefore unable to authentically feel anything without warning Fran first.

But eventually I pull myself together. Enough to let him know, "I mean, I did make that chicken joke that went viral. But three different producers rewrote it to make sure it was as funny as it could possibly be, and we did four takes to make sure I dropped the mic on my plate exactly right..."

I break off when I see the look on his face. "And I'm confusing you again. I'm sorry. But this is who I have to be when I'm here. I've got to talk back to my dad. I have to pretend I actually give two shits about my closeted, gay ex-boyfriend's new beard. And I've got to go with Dad to the VMH music awards tonight. Because here's a funny story: Dad's actually been nominated this year for a song he did with your favorite country singer, Colin Fairgood. But you need to understand, it's not really me. None of this is me. And that's why I didn't tell you. Because I didn't want you to believe I was like this, and I definitely didn't want you to get roped into any of this craziness."

I let out a sad breath, the dream of him never having to know about my past long gone.

"But don't worry," I tell him, circling a hand around his new sexy tux look. "I'll tell Sandy you're not signing any of her releases. Then I'll go do my duty tonight. I've got one more segment where I shop with Dad for their big thirtieth anniversary wedding renewal ceremony tomorrow, and then..."

I grab him by both hands to promise this next thing, "And then we're going to leave for Seattle and pretend none of this *ever happened*. It's just one more episode and then my contract on this show is done, okay? It has nothing to do with us, or the life we're going to live together."

But he shakes his head. "That ain't going to work."

Oh God. My heart clogs my throat. Yes, I realize I'm the one in the wrong. The one who purposefully kept things from him, the one who remained stingy with her love until he forced the truth out of me, the one who didn't take the time to prepare him properly for a life as the husband of one of the most notorious bitches on reality TV.

But now I finally get what it feels like to have your behavior backfire on you. Every single time I've ever misbehaved, the show's gotten higher ratings, but now the only man I've ever loved—for real love, not pretend love—is heading for the door. Walking out of my life for good.

Or at least I think that's what's going on, until he stops at the grand piano that sits between where I'm standing and the entryway.

"Now that I know this ex-boyfriend of yours Sandy wants me to make jealous is gay, I'm going for sure, Doc."

He leans over the piano, which I can now see has one of our show's standard guest star contracts.

He carefully signs it with the fountain pen Sandy left behind. Then he walks back over to where I'm standing and says, "I guess I really am part of your family now."

And all I can do is press my knuckles to my lips and laugh when he holds up the last page of the contract for me to see. The signature reads, WOODS MELLO.

He chuckles, too, but then he sobers to say, "I'm your husband now, Doc. Where you go, I go. Even when you're pretending to be somebody you obviously ain't."

I have never in my life loved anyone as much as I do Woods in that moment. I throw my arms around his neck and kiss him with more passion than bitchy Nitra Mello is ever supposed to show. I can't help myself. He's my husband and he's accepted my whole package. Bitchy reality show diva and all. I know then that I'll never be able to wrap my head around how I got so lucky to find a man like him. A man who now knows me like no one else in all of America ever has or ever will.

23

The Dolby Theater, formerly the Kodak, is one of the best known event venues in the world thanks to hosting the Oscars, the VMH "Vemmies" Award Show, and the season finale competitions for a few popular reality shows. So it's no surprise that some of the biggest music, movie, and TV stars in the world are already on the red carpet when the limo drops the three of us off.

However as my family, which now includes rapper C-Mello, Woods, and a grandchild I'm not telling anyone about yet, starts making their way across the red carpet, paparazzi and talent wranglers from several news outlets start yelling out to us.

There are bigger stars, I suppose, but none of them got promise married in Vegas yesterday.

"Oh, this right here's about to get nuts," my dad all but promises us as we wave at the fans.

Per Sandy's instructions, we don't stop for anyone, just keep walking until we get to the four-panel step and repeat embla-zoned with VMH's logo.

Not surprisingly, we find Lane Anderson, the same guy who hosts all of our season reunion specials, waiting for us with a mic.

"Nitra Mello!" Lane squeals, as if I've taken him totally by surprise. Even as my father keeps going—as instructed earlier—to the next panel to join Colin Fairgood for an interview with another VMH on-air personality.

"*You got married*??? What are you doing? What are you doing, babe?"

"I don't know," I answer with a laugh. "I guess I'm in love. You know, it ain't just thugs. Bitches need love, too."

Lane laughs. "So it's true, you actually got married in Las Vegas?!?!"

Shocking, I know, since my father and mother were, until now, the only couple on *Rap Star Wives* who are actually formally married.

"True, true, it's all true," I answer. "I mean, Vegas! How else you going to do?"

"Well, I know this is certainly a shock to all of us here at VMH. I wonder how Terrell's handling the news."

I roll my eyes and suck my teeth, the very picture of an unrepentant woman in Versace. "You know, I ain't even thinking about that little boy and his..."

I trail off, unable to say all the phrases that used to fall out of Nitra's mouth when it came to talking about Grenada, the other *RSW College Mic Drop* castmate who supposedly "stole" my boyfriend and upset me so bad, I left the coast. My usual go-to words are hussy, side-piece, ghetto ho—even though she, like me, had been privately tutored around shooting hours, and neither of us would ever really use words like that outside the show in our real-life interactions.

Tonight, standing next to Woods with his hand wrapped around mine, reminding me who I really am...well, I just can't.

"You know what? I'm here with Woods, and that's all that matters to me," I say to Lane. "Now if you'll excuse us, we should go find our seats before the show starts."

"Okay..." Lane says agreeably enough. But he looks over my shoulder at the red carpet talent wrangler, while flashing two fingers at me below the camera's field of vision. I'm supposed to do a full two minutes with Lane, and he's got to be pissed that I'm trying to leave before he's had the chance to properly turn the microphone on Woods.

In fact, the talent wrangler he signaled is already texting, so I'm more than certain I'll be hearing from Sandy about this.

But like a true pro, Lane maintains his bright smile as he switches the direction of his mic toward Woods. "And Woods, how does it feel to be married to the Mic Drop Princess? Any concerns Terrell might try to steal her back tonight?"

"It feels like I'm the luckiest man in the world," he answers with a lazy smile. "And the answer to your second question is no."

As it turns out, Woods is a lot better at the reality show game than I would have thought. His utter confidence plays well into the conceit of my ongoing drama with Terrell without him actually having to play along with it.

"Good job staying true to yourself," I murmur as we walk away from Lane after our mandatory two minutes.

As we move past all the step and repeats, I glance back at Colin and Dad who are still talking with the female half of VMH's red carpet team. Only to mind stutter a little bit when I find Colin looking straight at me.

Strange, he seems more interested in our departure than his on-carpet interview. Old habit makes me seek out his songwriter wife, Kyra Fairgood, standing dutifully on the other side of the carpet, a good six or seven months pregnant if her baby bump is any indication. She's not famous enough and probably not interested enough to stand with him in the spotlight, and like most of the non-famous celebrity spouses, she's texting while she waits for her famous half to be done with all this red carpet nonsense. She either doesn't notice or care that Colin's looking hard at another woman right now.

"Nitra!!!!"

The squeal of my "best friend" Dyana—at least on TV—cuts into my confused observation of Colin Fairgood and his wife. She comes running up, checking to make sure at least a few of the standing red carpet cameras see us, before stopping right in front of me for as affectionate a hug as two women who are trying to avoid all face contact can give.

"Did you see what that bitch is wearing?" she asks, taking me by the arm. "The same dress as you! You know she did it on purpose!"

I have to resist the urge to roll my eyes. Instead I hold on to Wood's hand as tightly as I can. Letting him anchor me in the real on one side, while Dyana drags me into fake drama on the other.

Unlike the Mellos, Dyana's family was kicked off the show years ago. So now she rarely gets any camera time unless we're at the same event. It's never bothered me before, but holding Woods' hand while listening to her throw outsized shade at Grenada...it makes me queasy with shame.

And of course Grenada and Terrell are seated right next to us when we're directed to our seats.

"It's not real," I promise Woods, right before I do what I have to do.

"I know," he whispers back.

He squeezes my hand before letting it go, so I can charge up to Grenada and demand, "Are you serious with this shit?"

For once, I don't call her a bitch, but we both do a good job of getting up in each other's face as we argue about which one of us actually chose the dresses our stylists picked out in real life along with the show's costume designer.

So good, I can practically feel Woods' twinkling blue eyes on me as he watches his formerly overly constrained doctor act a straight fool in public.

With perfect timing, he and Terrell pull us away from each other, and after checking that the million cameras that panned over to shoot the almost-fight got their footage, we all sit down. Each couple—both the fake and the real one—on either side of Dyana.

"That's it for our part of the night," I whisper to Woods with a mean smile on my lips, so it looks like I'm talking about Grenada as opposed to expressing my relief at not having to ever talk to her again. "Now they just need some reaction shots from us after Dad and Colin perform and have their awards announced. Then we're out of here."

"Good," he answers with a sincere smile. "I'm missing my wife. My *real* wife."

Thank God the duet award is scheduled early, as is Dad and Colin's performance. I'm exhausted and can't imagine making it through another hour, much less the entire three-hour ceremony.

But Colin and Dad are the first to perform, and they kill it onstage. The fact that a country singer would enlist C-Mello for his album speaks volumes to the iconic status Dad has managed to achieve in all parts of the music world. But the tall and lanky blond singer matches Dad swagger for swagger, strutting across the stage with the neck of his fiddle in one hand and performing hype man duties as my dad spits out his verse.

I come to my feet, goosebumps rising on my arms, when they take on the last chorus together, their well-known voices cater-wauling and crooning in perfect harmony until auto-tune takes over the last note, echoing their voices out across the crowd as the song finishes.

Fatigue forgotten, I clap and wolf-whistle along with the rest of the *Rap Star Wives* cast as Colin and Dad wave and touch hands with the cheering crowd of concert goers below their feet.

Dad looks so happy on stage, being adored by fans. And even though I don't want anything else to do with this circus my family calls a life, I hope he gets what he wants. That the drama I provided is enough to get the contract renewal he's hoping for.

As if sensing my good wishes, he finds me in the seats and points to me. I blow back kisses I know he can't see, but will treasure later on camera.

Yeah, we're a very strange and crazy family, I think after sinking back into my seat. But there's one thing *Rap Stars Wives* got right about us from the beginning: we truly love each other and I could not be more proud of my dad.

"That wasn't half bad, Doc." Woods murmurs in my ear before kissing my temple.

Flashes go off, and I can tell the photogs are eating this up, along with the two close-up cameras that panned across the audience to get our reaction shots to Dad and Colin's performance. Sandy will definitely be pulling this footage from the network's camera feed. And if the show plays their contacts right, the pic of Woods kissing me in his patented way will appear between the covers of at least a few gossip rags on Tuesday. I can almost see the headline now, "Secretly Married to a Mysterious Hottie!"

And though I thought I'd become used to being watched in this way, my muscles tense under all the camera attention. I love the way Woods treasures me, but I hate sharing the real us so openly. A feeling of wanting to get out of here and on the road to Seattle overtakes me. And my heart aches with the wish that we could hide together. Somewhere where no photogs or backwoods motorcycle gangs or reality show producers will ever look for us.

So it comes as a huge relief when I'm back on my feet ten minutes later. This time jumping up and down as I cheer Dad and Colin's Best Duet win.

As soon as they walk off stage with their golden microphones, I tell Woods, "I'm tired. Mind if we go home?"

This much is true. I'm barely standing in my heels at this point, but thanks to all my TV training, I know to keep the smile on my face to prevent the possibility of a picture being taken that could be used for an "On the Edge of a Nervous Breakdown?" story.

"Not at all, Doc." He doesn't have any camera training, so he looks down at me with sincere worry which I'm pretty sure will be construed by at least one blog as "Trouble in Paradise?"

No longer caring about my makeup, I grab ahold of his Prada and close the distance between our mouths to give him a kiss.

"I'm sorry for dragging you into all this craziness," I whisper as I wipe off all the purple I left behind on his lips with my thumb.

But before he can answer, my special phone rings directly to the smart watch I'm wearing as part of a branding agreement with the show.

It's Sandy.

"Showtime," her message says. *"Colin Fairgood wants you and your man to come up to his suite for celebration drinks."*

I sigh, not really wanting to go, but I did promise Woods I'd introduce him to Colin. And it is my last show...

"Okay," I say, rallying. "First we need to go up to the hotel and then you need to take me home and put me underneath you. Is that okay?"

He frowns. "There's a whole theater *and* a hotel in this mall?"

I can only grin at his befuddlement and say for the second time that day, "Welcome to L.A."

24

I think people must assume I'm presenting because no one even attempts to stop us as we walk to the set of elevators that will take us directly up to the penthouse suites on the top floor. Or maybe it's because a couple of guys from *Devil Riders*, VMH's popular unscripted show about a southern motorcycle gang, are right behind us. As per usual, they haven't bothered to get dressed up, or even attend the awards show, and they cut quite an intimidating picture in their leathers and denim as they crowd into the elevator with us.

At least they do until one of them says, "Hey, Nitra! Congrats on your old man's win."

"Thanks," I answer as we get off the elevator. "We're going to celebrate with them now."

"We ain't got nothing to celebrate ourselves," Jake Nicholl, the show's handsome young star says, grinning at me. "But I'm sure we'll figure something out after a couple of drinks."

I chuckle. "I'm sure you will."

The show's cast is known for their hard partying ways. I imagine there will be stories to tell when they're done at VMH's after-party, which is already thumping with Colin and Dad's song when we get upstairs.

"You coming?" Jake asks, eyeing my dress appreciatively as we file out of the elevator.

Even if Colin didn't have his own suite, I would have turned down the invitation. I can tell by the way Woods loops an arm around my shoulder and eyes Jake hard that he's not one of those L.A. guys who gets any sort of kick out of famous guys ogling his woman.

I clasp Woods' hand, reassuring him without words as I say out loud, "My husband and I have another party to go to, but have fun!"

"I most definitely will," Jake assures me with a wicked grin, and I have a feeling he'll be on to the next girl within the next five minutes. "Congrats, brother," he says, nodding at Woods.

Woods doesn't answer him, just asks, "Which one we going to?" when the bikers are out of earshot.

As if in response to his question, a huge bodyguard standing in front of a door on the other side of the carpeted courtyard calls out to us, "Miss Mello, right this way. Fairgood's expecting you."

We walk over, only to be taken by surprise when, instead of stepping aside to let us through the penthouse suite's doors, the bodyguard pats Woods down without any warning.

"Hey, sir," I protest on Woods behalf. "Colin invited us up here."

If I'm expecting any remorse from the guard, I don't get it. He just stone-faces Woods and says, "Alright, you can go on in. But you start something with my boy and I'm going to end it. Understand, son?"

My eyes widen. Did he seriously just threaten my husband?

But Woods just crooks his head to the side as if he's nothing but amused by the guard's words.

"I'm not your son, sir. But yeah, sure, I understand," he says in a way that makes me feel like he's merely humoring the much larger man.

The guard grunts, but finally steps aside so we can walk through the door.

Weird, I think as we go in. Colin's is the only door with a guard. Even the network party seems to think the security downstairs is enough to handle any would-be party crashers.

Still, I school my face into my best Nitra Mello when I see Colin waiting for us in the suite's sitting area. "You won, bitch! You won!!!" I call out like we're old friends, as opposed to people who have met exactly once for, like, two seconds at a Grammy party over seven years ago.

But I know Colin. He makes Blake Shelton look like he's never seen a camera before, and I imagine he'll embrace me warmly and say something about how I'm all grown up now.

Yet I stop short inside the aggressively modern suite with its "fuck you poor people" views of Hollywood. The large suite is as beautiful as you'd expect...but save for one person, it's completely empty.

"Hello, Nitra," says Colin. The only person here.

"Hi," I answer, still looking around the suite. Not understanding at all. "Where's my dad?" I ask Colin.

"At the network party," he answers. "So's my wife. I told them to meet me there later."

That's when his eyes shift from me to Woods. "I didn't want to do this any place but in private."

Oooh-kay, I think as his words sink in and Woods' hands fall out of mine.

I'd heard rumors that Colin kept his relationships out of the press before he got married because he was super kinky. And now I'm wondering how I can explain this situation to Woods without it ending in a fight.

"Listen," I say to Colin. "I know there's still a lot of confusion going around after I kissed Dyana in that one episode. But that was just for show. I'm not into threesomes or swinging or whatever it is you thought I might be good for when you had Sandy arrange this, ah..." I'm not sure what to call it now, so I settle for, "meeting."

"That was a good episode," Colin says, an appreciative note tinting his voice, "But I didn't invite you up here to have sex with you."

Woods' expression goes from hard to granite, and my eyes widen as I say, "Oh, you want to...?" I look from Colin to Woods and grimace because they're both so ridic hot, I have to admit if it were anyone but my husband involved in this hypothetical, I'd be crazy turned on by the thought of them going at it right now.

But since this is my Woods he's talking about, I say, "Oh no, Colin. This isn't a Terrell situation. Woods doesn't swing that way."

Then I rush into a formal introduction so we can change the subject. "This is my husband, Woods," I say to Colin. "He's a really big fan of yours…" Then I trail off yet again, because oops, yeah I heard it.

"Of your music," I quickly edit. "He's a really big fan *of your music.*"

But instead of taking the compliment, Colin's eyes go all squinty and angry on Woods. "You really going to do this, man?" he asks. "How far are you willing to take this?"

"What do you mean?" I ask, looking between Woods and Colin with real alarm.

"He's old," Woods says.

His voice is quiet. But the two words erupt inside the room, blowing up my initial perception of the situation as I realize Colin knows who Woods is. He *knows* him.

But Colin jerks his head back as if Woods has physically punched him, "Okay, first you have the nerve to show up here, and now you're calling me old?!"

"No, that's just the way he talks," I answer for Woods. "Because of a very long and involved story. But him calling you 'old' is actually a good thing, because you're the first person he's met that he's actually said that about. And, oh my gosh…!"

I grab my almost-husband's hand and say, "He actually knows who you are! Like in real life. Maybe that's why you were playing his song on the guitar."

"Stop right there," Colin says, holding up one hand to me while he says to Woods, "You been playing a song of mine on the guitar? Why the hell would you be doing that?!"

And at that point I have to ask Colin, "Um, are you and Woods some kind of rivals? Did he win some award you really wanted or something?"

Truth is, save for the crossover acts, I don't know a ton about country other than the indisputable fact that Dolly Parton is a national treasure. But I'm well aware of how vicious the music business can be even when it's served up in a baseball hat and plaid shirt. And right now, I doubt Colin has a gun on him, but I can definitely see he and Woods—or whoever Woods used to be —have some major beef.

But Colin continues to glare at Woods as he says, "No, he ain't my rival, he's my half-brother. And by the way, I don't know what lies he's told you in order to get this close to me, but his name ain't Woods. It's Dixon. Dixon Fairgood."

25

*D*ixon Fairgood. We finally had a name. And that's wonderful. Even if neither Colin nor Woods—no, Dixon—seem to think so at the moment.

The two are staring each other down like a rap battle is about to go off, but I can totally see the resemblance now that I'm looking for it. Colin's more muscular, but they're both around the same height with the same lanky build. Also, they have the same set of crystal blue eyes.

However while Woods', uh, Dixon's are completely cold, Colin's are glittering with red-hot hate.

"Why are you here?" Colin demands, his voice harsh.

"I don't like you," Dixon realizes this out loud, in a way I've become familiar with. But Colin reacts like his half-brother straight stepped to him.

"You think I care what you think of me, Dixon?" he demands, stepping towards the man I'm assuming is his younger brother in the time-honored tradition of men getting all the way up in each other's faces. "You think I won't have my security guard beat you within an inch of your life if you ever try to come anywhere near me and mine again, you piece of shit?" he demands. "I already told you lot how I feel about you coming near me. And I think my choice of life partner ought to have cemented my position on these matters loud and clear. Although, obviously you're snake enough to trick this poor girl into bringing you here—"

"Wait, wait, wait!" I say, squeezing between them and putting a hand on each of their chests.

"I don't know what you think is going on here or what's gone down between you in the past, but Woods—I mean, *Dixon*—has amnesia. He didn't lie to me about his name. He's never lied to me."

But Colin shakes his head at me. "What? No. He lied to you."

Exasperated, I ask, "Do you watch *Rap Star Wives* for real? Or was that just a joke you were making earlier?"

Colin squints in a manner so similar to Woods, it's a wonder I didn't recognize them as kin from the door. Then he admits, "Maybe an episode or two. My wife loves that show."

I don't bother to tell him we have a near 50% male viewer share and only a few percentage points worth are actually unabashed gay male fans. The rest are men who claim to only be watching the show because their wives or girlfriends do.

Instead, I continue with my explanation. "So then you know I've been in West Virginia for the last few years, and now I'm a doctor in real life. I know it sounds crazy, but I swear it's true. I met your half-brother at the hospital where I work. He has a severe case of amnesia. I swear to you he does not know who you are to him, and he really doesn't remember whatever caused this beef between you two. So please, I need you to set aside whatever happened and tell him exactly who he is. Right now."

Colin shakes his head in denial. But then he gives me a considering look—again so similar to Dixon's I feel a chill go down my spine. And my words must sink in, because eventually his face softens as he asks, "Dixon, is this true, man? Do you really have amnesia or is this some elaborate scheme Uncle Fred put together?"

Dixon steps forward, tucking me under his arm. Despite his confusion, his first priority still seems to be protecting me, even now.

"Yeah, it's true," he answers, voice cold. "I get that you don't like me and I don't like you. That's old. But I can't remember the reason."

Now Colin looks down at me, his eyes wide. "And, oh hell, is the rest of what they've been saying all night true, too? You married —actually married Nitra fucking Mello?"

Okay, I get that to just about everyone in the entire world who's ever seen an episode of *Rap Star Wives*, I'm not exactly a catch. But I feel compelled to point out to Colin, "You know that's not the real me. Your half-brother is now married to a doctor with nothing but good intentions toward everyone she meets. Nitra Mello is a character I play on a TV show."

But Colin scrapes two hands through his hair and says, "Oh hell, Dixon. I can't even wrap my mind around what is happening here."

Something is wrong, I realize from inside Dixon's arm. I wasn't expecting Colin to be like, "Okay, yeah, I get it. That's cool." But there's something a little outsized and a lot off about his reaction.

And only my medical training keeps my voice level as I ask, "Seriously, can you please just tell us, Colin? What the hell is going on here? Why are you so upset about—?"

My many questions are interrupted by the sound of loud voices outside.

"What the...?"

But both Colin and Dixon must recognize the voice of whoever is yelling at Colin's bodyguard, because Dixon grits out an, "Old" just as Colin says. "Oh, fucking hell..."

He turns to Dixon with an apologetic look. "I didn't think. When I saw you down there, I called Mason and left him a voicemail, telling him off. But he must have already been in the area if he got here this quick."

I'm a reality star, but at that moment, I feel like I've switched genres. Listening to both Colin and the commotion outside the door, I find myself shaking my head in horror.

The yelling cuts off abruptly, followed by the unmistakable dull smack of fist against skin.

"Fuck," Dixon says, then, "Doc, get behind me."

"Me too," Colin says grimly as he comes to stand beside his half-brother.

But before I can even consider doing as they say, the door bangs open, admitting two men dressed in sleeveless leather motorcycle jackets, black jeans, and long-sleeved tees. In what feels like a strange recasting of the West Virginia diner showdown, one is stocky and older, with a full head of gray hair. He immediately puts me in mind of a rattlesnake with his weathered skin and mean glare. But he doesn't scare me nearly as much as the younger one.

He's larger than life. The largest, nastiest thing I've ever seen. With tattoos completely covering his meaty forearms and snaking from places unknown over his neck. Beautiful tattoos, like nothing I've ever seen before. But completely without color. A mish mash of black covering white skin so I can barely make out any of what they say.

I'm not quite sure what to make of him. Can only assume he got up here because security thought he was part of the *Devil Rider's* cast. But I've met most of those guys, and they're total sweeties in real life.

These two are definitely not.

Neither of them are blond, but I can immediately tell by their light blue-eyed squints that they're also Fairgoods. Like tigers and lions. Part of the same family.

And I'm standing directly between both sides.

I look to Dixon, who's staring at these guys like he stared at those motorcycle gang members back in West Virginia. Like he's afraid they're going to hurt me. Like he's willing to do anything to prevent that from happening.

"Who...?" I have to swallow when my voice comes out as little more than a croak. "Who are they?" I ask Colin.

Colin answers, his voice grim and dark. "Our cousin, Mason, and our Uncle Fred."

Then before I can respond to that bomb drop, Mason growls, "Where's our money, D?"

At the same time his uncle asks. "Is it true? Did you really marry this nigger bitch?"

26

*D*espite my years spent in the reality show business, I've never understood the term "all hell broke loose" until now. On my show, the fights are pre-planned and sometimes even coordinated for the best camera angles and effects.

But Dixon jumps on the older man so fast, the first punch is being thrown before I can even think to stop him. His uncle takes the punch and throws one of his own, which Dixon narrowly avoids by canting to the side. But then Mason spins him around, one meaty fist already raised...

"No!" I scream at Mason. "Please don't hurt him."

Thank God for Colin. He jumps Mason from behind, sending the biker stumbling backwards.

"Run!" I yell at Dixon.

But instead of running, Dixon follows Mason's backward stumble. Seemingly hell bent on punching him out, too.

The doctor in me is about to have a brain aneurysm at the thought of the many relapses and injuries Dixon's setting himself up for. But my heart un-seizes when I hear the sound of running feet....

Only to curdle right back up when I see who it is: My dad, Sandy, and a camera guy, probably dragged out of the VMH shindig where he was supposed to be shooting advanced footage for the Vemmie's after-party news story.

Dad stops for a second to assess the situation, then faster than you can say "ratings gold," he's in the mix, too. Showing his true street nature and throwing punches right alongside Dixon, like a man who's been leashed up in his gilded cage for way too long.

"Stop it! Stop it!" I scream. The knowledge that I could hurt the baby is the only thing keeping me out of the fray.

In a burst of strategy, I get in front of the camera, blocking the shot. "He has a head injury. Please stop! Please stop rolling and make them stop fighting!!!" I scream loud enough for the entire legal department of VMH to hear in their matching Brentwood homes.

Me breaking the fourth wall and pretty much ruining the take is Sandy's cue to act like an actual human. "Okay, that's enough, Curtis!" she informs my father. "We need Woods out of this fight."

Like an impeccably trained actor, C-Mello immediately stops fighting and starts yelling. "Okay, okay shut this shit down right now. This supposed to be a celebration. What the fuck you all doing fighting up in here?"

Dixon's uncle, whose nose is pretty much bleeding and broken, replies, "You think I'm going to listen to you? You ain't nothing but a..." And that's when Uncle Fred drops another N-bomb on my dad.

Having grown up on the mean but mostly black streets of Compton, I realize at that moment that the well-known rapper may not have ever been called that particular word in his life by an actual white Southerner.

Dad squints at the bloody nosed biker and his voice drops about two registers deeper than I've heard it in over a decade as he asks, "*What* did you just call me?"

"He has amnesia!" I yell, running to get between the two factions before they can start fighting again. "He has amnesia. I don't know what you all are so mad at him about, but whatever it is, he doesn't remember. So please stop this before you seriously hurt him. Please!"

Mason, who was just gearing up to throw another punch at Dixon now that Colin is finally off his back, lets his arm drop.

"What?" he asks.

I would have done anything to not have this go down with cameras rolling. Anything. But my reality life and my real life have finally collided and I find myself with no choice but to step forward and explain, on camera, for all of America to hear: "I don't know who you are, but whatever you believe this man has done to you is a mistake. He didn't steal your money. He has amnesia. He presented in my hospital a few months ago with no recollection of who he is or why he was in West Virginia."

Mason steps back, both fist uncurling as he asks, "That true, D. You don't got any memory of me? Or you?"

Dixon just looks at him, fists still raised. But he admits, "You're old."

Before Mason can get offended like Colin did, I explain, "That's his way of saying he knows you have a place in his past, but he doesn't remember who you are or what you mean to him. When we first met he called me new. In fact, everyone he's met has been new up until tonight."

"I bet. You're real new," Mason snarls at me. Then he turns back to Dixon. "Tell me you didn't really marry her like we heard on the news."

I peek over at Dixon. Considering how his family is taking this news, this might be a good time for him to confess that we're not legally married, just promised.

But Dixon glares at his cousin, brow pulled low. "I don't care what kind of kin you are to me. She's my wife, and if you say another word against her, I promise I will end you."

For a full second, Mason only stares back at him, mouth agape. Not with anger, I now realize, watching him watch Dixon, but with true confusion. As if Dixon has just said the most preposterous thing he's ever heard.

"You cannot feel that way about her, D. You cannot stay with her," he explains like Dixon is a slow child. "That is not an option for you."

"Why, because you said so?" Dixon asks in a way that doesn't leave much in the way of doubt about his unwillingness to do anything his cousin says.

Mason shakes his head. "No, dickweed! Because you're the president of our motorcycle gang, the Southern Freedom Knights."

Oh no, I think, *he's the leader of a gang.* And that's all I'm thinking in the moment.

Forgive me. This is a lot to take in, following the chaos of the fight and all the jaw-dropping reveals. That Woods' name is really Dixon. That he's related by blood to one of biggest singers in country music. That he's apparently the head of—if Mason is any indicator—a really gnarly, redneck motorcycle gang.

So maybe you can see why it takes so long for the other shoe to drop. Why I don't get the implication of his and his cousin's names until my dad says, "Wait a minute, you talking about that fucked up white supremacist gang? *Them* Southern Freedom Knights?"

"Yeah, *them* Southern Freedom Knights," Dixon's uncle answers without any embarrassment whatsoever. Then he turns his horrible gaze back to Dixon to say, "We don't believe in race-mixing of any kind. In fact, the only way any of us would agree to be with one of her kind," he jerks his head at me, "is if he had a goddamn case of amnesia."

27

*T*he world spins.

Not because I'm pregnant.

This isn't another fainting spell, but the kind of mental whiplash you get when a ride spinning so fast one way suddenly decides to go in the opposite direction. A sickening reversal from when John Doe kissed me in my apartment, and made every wish I wouldn't have admitted to harboring—being known only as a doctor by somebody, being kissed for real, not for ratings, experiencing actual attraction for the very first time—come true.

Our story, the story I thought would be wrapped up with a happily ever after bow when we left for Seattle in two days, unravels as my world spins backwards. And this time, when the spinning stops, I'm not a doctor falling hard for an amnesia patient who needs my help, but a crazy reality star who has let the unthinkable into her heart. Into her womb...

"No," I whisper, even as I look at him and see in his eyes that this concept is not new. That it is, in fact, old.

"Doc," he whispers. Then stops, wincing as if something painful is happening inside his head. "I don't know...I don't understand. But I don't care what they say, I love you and I want to be with you."

Sandy has been a producer for too many years. She must have pulled out her phone and started researching as soon as Mason started talking, because she's suddenly standing beside me. Silently shoving a phone into my hands, then quickly stepping back so the camera can get a clean reaction shot.

On her phone, Dixon is dressed in what my mother would call a Sunday Suit. He's clean cut with the kind of neat, contoured pompadour one associates with upstanding Christian men. My mom would totally approve...

If he weren't also waxing poetically and convincingly about subjects so vile, I drop the phone only a minute into it.

"What the fuck is this?" Dad says as I cover my mouth for fear I will throw up all over my evening gown.

"Oh my God...Oh my God..." I say. Still not understanding anything, but somehow getting everything. The mystery of who he is has finally been solved. In under two minutes of YouTube footage.

I look at Woods—no Dixon, as in the freaking *Mason Dixon* line. His name, and his cousin's, and all the implications are suddenly as clear to me as a good-bye song in a musical.

The man standing in front of me is shaking his head like he doesn't understand any of this. But the man on the fallen phone is steadily extolling his viewers to believe, as he and the Southern Knights of Freedom do, in the separation of races.

"That's not me," Dixon insists, his voice harsh with emotion. "He looks like me and he sounds like me. And what he's saying—that's old. I can feel that now. But he's not me, Doc..."

He reaches out for me and I scream, "Don't touch me! Oh my God, don't touch me...!"

And though I'm the one screaming, the one who just found out the guy she fell in love with is the very well-spoken leader of a white supremacist motorcycle gang, he's the one who looks like he's about to cry. "Doc, no...you've got to listen to me. You've got to—"

"She don't got to do nothing but get the hell out of here," my father answers in my stead. "Sandy, cut them mother fucking cameras."

"But this is a rating wonder bomb," Sandy starts. "When the network sees this, they'll renew your contracts for sure. You'll be able to name your price—"

"I said cut them!" Dad yells at her, his face blazing with 100% real anger.

With a disgusted sound, Sandy gives the hand signal and the op lowers the camera.

"C'mon, baby," Dad says, putting a protective arm around me and starting toward the door.

But Dixon gets in front of us. "No! She is my wife!" he says to my dad. "She is carrying my baby."

"What!?!?" both Dad and Dixon's uncle roar.

And fuck orders, the op raises the camera and starts rolling again.

Just in time to watch Dixon fall to his knees in front of me.

"What are you doing?" his uncle demands. "Get off your knees. We done told you how it is. How dare you defile yourself like this over a...!"

Yet another n-word drop, but I'm not sure Dixon even hears the hate his uncle is spewing, his eyes are so intense on me.

"Doc! Doc!" he implores desperately. "It's still you and me. I still love you more than anything. I know this is scary. What I used to be is scary. But you've got to believe in me, in us."

My stomach lurches. I'm torn between so many feelings. I don't want to be on television anymore. I really, really don't want to be anywhere near it. Dixon is a monster—a true monster by both belief and trade. And me...I'm the stupid, stupid woman who fell in love with him. Whose heart can't help but squeeze at the desperate tone of his words, even though I completely understand who he is now.

Tears well up in my eyes, but this time I don't let them fall.

I'm a reality star. I'm a doctor. And now it's time to stop being a fool.

I uncover my mouth and pick the tattooed behemoth he was apparently named beside out of the small crowd. "Hold him back. Hold him back, or he'll try to follow me."

Then in a sweep of heavy evening gown, I head to the door without waiting for their responses.

But Mason, I can tell, is a very, very good soldier for his cause. I hear but don't see him grab Dixon in some kind of chokehold clinch that makes his, "No, Doc! Doc! Doc!" come out strangled.

Yet Dixon still manages to yell after me. So loud, I can hear him begging me not to go, yelling how much I mean to him, how much he loves me. How that's his baby I'm carrying.

"You two belong with me! We're a family! You said you would be my family," I hear him yell as I run for the elevators.

Then and long after the elevator doors have closed.

---

28

*I*n the days that follow what a few online sites dubbed the "Penthouse Showdown," I've read enough to last me a century about Dixon Fairgood.

I now know that the Southern Freedom Knights are an organization so old, they started off on horseback and count themselves among the very first motorcycle "clubs" in the country, begun right after World War I. Dixon's father was actually pretty low on the club's totem pole, and by all accounts a reckless alcoholic who could barely hold down a job, even a criminal one. He never even made it onto the SFK's board. But Dixon's maternal grandfather was the club's president, and his father's brother was the club's Vice President. They along with the rest of the board recognized something in Dixon from a very young age, and he'd basically been groomed to become the president after his grandfather .

Unlike my father who's built an entire bragadocious rap career from a one-year stint selling drugs on the street, the Southern Freedom Knights are actually real-deal criminals. The Feds and the state of Tennessee have them under investigation for all types of shit: from selling meth to running guns.

Colin and Dixon's father actually did a few stints in jail, but the authorities could never make anything stick.

In any case, Dixon Fairgood had been doing a much better job in his inherited position. No blond-haired, blue-eyed Aryan babies to show for it by the age of twenty-eight, but that speech, which he'd made at a "Whites Right Rally" a few years back, with his grandfather's encouragement had gone viral. And he'd apparently done a much better job than his grandfather of connecting and working with disparate supremacist gangs throughout the country. The SFK has been allegedly running their various lucrative underground businesses investigation-free ever since Dixon took over.

Colin might not have liked him very much, even going so far as to declare in one interview he didn't consider him so much a brother as a man who'd been tragically brainwashed. However, there had been no doubt in either Dixon's supporters or detractors minds that he'd eventually go on to be the most famous leader the SFK has ever had.

"Dangerously likeable" one left-leaning political blog described him. Handsome, well-spoken, and smart enough not to "adopt the look," so he blended in with the rest of the populace. A few bloggers spoke of the possibility of him going the David Duke route and eventually running for public office. Sadly, in the rural part of Tennessee the club called home, it wouldn't be hard for him to find enough like-minded people to garner a congressional seat.

And no wonder he'd loved the sweats I'd gotten him. According to the many pictures and reports swirling around on the internet, he'd only worn two uniforms: a full suit or full leathers.

Being able to walk around in sweats all day probably blew his mind.

My mama had warned her stadium congregations in more than one sermon that the devil came in many disguises, and in Dixon's case, it had been a pair of hospital issue sweats.

This is bad. So bad.

So bad, Sola calls me shrieking, only to offer to abandon her Moscow Opera directorial debut after I explain what happened. So bad, she also offers to send in her extremely large husband to "handle" Dixon and the rest of his crew.

I turn down both offers, still too sad and broken-hearted to do anything more than lie in bed most days.

It's so, so bad.

So bad, my mother, who never comes off tour, comes off tour. As does Curt Jr, even though he's also on tour and has been calculatedly throwing Twitter into a tweeting frenzy with hints that he may debut a character based on his mother when both their tours collided—with cameras rolling of course—in Chicago that weekend.

But instead of making the reality TV ratings they need to get their contracts renewed, they both fly home to California. And I know it's really bad when all three of them enter my gigantic bedroom without any film crew, although it was designed specifically for that purpose.

According to Sandy's many texts, my story is scheduled for the front covers of no less than four major gossip magazines, and the network is even talking about pushing forward the season so they can take advantage of the press the Penthouse Showdown is getting.

But I know it's epically bad when my family doesn't say, "Wow, you done fucked up." Or even, "That was some good TV you just made, Nitra!"

Instead, they all crawl into bed with me, like we used to pile in bed together back in the day.

When we still lived in Compton, because Mom's fledgling church was there, and Dad was steady bent on keeping it real. On TV, we're known for having cozy little conversations in our oversized beds, which are all big enough to fit five people. Conversations ranging from what happened that day to what we'd do if a motherfucking alien tried to come at us and we didn't have a gun.

But that was just on the show. In real life, we often used to lie there. Quiet and exhausted and grateful to be part of such an accepting and loving family at the end of a struggle-filled day.

I know it's bad, because instead of talking, we lie like we used to for a very, very long time. So long, I wonder if we'll ever leave the relative safety of where we've ended up.

But eventually Dad says, "I talked with Sandy earlier today. Told her not to bother with contract renewal negotiations. We ain't coming back."

That's an awfully big decision. One most men would have been expected to discuss with their family before making.

But my brother tucks a lock of his wig hair behind his ear before quietly agreeing, "Yeah, I think this is a real good place to end this shit show."

However, I can't let them do this. Can't let them throw away the life they love just to protect me. "No, Dad, you don't have to do that. This is all my fault. I can't let you lose your renewal because of what I did. What I let happen."

Dad looks at me like I'm crazy. Then he says, "Bitch, is you out your monkey-ass mind? This family 300! I don't care what you bitches do or why you do it. We in this together. Ride or mother-fuckin' die." But then Dad's face saddens, as he seems to realize out loud, "That's what I should have told you the first time you tried to quit the show."

"That's right!" Curt Jr. calls out from the other side of my parents, like we're at church. "We family. No matter what happens, Nitra. And you know we have your back no matter what, just like you've always had ours."

When he says this, I know he's talking about when he came out as someone just south of transgender when he was twelve. The "unconditional acceptance on top of unending profanity" that made us such a fascinating docu-drama series hadn't been as automatic as the public was led to believe. And my intractable bitchiness on all subjects from veganism to whether Grenada bought off the rack had come in most handy when wearing both my evangelical mother and my just plain homophobic father down on the subject of letting their only son walk his own path.

However, I truly believe Curt Jr. deserves to live his life however he sees fit. Me getting knocked up by a white supremacist biker? That's on a whole 'nother level.

There's also the other elephant in the bed. My mother and her expectations.

"You can be as bitchy as you want, Nitra Mello. But not with our God. Not with your God!" she told me the one time I tried to float the idea of not going to church with her on TV. "Now get your narrow ass up them steps and get ready for church!"

Right now, I can't help but feel like the biggest disappointment in the world to the woman who raised me to be both practical and responsible, to separate show life from spiritual life, to respect my body enough not to let anyone I don't love into my temple.

This feels way beyond the string of one-night stands I engaged in with regular boys once the cameras were turned off.

And I turn over to look at her, so she knows I mean it from the bottom of my regretful heart when I say, "I'm sorry, Mommy. I'm so sorry."

My mom doesn't cry. She's a shepherd of the Lord, here to do his work without getting distracted by the laments of life. But right now she looks as close to tears as I've ever seen her. And I get the shameful feeling she's forcing herself to meet my gaze after my apology.

But then she pushes my weaved in locks out of my eyes, making me feel like I'm ten again. Like before the show, when she used to talk with me quietly, without "a very special moment" music playing over her words.

"You know where I draw the line when it comes to life," she tells me, voice tight. But then her voice softens as she adds, "But no matter what you decide to do, your daddy's right. I'm with *you*.

I've got your back, too, baby. Because you're my daughter, and I love you."

"I know, Mommy," I say, though I don't think I really did. Not until now, in my darkest moment.

And though I haven't trusted them for a very long time, though I've kept so many things to myself for fear of what they'd do with the news, I tell them now, "I'm keeping this baby."

Mom expels a relieved sigh. She is a true shepherd of the Lord, but I think a drag queen son and a dead daughter is enough for one pastor to have to deal with in a lifetime. I appreciate her bravery and commitment, but I'm not going to add the abortion of her very first grandchild to her lists of woes. Also...

"I loved it before I found out what kind of evil its daddy really was, and I still love it now."

"That's right," both my dad and brother co-sign as Mom nods in full agreement.

"I'm going to pray over you and this baby," she promises me. "And after I come off this tour, me and Daddy will be coming right up there to you in Seattle. You won't have to worry about a thing. Because we're going to help you raise this baby right with the Lord and love."

"And if my little nephew or niece shows any interest in high heels, you know I'll be coming right on up there with a starter set!" my brother promises.

As my mother often does with my brother, she goes silent before making the very wise decision not to respond to his (most likely super true) declaration.

"The point is, it doesn't matter who this baby's daddy is. I hope you know that, pumpkin."

I nod. Knowing but not quite agreeing. Because I know in my most secret of hearts I'm not just keeping it because I love it, but also because it's the only thing I have left of the only man I've truly ever loved. A man who walked into Colin's penthouse suite with me, but didn't come out. The man whose ring I still haven't managed to take off. Even though I know he's not my real husband, could never be my true family after the things his real self has done and said about people like us. No matter how loudly he called after me that we were a family. That he loved me.

Now I let my real family hold me, making the greatest sacrifice they know how to make in order to keep me safe and sane.

Now I cry for all the stupid decisions I've made over the past two months—the ones that felt like falling in love.

And now the mom I thought had been left behind in Compton holds me as she says, "Ssshh! It's going to be all right, baby. We're going to get through this."

29

But I can't stay in the bed with my family forever. For one thing, I have a job I'm supposed to be starting in Seattle next week, and I've already spent three-and-a-half of the four adjustment weeks I'd given myself, hidden away in my family's Hollywood home. For another, the cameras will be back in a few days to film my father going back into the studio to record a love song for my mom in preparation for the huge vow renewal ceremony that's supposed to end their season arc.

Still, my dad doesn't love the idea of me leaving, especially at night. We can be sure there aren't any paparazzi lurking about, even in the trees. So no one will follow me off the property. But...

"I don't think you should be driving by yourself at night."

"It's just to Sola's old place in Valencia," I assure him. "I'll be there in less than an hour, and then I'll wait until daylight to start driving again. I promise."

I wonder if I'll ever get used to this version of my father. The one who became an only slightly nutty, and not nearly so foul-mouthed, forty-something as soon as he decided he was done with the cameras for a while.

I hug him, and then Curt Jr. who's kitted out in full Beyonce drag, yet still managed to get my large suitcase into the back of my Prius in mile-high stilettos.

After he's done, my brother pulls me into a hug. "You sure you don't want me to drive you?" he asks for the millionth time.

I laugh. "Somehow I don't think I'm going to do as good of a job of staying under the press's radar with BuhBounceye in the driver's seat."

"Girl, that ain't nothing but an outfit change," Curt Jr. assures me. "I got a Ruby Dee upstairs ain't nobody going to question."

"Okay, sweetie," I say, kissing him on both cheeks. "I think it's time for both you and Mom to get back to your tours, and for me to start pretending the last two months never happened."

"That's gonna be a stretch even for you, Nitra," Dad says.

But Mom pulls me into her arms and says, "Text us as soon as you get to Sola's house."

"I will," I promise.

And I do, sending out a group text before I stop in at the main house to say hello to Brian.

Brian is Sola's mentor and second father. Literally the man who gave her away at her wedding to Ivan Rustanov. In fact, he's leaving early the next morning to attend the opening night performance of her Moscow Opera directorial debut, but he still stayed up late to make sure I got into Sola's old guest house okay.

"Not at all, my dear girl," Brian insists when I try to thank him for his consideration. "I don't sleep much these days anyway. Consequence of getting old and sober."

We have a cup of organic loose leaf tea and talk about the weather in L.A. as opposed to West Virginia. My new job at the Children's Hospital of Seattle. The relatively light traffic on the 5 this time of night.

Everything except what's most weighing on our minds. My huge scandal, and the recent death of Brian's husband.

The closest we come to it is when he walks me to the back door and clasps my hand between both of his. "You'll be doing good work up there in Seattle, young Anitra. Even though you've abandoned the arts, I want you to know both Sola and I remain proud of you."

His words mean a lot to me. But the truth is, as I sink into bed in Sola's old bedroom, I feel closer to turning fifty in July than twenty-six. I'm weary in a way that probably has nothing to do with the life I'm carrying inside me. I think about the one time I pushed the man I originally knew as John Doe to get help, and wonder how long I can go before I'll have to consider taking my own advice.

Then I welcome the black of sleep, dropping a curtain down on both the reality show and real life.

∼

I FALL asleep in Sola's bed...

...but I don't wake up there.

Instead I come awake with a gasp in the harsh early morning sun. The wind whipping through my weave, my hands tied in front of me. There are wooden planks instead of Sola's carpet all around me, and beyond that, lots and lots of stone blue water as far as my eyes can see.

There's also a metal banister in my direct sightline. It's the only thing standing between me and the grayish blue water. That's when I realize I'm on the deck of a large but ancient tugboat, sitting on a bench originally meant to seat fisherman. But why do my feet feel so heavy...?

My eyes widen with horror when I look down. My legs are also tied, nylon rope binding them to what looks like some kind of small, rusty engine...

A motorcycle engine, I realize with a start.

"She's awake," a gruff voice says. And then comes the sound of booted feet approaching.

I get most of my answers then with one tilt of my head upwards. A bunch of bikers in leather vests and thick sweatshirts are now standing in front of me.

There has to be at least eight men surrounding me, all dressed in leather, all with different degrees of extreme hate etched across their faces.

Mason's there. As well as his father. But the only one of these men I really care about is standing in the middle of their ranks. And that's when my heart totally flatlines.

Because I don't recognize this man.

This man has the same blue eyes as the John Doe I met two months ago, but now he's clean-cut with the same haircut as the man in the video I watched that night in Colin's penthouse suite. He's also wearing a leather jacket with a patch that declares him the President of the Southern Freedom Knights.

Woods is gone. I can see that now. Killed and buried under his true identity. And Dixon Fairgood—the real Dixon Fairgood—has taken his place. He stands like a boss among these vile men, glaring at me with the same glittering hatred in his eyes.

"Your memory's come back," I whisper.

He looks me up and down, lets a full disgusted second pass by before answering, "That it has, race traitor. That it has."

30

*H*e remembers.

I'm almost more horrified for him than myself, even though I'm the one tied up. Because now he remembers everything. And now he hates me just as much as he would have if he'd met me before his accident.

No worse, because now he also hates what we did together. And the baby we made.

It feels like I spend hours inside Dixon's hateful blue stare. But in actuality, it's only seconds. Seconds of him glaring at me in the exact same deadly way he glared at those West Virginia bikers. Associates of his, I can now see clearly, with the 20/20 hindsight of true knowledge. That must have been how he just "knew" they were there about his backpack.

Back then, those guys were the enemy and I was the woman he was trying to protect. But now...

Now his uncle asks, "You ready to wipe this impurity and her mulatto abomination from the Earth?"

And I'm so busy looking for any trace whatsoever of Woods inside Dixon Fairgood, that it doesn't even occur to me to process or protest what his uncle just said.

But then Dixon issues a stony, "Mason."

And like a leather clad automaton on voice control, his cousin moves toward me.

"No!" I scream. Finally understanding, but still not quite able to believe Dixon is going to kill me along with our unborn baby because of his hateful views. "No!!!"

But then it's too late. Mason lifts me from the bench like I weigh no more than my one word of protest. Then I'm sailing through the air. Into a place where no sound or safety exists, right before I crash into the water.

I struggle against my fate, even as I realize I'm going to die.

I keep my eyes open against the sting of the cold salt water, fighting my inevitable death with everything I have, even though I know it's hopeless.

I fight and fight. Until the ropes around my hands suddenly give way, the knot coming undone as easily as a shoe lace.

My arms are free!

Now I really start struggling, pushing my arms against the water, trying to get up to the sweet, sweet air. But the engine tied around my legs is heavy, and despite my adrenaline and desperation, my arms are starting to weaken. I'm simply not strong enough to—

My desperate thoughts are interrupted by a cannonball hitting the water.

No, not a cannonball, but...

My eyes widen. Confusion temporarily shorting out my panic as I see a man whip around, searching...until he sees me and makes a beeline.

I haven't made much progress, but I'm close enough to the light above the water's surface to realize that it's Mason. And he's got a huge knife in his hand.

What the...? Oh no!

He reaches out to me, and I fight him. But I'm no match. He easily grabs me around the waist, pulling me in close with one arm. And my soul cries out, because I know he's going to put that knife through my stomach, but then...

I'm suddenly lighter, and just like that, we're rising. Getting closer and closer to the surface on the power of Mason's kicks.

And things only get stranger after we break the surface. I'm busy trying to cough up water and breathe and tread at the same time. But he seems intent on some kind of mission. He only gives me a few moments to finish coughing before pulling me backwards into a rescue hold. He paddles us back toward the old tugboat and doesn't stop until we reach the place where a short metal ladder hangs down from the side.

I grab ahold of the structure gratefully, still coughing up water. But the oxygen must have brought back my rational brain, because I pause halfway up, not sure what to do.

On the one hand, I don't want to take my chances back in the ocean, especially with no land whatsoever in sight. On the other hand, the last time I checked, the only thing on this tugboat was a group of bikers who wanted me dead. Including the father of my baby.

"Go!" Mason shouts behind me, ending my indecision. "Get back on the fucking boat!"

I climb, liking my odds on the boat way better than down in the water, especially now that my hands are untied and my feet are weight free.

And just as I'm about to crest the top of the ladder, a familiar hand reaches out. One that's touched every single part of my body.

I take it, more out of surprise than anything.

And Dixon hauls me back onto the boat, gathering me into his arms in a way that feels both foreign and familiar. Yes, I remember the hug, but the leather jacket he's wearing is cold and unforgiving against my cheek.

He takes the jacket off and tries to wrap it around me. But I shake my head. Even as cold as I am, I do not want that thing anywhere near my body.

"Mason, get her a blanket," he calls out. And a moment later, I'm wrapped up in a blanket even warmer than Dixon's arms.

He takes my face in both his hands, "You okay?" he demands. "Are you okay?"

"Wh-what did you drug me with to get me out here?"

He gives me the name of the same anesthesia I'd seen used to put pregnant women under when they need gallbladder surgery.

"How much?"

Again he answers with a dosage number I can live with. "Okay," I say, releasing a shaky breath. "I was only down there for a few minutes. At this early stage I'm most likely fine, like I just took a swim. But I'll schedule an ultrasound to make sure on Monday."

"Thank God." He hugs me again. "It was the only way to get you clear while I took care of them. Or else I never wouldn't have chanced it."

The only way? Now that my initial diagnosis is done, my trembling mind struggles to process his words. What reason could he possibly have for kidnapping me? Having me tossed in the ocean? Taking such a chance with two lives, one of which is still extremely fragile?

As if hearing my questions spoken out loud, he tells me, "They were going to come after you. I had to play along. Get them out here. Then get you clear, so I could make sure they never threatened you or the baby again."

I pull out of his embrace, because I still don't understand, much less comprehend his words. Until suddenly I can, because that's when I see what I couldn't when his arms were around me...

All the dead bodies now strewn across the tugboat's floor.

"Don't look," he implores me.

But how can I not? Every single biker from before, every single biker other than Mason, is now dead on the boat's deck.

31

It was the only way.

We drive back to Sola's place in the same white conversion van I was apparently driven away in. Like the boat, the van is also old. A loaner from a local club.

California has white supremacist gangs? I almost ask, before realizing I've been coddled for far too long. Outside my rarefied world, there's real life hate, not staged hate. As it is, I'm finding it hard to feel anything but neutral about the deaths of what Dixon referred to as "his board" when he came to get me out of the tugboat's inner cabinet.

By the time Mason and Dixon are done disposing and cleaning-up after the eight dead bodies, I'm dressed in dry clothes, warm, and totally okay with Dixon's logic. He's right. As crazed as his gang was, there would have been nothing Dixon could have said to them to get them to leave me alone and let me have their president's mixed-race baby. This wasn't the only way, but yes, it was probably the best way to eliminate the threat as quickly, quietly, and efficiently as possible.

Which is how I find myself hesitating when we pull into the driveway and it's time to get out of the van.

When he comes around to the passenger side after fetching my suitcase—you know, the one he and his gang stole from the guest house when they drugged and kidnapped me in the middle of the night—I realize what I should do is take it and run, never looking back.

But instead, I find myself pulling Ivan's business card out of the Virkin PETA gifted me with a few years ago. "Here," I tell him.

He lets go of my suitcase handle and takes the card from me. "Ivan Rustanov. Who's this?"

"My best friend's husband. He's part of a powerful Russian family. If anyone can help you with fallout control, it's him."

His eyes flick from the card back up to me. "You still worrying about me?"

I put a lot of effort into not letting him trap me in his gaze again. We're no longer those strangers who met in West Virginia. "I don't want you hurt or dead, if that's what you're asking."

"No, Doc, that ain't what I'm asking."

He looks at me and I can't help but look back at him while tension that should no longer be there crackles between us.

But...

"You really remember?" I ask him, voice so faint, I wonder if it won't be drowned out by the birds chirping over head.

He looks down, then seems to decide to meet my eyes. "Yeah. Not at first. They took me back to Tennessee. Back to our family farm. Couple of days in, I was drinking a Shiner Bock and cleaning my bike and it all just came back to me. The deal with the New Rebels, the accident, everything before it."

"Spontaneous recovery," I say, unable to stop myself from labeling what happened to him. Back when I'd been trying to help the John Doe in the hospital, I'd read how the reminder effect often didn't help with retrograde amnesia, but sometimes classic association did. The act of doing something you'd done a million times before—like drinking a local beer while you clean your bike—bringing back a flood of memories in a way that simply being shown or told something hadn't.

"Yeah, I guess that's what you'd call it."

"So you remember saying those things in the video now?"

Again he looks downs, jaw ticking before he admits, "Yeah, I do. I don't know what to say to you about that now."

He looks back up at me then. Eyes still so honest. But clear and no longer those of my innocent John Doe. "I'm trying to fix this. Trying to fix it the best I can."

I can see that, and I release the breath I didn't realize I was holding. "Okay," I say. "Call Ivan. He can help you fix it, and keep it fixed."

Dixon nods. "If that's what you want me to do, then that's what I'll do."

I'll do anything you want me to do. You know that, right?

His words from just a few weeks ago float into my mind. Hurting me more than getting thrown into the water.

I want to touch him. I want to knuckle his face like he used to knuckle mine.

Instead I grab the handle of my suitcase. "I should go," I tell him.

Because I really should before I add one more ill-advised thing to the list of "Dumb Shit I've Done Since Meeting Dixon Fairgood."

Dixon runs a hand over his face. And he's still so handsome, but there are dark circles under his eyes now. Like me, he now reads a few years older than when the biggest secret between us was some silly reality show.

Still, he smiles at me. "Don't worry, Doc. I'm going to make sure you're safe. And thanks for this," he says, waving the card.

He's no longer a John Doe.

He's the president of a white supremacist motorcycle gang.

He remembers everything now.

He had to have me kidnapped and thrown into the ocean to protect me from all the people who want to hurt me because of the baby inside my womb.

Yet, it feels like I'm at the door of his hospital room again, heart beating fast, because I know I'm somewhere I shouldn't be.

But this time, I don't come in and take a seat. This time, I take my suitcase and rush into the guest house without saying good-bye. For fear of what will come out of my mouth if I let myself stay there even a moment longer.

32

I wasn't trying to assuage Dixon when I told him I thought I was okay. Knock-out drugs withstanding, I can sense the baby inside my body will be fine after this. And when I walk back into the guest house, it feels like I've taken a very scary dip in the water. Ultimately not harmful, but emotionally exhausting.

I end up falling back into Sola's bed for a very long time, and this time when I wake up, I'm still in it. It's also morning again.

If not for the fact that I'm dressed in an entirely new outfit, the same yoga pants and long-sleeved top I put on in the tugboat's cabin, I would have thought the whole thing a nightmare.

But it wasn't. If I didn't know that for sure before I take a shower and repack the few things I took out of my suitcase, then I definitely know it when I walk out to the living room...

And find Mason sitting on the couch, flipping through an old issue of *Vanidades* magazine. He's once again dressed in dark jeans. But this morning he's paired them with a simple waffle shirt. Unlike the last time I saw him, he's not dripping wet, and his Southern Freedom Knights jacket is nowhere to be seen.

"How did you get in here?' I demand.

Mason grunts and throws the magazine back down on the coffee table. "You ready to go?"

Seriously, why is he in Sola's living room? But I also feel compelled to ask, "You know Spanish?"

"A little," he admits with a frown. "Enough to do deals with the wet—"

He stops himself and replaces it with the word, "Hispanics. Dixon couldn't be seen doing deals with them. He was the one they sent to do deals with our kind without attracting too much attention. I'm the one they used for the people they didn't want to be associated with."

"Okay, well thanks for that disturbing bit of information. And for looking out for me while I slept, I guess." I start toward the door. "I'm going now, so you can also be on your way.

"Ain't good-bye yet," he informs me, standing up and blocking my path to door. "Not 'til we get to Seattle."

I shake my head. "I can get my own self to Seattle."

"Probably," Mason agrees. "But D. told me to take you, so that's what I'm going to do."

"Seriously, I'd rather drive myself. And no offense, but the thought of spending a day-and-a-half in a car with a virulent racist murderer really doesn't appeal to me."

"No offense back, I don't give two fucks how you feel about being in a car with me. D. said I was taking you, so that's what I'm going to do. Now, you can stand here and flap your mouth some more or hand over your keys, unless you want to do this the hard way."

Against my better judgment I ask, "And the hard way is?"

His mouth hitches into a lazy smile, just the same as Dixon's. "I don't know for sure how you're going to like spending a day and a half on the back of my bike with your arms handcuffed around my waist, but I suspect it ain't going to appeal to you. Plus, we'd have to leave your suitcase behind. But if that's how you want to do it…"

So that's how I end up spending the next several hours in the passenger seat of my own car. Arms crossed in grudging silence, until we get to San Francisco.

Mason scans the horizon, his light blue eyes taking in the city. "Guess we'll stop here for the night," he doesn't sound at all happy about the prospect. "Have to check in with Dixon and tell him we got here safe."

"Are you afraid your gang will come after us in San Francisco?" I ask him.

"No, the board hasn't been missing long enough for them to worry yet. And they don't have the resources. D. emptied the accounts, and most of them don't have two nickels to rub together without the club. I just hate cities, that's all."

"I think Dixon hates them, too," I say, thinking back to how he spent his time during the month he lived with me. "He really likes being outside."

"Yeah, his old man was a piece of work, and he only got worse after D's mom died. Drank a bunch. Me and D. would meet up and camp out for days. A lot of times, outside was the safest place to be."

"Did his father smoke," I ask, remembering the episode with the neuro res and the cane.

"Three packs a day and sometimes he used D. to put them out. D. sure wasn't crying at the funeral after the bastard's liver finally gave out."

"And you?" I find myself asking.

"And me what?"

"Was your dad a piece of work, too?" The memory of Dixon's uncle, dead on the deck floats into my mind. Of hearing Mason say at one point during the clean-up, "Well, my old man was right about this being a good place to dump a body." With no emotion whatsoever.

"I ain't sad D. killed him if that's what you're asking."

I think back to Dixon's response to my similar feint yesterday. *No, Doc, that ain't what I'm asking.*

And I wonder how many old broken bones an x-ray scan would find under Mason's otherwise massive body.

"Is that why you're going against everything you know to help Dixon?" I ask him. "Because your father was abusive?"

"Yeah, sure, I guess. Let's go with that and stop talking about it," Mason answers in a way that tells me that's all I'm going to get from him on the subject. Then he pulls into the garage of the first hotel he sees.

I THINK about running away in the night. But Mason still has my keys and I'm not even sure the hotel will let me have my own car back since Mason checked us in with the valet.

So instead, I end up sharing continental breakfast with a much less chatty Fairgood. One who answers every question I have with little more than monosyllabic words and grunts.

I'm almost happy when we get back on the road, because it means I'm that much closer to not having to spend any more time with Mason.

Still, I find myself peeping over at him. Unable to resist the temptation to diagnose his behavior despite how very little he's given me to go on.

"So you just do whatever Dixon tells you?" I ask, trying a different tact. "Up to and including driving his black baby mama to Seattle?"

Mason grips and ungrips the steering wheel. "You're more to him than that," he eventually answers. "Maybe you ain't as smart as he says you are, because you ought to have figured that much out after seeing all them dead bodies on the boat."

I shift in my seat, not wanting to believe, but having to ask. "So you're saying he still has feelings for me. Even though I'm black?"

"Yeah, even though. Or maybe because of it. Hell, I don't know." He grunts and refocuses on the road. "You grow up all your life being told you can't have a thing, it's going to make you wonder. Then you take a bad hit to the head? I dunno, shit happens, I guess."

I can tell he more than wants to be done with this conversation. But my now inherent sixth sense for latent drama detection won't let me let it be.

"This isn't about Dixon and me, is it?" I guess out loud.

Now he looks over at me like I'm an idiot. "Of course it's about you and Dixon. Who else would it be about? You think I'd be driving you around in this fucking golf cart disguised as a real car if it wasn't about you and him?"

He's trying to make me feel dumb, intimidate me into shutting up. But at the end of the day, he's unwittingly made an appearance on exactly one episode of a drama-filled reality show, while I've been contracted for over one hundred—not including reunion specials. I'm just plain old better at uncovering drama than he is at keeping it hidden.

"No," I answer after carefully considering his words. "I really don't. It's taken me seven years to outgrow my reality show values, and I didn't even start off on *Rap Star Wives*. You and Dixon were born into this. So no, I don't think you'd let him kill your father and explode your legacy just because he asked you to...not unless there was something else in it for you. Or..."

My drama sensor finally goes off like it's hit pay dirt as I realize out loud, "*Or someone else.*"

Mason doesn't answer, but his hands are gripping my Prius's steering wheel so tight, I can tell I hit a nerve. And that sends my mind down all sorts of different paths. Wondering what girl could have caused Mason to reconsider his value system after all this time. Who is she? And perhaps more importantly, what will he do now that he's no longer a Southern Freedom Knight?

But then Mason explodes. "You know what? Me and Dixon have been through a lot together! We were born the same exact week, so we're more like brothers than cousins. So if he says it's time to dismantle the SFK, I do it. If he says he needs me to drive his big-mouthed girl to Seattle, I do it. That's the whole story. The end of the story. Now shut the fuck up!"

Oooh, I've made someone very mad! I waggle my eyebrows, Nitra Mello on total fleek, even as I agree with an easy going tone, "Okay, I'll be quiet, but if you ever want to talk about this girl with somebody..."

"I swear to fucking God, I will put you in the trunk of this car and duct tape your mouth shut," he threatens. "D. just said I had to drive you. He didn't say how."

I don't think Mason would really do it. But there's a rather thin line between think and know. So I clamp my mouth shut on a smile, and settle for silently knowing what I'm pretty sure I now know.

This goes on for a few minutes before Mason cuts into my thoughts with a growled, "Fuck, we need gas."

He pulls into the first gas station he sees. "Fucking take a piss now, because I ain't stopping again until we get to Seattle."

Again I decide to err on the side of preventative belief.

"May I give you money for gas?" I ask when I come back from the bathroom and find him at the pump.

His eyes narrow. "Funny, you don't sound anything like you did on TV."

I look at him, thinking that's why I liked his cousin. He's the only real life love interest I've ever had who hasn't expressed surprise that I don't actually sound like a reality show stereotype in real life.

"I'm not Nitra Mello anymore. I'm Dr. Anitra Dunhill full time from now on," I tell Mason.

"Well, I don't need your money, Dr. Dunhill," Mason informs me. "But as long as you're on this side of the car…"

He opens the Prius's back door and half his body disappears inside.

When he re-emerges, he has a manila envelope in his hand. "Here, read this instead of bothering me for the rest of the trip."

"What is this—?" I start to ask.

But he turns away, walking toward the station's restrooms before I can finish my question. "Gonna take a piss," he calls back to me as if I need to know that.

33

$\mathcal{B}$ack inside the car, I open the envelope and find…

A brown craft paper journal, with the words UWV/Mercy Mental Health Services emblazoned across the front. I pull it out along with several pages that have obviously been torn out of an indexed notebook. A letter, I realize when I see the words written at the top of the first page.

Dear Doc,

I'm known in my circles to be eloquent with my words. But I guess that's a lie, because standing outside that van with you, I still didn't have the words to explain who I used to be. So I'm doing what the head doctor said I should back when I was a patient at your hospital. I'm writing everything down in the hopes I can make sense of it.

I could tell you I was born into this. As was my father, and his father before him. My father was an angry drunk who beat on anything stupid enough to love him, including my mom, but they agreed on one thing: that the races should stay separate. That we were superior. But I guess you already know that.

I grew up on a compound with people who believed the same as my parents did. In my whole life, I'd never said more than five or ten words to someone who didn't have the same skin color as me. We weren't allowed to watch TV. We weren't allowed to listen to anything but white country and Christian music. I play the guitar, but country and Christian is all I play. I also know a few things about doctoring, because my mother was the club's nurse. As the daughter of the Prez, part of her job was to patch up our club members, and sometimes I helped with that. I think that's part of the reason I was attracted to you in the first place. Because you remind me of the better aspects of her. The best ones.

I know that's a strange thing to say with you being black and all. But you have to understand, without these memories, without this care-fully cultivated hate inside of me, black ain't what I saw when I first laid eyes on you.

I saw you. The real you. Not that girl on TV. But the doctor I had mistaken for a nurse, teaching dying kids to sing. I can't begin to explain how beautiful I found you from the first moment I laid eyes on you. Skin color didn't have nothing to do with it.

As for the things I said. I can remember saying them now. And even worse, I can remember believing those words. But now...now I know you. Now you're carrying my baby. A little life we made together with love, not hate.

And when I watch myself saying those words I had memorized by heart, even though I remember giving those speeches, it feels like I'm watching someone else. Somebody young and ignorant, even though that was me just a few months ago.

So now I'm doing what needs to be done to keep you safe. To keep what we made together safe. I'm disbanding Southern Freedom Knights, and doing a few other things to ensure they never ride again. The Feds approached me and Mason a couple of times before my accident, and I turned them down. A few weeks ago, Mason and me had a long discussion, and we decided to approach them this time.

I know your father has a helluva lot of things to say about snitches, but in this case, I think he'll forgive me for working with the authorities to make sure our club never hurts an innocent again.

I signed our land over to the state, suggested they do something good with it.

And as for that money I was walking around with? Well, technically I got that and a motorcycle in exchange for a conversion van full of guns I drove up from Tennessee. That's why I wasn't carrying ID on me. It would have been too dangerous for the club if I'd gotten caught. So yeah, that money's plenty dirty, but I made it clean. It belongs to UWV/Mercy's Pediatrics Department now. An anonymous gift.

Why am I doing this? Why am I so determined to protect you and our baby given how I was brought up? That's what I'm going to try to make you understand now, Doc.

I was broken way before I ever landed in your hospital, and crazy as it sounds, I truly believe that TBI saved me. I truly believe your love healed all the things that were wrong with me. Doc, you're the one who fixed me.

I know it's impossible to believe feelings like the ones I used to have about race-mixing could go away overnight. That all these memories could come back to me and look like nothing but a bad TV show I don't want to be on no more. But that's the truth of it. The truth as I know it. Fuck everything I've been taught, I only want to be with you.

I love you, Doc. I still love you with everything inside me. I didn't want to scare you with it back in West Virginia. Didn't want you to think I was both brain-damaged and crazy. But I'm enclosing something that will hopefully explain the way I feel about you, how I felt about you from the start, in a way I can't with this one letter.

It's the journal my hospital head doctor told me to start keeping to help me with my memory recovery. He told me to do that two weeks before I met you. But I didn't pay attention. Not until I saw you.

I hope this helps you understand, Doc.

Yours forever,
Woods

FORGET MY TRAINING. With shaking hands, I put aside the letter and open the journal. Inside I find an unexpected bounty of words that begin with, *"Today I saw my future wife for the first time..."*

Unable to stop myself, I read a side of this tale that I'd never heard. About a thirty-something amnesia patient who didn't know anything of his past. Only what was in doctor's reports. He's miserable and confused and weak, which he hates. His misery makes him belligerent, and half his PT sessions end with him limping out in a snit. That is until his physical therapist takes him down to the chemo lounge, during one of his mandated walks. He hangs back on the wall, only watching for the excuse to not have to walk for a while. But then *she* comes into the lounge with her guitar. A nurse with the prettiest hair and eyes he's ever seen. He loves her the moment he sees her singing with those kids. But he's feeble at this point, "not half a man," so he watches from afar. Works harder at the PT. Biding his time for now, but knowing she's his.

Then one day he calls out to her, and what follows is pages and pages of every word I ever spoke to him. Of how he tries not to stare at my beautiful brown skin or fall into my dark eyes, but how he can't help himself. In this version of his story, every single thing I say and do means volumes to him. From bringing him lunch to telling him I'll be the family who can't be here for him.

"When I hear the word 'family,' I don't get the sense of it as a good thing. But when she says the word, it's all I can do not to grab her and kiss her the way I been wanting to all along."

He goes on and on like this. And yes, there's the map he drew for me that one day when we were doing cognitive exercises, with the label *"Drew this for her because she asked me to."* Then comes a dark moment with the cane and the smoking resident. He thinks he's scared me away forever, that I'll never come see him again. He's pondering how to find me downstairs now that his walking around privileges have been revoked. Trying to figure out how to convince me to come back to him when the journal entry abruptly cuts short. Only to pick up at the next entry proclaiming that I miraculously showed up in his room, *"more worried than scared."* And though I didn't come back after he kissed me, he knows. He just knows. *"If we could make it through that, we can make it through anything."*

My heart clenches reading the words, so indicative of the John Doe I knew. So sure of himself. But so naïve when it came to matters of love.

The journal ends the Monday after I take him home. *"I'm outside now. Not in the hospital's outside, but in <u>her</u> outside and down to my last page. She's brought me home. Maybe because she's a very good person. At least that's what she's probably telling herself. But I think she's feeling it, just like me. That we belong together. That now we've found each other, we ain't got no business ever being apart. She ain't my wife yet, but I know it's just a matter of time. We're going to be something to each other. She's going to agree she loves me, too, and at the end of this story, she will be mine. All I gotta do now is wait."*

BY THE TIME I'm done reading, the diary pages are damp with my tears. And the car, I realize, is still parked.

I look over at Mason. "Why are we still at the..."

I trail off before I can finish because I see we aren't still at the gas station. I was so absorbed in reading, I didn't notice that not only had we left the gas station, we've driven about forty miles. And now we are sitting outside of a building I'd only seen before in online images. A spaceship-like structure constructed of brushed aluminum and glass that looked as far from my little brick two-story apartment building in West Virginia as you could get.

Yet, on the steps sits a long, lean figure I still associate with West Virginia. Except he's not dressed in sweats now, nor leather.

Today he's wearing a simple Henley with jeans and he has a
piece of paper in his hand.

He stands as soon as I get out of the car.

"Dixon..." I say, not knowing what to make of the fact that he's
here at my new home. As if I conjured him out of thin air with
my tears.

But he shakes his head and holds up the document in his hand.

"I filed for a name change," he tells me from above. "My name—
my real name—is going to be Woods from now on."

He lowers the papers and says, "I ain't John Doe no more, Doc.
And I could never ask you to love Dixon Fairgood. But do you
think you could love Woods Mello? Because believe me, he loves
you more than anything else on this earth."

We stand there like that. Him above and me below. The ultimate
question hanging between us, along with both our pasts.
Waiting for my answer.

EPILOGUE

"*W*hat did you say?" Lilli, the new peds nurse, asks breathlessly after I finish my story.

I widen my eyes at her. "What do you think I said? I told him no freaking way! I don't care how many times you change your name. Ain't no way we are ever, ever getting back together."

Apparently Lilli's a lot more romantic than I am, because she looks absolutely crushed by my story's lack of a happy ending. "But what happened with the baby?" she demands. "And where'd he go after you said no?"

"Right on into her new apartment with her," a voice answers from the door.

"Damn it, Woods, I had her!" I complain as my husband strolls into the break room in a sweatshirt declaring him a medical student at Washington State University—Seattle. "She's been in Japan for the last few years, so this whole story is totally new to her. I could have kept it going until Sandy showed up in September!"

"Un-huh," Woods says, pressing a tender kiss into my forehead. "And what would you have done when I kept on showing up here for lunch every day during my school break?"

"Wondered why you weren't at home studying for the Step 1, just like I am now," I answer.

Woods lifts an eyebrow. "C'mon, Doc...you know how I feel about lying," he says. "And Taylor Swift quotes."

"More like teasing. A gentle hazing if you will," I answer. "And Taylor writes very quotable songs. What can I say?"

"Well for starters, you could tell..." he throws Lilli an apologetic look and she supplies, "Lilliana. Lilliana Tucker. But everybody calls me Lilli."

Wood sticks out his hand. "Nice to meet you, Lilli. I'm Woods Mello. Sorry my wife's been pulling your leg. What she should have said is after a whole lot of talking and some couples' counseling, we figured it out. And now we're very happy living in a big old house in Maple Valley with Nitra's parents and our little boy Curtis. I got accepted into the combined med school program over at WSUS, and somehow we're making it work. Our life is crazy, but it's good. In fact, it's better than anything either of us ever could have imagined."

"Yeah, I could have told her that," I agree, looking up at Woods with all my love. "But how funny would it have been when Sandy showed up with the cameras, and we were all like, 'Psyche! We living happily ever after, Lilli!"

Lilli shakes her head with a quizzical look. "Really? Because I don't see why that would be so much fun for you..."

Again Woods apologizes for me, "My wife will never admit it, but truth is, now that we're on a serious docu-drama that actually received a Peabody award last month, she's missing all the fake drama."

"Maybe," I concede. "But not any of the real stuff," I promise him. "I like our life just fine."

"I bet," says Lilli with a laugh. "Your story is crazy, but I'm glad you two figured it out. Can I ask what happened with Colin Fairgood? Oh, and how about Mason and the girl you think he might have been secretly in love with?"

I grimace while Woods whistles low.

"Well, Colin and his family are coming to visit us at Christmas, but Mason—that's a whole 'nother story," he tells Lilli.

One I'm perfectly willing to tell, since Woods is maybe totally right about me missing drama that doesn't involve coordinating schedules, potty training, and staving off ever more aggressive questions from my parents about when I'm going to give them another grandbaby to spoil. At this point, other people's gossip is just about the only thing I have left from my old life.

But before I can give Lilli the goods, Harriet Fields, the director of our hospital, sticks her head into the break room, looking all sorts of peeved.

"Miss Tucker, there is a possible Japanese donor in my office who would like to go over a few questions he has about the hospital with you."

"Um..." Lilli starts. "I only speak a little Japanese, and I also just started here a few weeks ago, so maybe I'm not the best choice..."

"Yes, I'm well aware of this, Miss Tucker," Harriet answers. "Nonetheless, he is here and asking for you. Specifically. He says you were... associates in Japan?"

Lilli starts. "Me?" Then she asks, "What is his name, exactly?"

"Norio Nakamura."

Lilli's mouth drops open, as if she's just heard the name of a ghost. A very scary ghost.

"Norio Nakamura," Woods repeats into Lilli's shocked silence. "Are you talking about that billionaire who just bought the Seattle Fishers?"

"He did what?!?!" Lilli asks, like Woods has shocked all the breath out of her.

"Yeah, I know, only in his 30s, and now he owns a major league baseball team. That's all they were talking about on sports radio this morning," he answers Lilli. Then he asks Harriet, "Are you talking about that guy? Because if so, that's a mighty big potential donor you got waiting in your office."

"Yes, he is," Harriet agrees, shooting Lilli a sour look. "So if you could follow me, Miss Tucker."

I can tell by the way Lilli stands there as if her feet are rooted to the ground that she doesn't necessarily want to see this mysterious billionaire claiming to be an associate of hers.

"Wait a minute, Lilli's on her lunch break," I protest on the stunned nurse's behalf. "Plus, we're having a very important conversation. You can't just come in here and tell her she has to go answer this guy's questions."

"Oh, yes, I most certainly can, Dr. Dunhill!" Harriet insists. "Do you know what kind of donation could be on the line here?"

I'm about to show our director my weird talent for getting as close as humanly possible without touching while shouting into another woman's face when Lilli suddenly unfreezes.

"It's okay," she assures both of us, or maybe just herself.

She expels another long breath, shaking her whole body out, before saying, "Yeah, yeah, I can do this. Sure, it's no problem for me to show him around."

I watch Lilli follow Harriet out of the room and down the hallway with my lips clamped together until Woods observes, "There you go again..."

"There I what again?" I ask, shifting my attention back to him.

He draws me into his arms with a lazy smile. "Worrying big about people you've only just met."

"Well, it worked out with you, didn't it? With just a little bit of drama in-between. At least so far."

"At least *forever*," Woods corrects, pressing another tender kiss to my forehead. "I don't care how much drama life throws our way, I ain't never giving up on us."

His commitment to our love and our family continues to make my heart beat faster two years, one adorable baby boy, an expensive house, and one very real reality show later.

But before I can let that thought guide me toward kissing him, I remember the question he never answered, "Seriously, why are you here? I thought you'd be studying for the Step 1 all summer break."

"Yeah, about that, Doc." He grimaces. "I got to thinking about spending the only six sunny weeks Seattle gets a year doing nothing but studying a test and not seeing much of you or Lil' Curt and I decided, "Nah, not for me."

"Not for you?" I repeat, shaking my head with real alarm. "What are you trying to say? Are you dropping out of med school? But I thought you loved it, even with the crazy class schedule and having to study all the time!"

"More like I decided to take the test without the studying all hours of the day part."

"What?!?!" I all but shout. "Tell me you did not take the most important test of your medical school career early, just to get out of studying!!"

"And to see you and Lil' Curt more," Woods reminds me.

"Woods, tell me you didn't do that for *any* reason...!"

Woods wags his head from side to side. "I would tell you that, Doc. But remember those vows we exchanged about being honest with each other at our real wedding?"

"Oh my God! You know they don't let you re-sit the exam if you get a low score. And this could affect all your matches!"

"There you go thinking again, Doc," he answers with a lazy smile.

"No, Woods, this is serious! Don't try to distract me with all your cuteness. We need to figure this out. I guess we'll just have to wait until your score comes back to see what you got..."

Another grimace. "That's kind of why I'm here. I just got my scores back."

"What?!?!" I shout again, even louder this time. "But you just finished your academic year last week. How are you already getting your scores back?"

Usually I can't help but laugh when my lethal husband screws up his face like he's afraid of getting hit by little ol' me. But it's not so funny when he does it as he answers, "Because I took the test during spring break."

"You...you...?" I'm too flabbergasted to even repeat the words that came out of his mouth or believe my husband took a life-changing test he didn't study for before he was even done with his second year of classes.

But he seems to get the gist of what I'm trying to ask. "Well, you were scheduled to work all week. And your parents took Lil' Curt with them to visit your brother. Figured why not?"

I open my mouth to tell him all the reasons why not. But then I remember who we are. Family 300, all the way, through and through.

"Okay," I say on a sigh. "This is okay. Whatever happens it's okay. We're going to be okay."

Woods rubs the back of his neck with a chagrined smile. "I'm glad you feel that way, Doc, because...I got a 267."

I'm pretty sure even the people on the bottom floor of the hospital can hear my happy scream all the way on the top.

Just in case you're not a subscriber to the *Miserable Medical Student Times*, 267 is pretty much the best score you can get without possible match residencies flagging you for maybe being too academically advanced to work well with patients.

This score, along with the notoriety our award-winning show has brought him, means when it comes time to be matched with a residency program, he'll have a very good chance of getting into one right here with me in Seattle.

In any case, a few minutes after his announcement, I find myself owing Shonda Rhimes yet another apology letter.

I never knew or heard of anyone having sex in the call rooms at UWV/Mercy, but as for the hospital I work in? Well, let's just say it definitely has something in common with the fictional Seattle Grace other than a city.

The rest of my lunch hour is spent underneath Woods in the on-call room. Receiving tender kisses as he roughly drags his hips into mine.

"You want this?" he asks me. "You glad I made you my wife? You and me going to do this happy ending thing to the day we die, Doc?"

Without waiting for an answer, he takes me to paradise with one last grinding thrust, then pulses his hips inside me as I scream into his shoulder, ferrying me through my climax before picking up the pace and finding his own release.

He's still so crazy. So much wilder than any reality show.

Because I know for certain my answer to all his questions is and will always be yes.

$$\sim$$

Girl, girl, *gurrrrrrl!*

Dude, I don't even know what to say here. Anitra and Woods are my most surprising couple yet. Our hero was pretty straight forward about who he really was when he presented for this story, but can you believe Anitra kept her reality show life a secret from me until the very last rough draft minute??? What a minx! And, oh man, what a ride. I'm a true believer in the healing power of love, and I hope this couple proves that.

I also super hope you enjoyed their story and didn't get too much whiplash from all those twists in turns. I'm thinking I might have to go see a chiropractor before I start the next book! But if you're well enough, please consider posting a review, so others might find this story, too. And remember: Sssh!!! Don't tell anybody who Anitra and Woods really are! *Keep the secret*!

So much love,
Theodora Taylor

P.S. — If you loved Woods and Anitra, check out, *HER RUSSIAN BRUTE*, the story of her best friend Sola and Ivan Rustanov.

P.S.S. — Wondering if Anitra is right about Mason's motivation? Keep reading for a sneak peek at HIS TO OWN.

WHAT READERS ARE SAYING about *HIS TO OWN*:

★★★★★THIS couple was EVERYTHING!

★★★★★ I am so glad I started to read this on my day off because I couldn't put it down.

★★★★★Unforgettable and Amazing

★★★★★I absolutely loved their story.

And make sure to read the complete
Very Bad Fairgoods series!

His for Keeps
His Forbidden Bride
His to Own

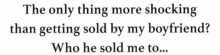

**The only thing more shocking
than getting sold by my boyfriend?
Who he sold me to...**

JUNE: Over the years with Razo, I've learned to keep my mouth shut. Learned not to fight back. Learned that talking only makes it bad...fighting only makes it worse. I shut down my feelings long ago. Because it's the only way to survive.

But then Razo sells me...

...to a dangerous biker with zero morals and a sick upbringing. A psycho who makes me feel like I have a flock of ravens inside my stomach. He never hesitates to remind me: I belong to him now.

And he'll do just about anything to keep me.

Crazy. Psycho. Killer.

MASON: I know I'm crazy. I know I'm scary. And I definitely know I don't got no business buying some girl off a gang leader I'm supposed to be selling guns to. Fact is, her kind and my kind...we ain't never supposed to mix.

See, I know all this. But I don't care.

She belongs to me now. Don't matter how I got her, only that I'm keepin' her. And no matter what it takes, I'm going to make her mine in all the ways that count.

Nobody and nothing is going to keep us apart.

FUCK if he isn't going to have to end this deal with a body count. Mason silently tallies the number of Hijos de la Muertes standing in front of him, while pretending to listen to their leader's ridiculous "request." How they'd like fifteen more glocks added to their order. On the house, of course. Blah, blah, no fucking way, blah.

Mason's got plenty of time to run diagnostics on the situation. The head guy likes to talk. A real pompous ass. He ain't wearing a shirt—maybe because it's summer. But more likely because the front of his torso is entirely covered in what has to be thousands of dollars' worth of quality ink. Beneath two beautifully rendered tattoos of ornate Mexican cartel revolvers, the boss man's pecs stay puffed up like he's part rooster.

Mason knows the soon-to-be-dead fuck's name is Razo. Not because he introduces himself proper or anything like that, but because the asshole's name is inked clear across his stomach in large, ornate script: RAZO. And Mason has to admit it looks pretty slick beneath the huge HIJOS DE LA MUERTES etched along the guy's collar bone. Every single bit of his front torso, including his arms, have been turned into a living canvas. Mason spots a few less skillful tattoos buried under the quality stuff, but he can see that somewhere down the line, Razo got real smart about his body art. Hooked himself up with a talented visionary. A *real* artist...nothing like the washed out old man Mason knows back at the SFK clubhouse, the one who inks new members with the official SFK seal.

Given that Razo is a full foot shorter than Mason, he's sure the little bitch shows up shirtless to every deal. After all, the tats make him look more bad ass in every way. Tougher, bigger, more powerful. Like the overlord of a serious Mexican drug cartel rather than the leader of a small-time Latino street gang. The intimidating ink combined with the handle of the GAT sticking prominently out of Razo's pants have most definitely convinced other sellers to give him what he wanted.

But not tonight. Because now this beaner prick is dealing with Mason Fairgood.

"Sorry, hombre. Southern Freedom Knights don't do nothing on the house," Mason answers when Razo's finally done flapping his lips. And he doesn't bother to sugarcoat his words with a friendly tone, like his cousin D might have done. No, Mason's voice is flatter than all those miles of highway he traveled to get here from Tennessee.

The Hijos de la Muertes have holed up in what the SFK often refer to as a roach town. The brown roaches move in, and the whites move out. Ceding their pretty properties to beaner scum in favor of new and improved—and as yet un-infested—suburbs. What was once a nice neighborhood is now completely occupied by Razo's crew. Their distinctive graffiti tags cover every street sign, dividing wall, fire hydrant, and sidewalk. Damn shame.

But there are only three guys standing behind Razo. Likely his most trusted and strongest gang members. Not that it really matters. Nobody beats Mason in a fight. Not even hardened street cholos like these. No, the odds aren't fair for Razo and his men. They might look tough but Mason knows these inner city gangs don't weapon train for shit. No mandatory time spent in target practice. No game hunting in the woods. Just time spent shooting at each other in brief street skirmishes, like something out of a lame-ass video game, using illegal weapons provided by the SFK and other distributors.

The thought of these pussies referring to themselves as "soldiers" turns Mason's stomach. But whatever, at least it gives him the advantage in close situations like these. He supposes he ought to be grateful that these low-rent assholes lack basic shooting and hunting skills, even as more and more of them sprout up across the country. More gangs equal more business opportunities. And more target practice for Mason.

The only Hijos he really has to worry about are the five or six guys milling around on the front porch of the house Razo exited to do this deal with Mason. There could also be a few men hidden in the surrounding cul-de-sac.

And if any them actually have something with a sight on it, well...hello bullet straight to the head. Even a kid could hit a moving target with that kind of set up.

"You Knights don't do nothing on the house?" Razo asks. "That ain't what I heard, man. I heard your cuz gave the Lightning Bolts in Little Rock a couple of AKs. Like as a bonus and shit."

Mason shrugs. "My cousin and I handle things different."

Unspoken: *Also, I'm white and you ain't. Which means no extras as far as any business deals go.* The truth is, the SFK board doesn't exactly like to advertise that they do business with buyers who don't—how to put it—match their preferred client profile.

But the SFK likes money, and thanks to the growing heroin problem across the Midwest and Deep South, these fucking beaner gangs are flush with cash. Too much to just leave on the table.

So the SFK board decided to strategically split off the gun sales. They sent Dixon, Mason's pretty boy cousin—who also happens to be the gang's prez—to make deals with preferred customers (read: white gangs). And they sent Mason, the enforcer, to run all the beaner deals. Well, at least that was the original plan. Until D up and disappeared a few months back. Ever since, Mason's had to handle both sides of the coin for the SFKs.

But that's a whole 'nother shit show. So to Razo, all Mason says is, "You're dealing with me now. Not my cousin."

He doesn't notice the hand-rolled cigarette Razo's smoking until the shorter man puts it to his lips. He takes a long, thoughtful drag before pointing out, "This is a big order, *bolillo*." Razo nods towards the suitcase of money one of his men handed Mason a few minutes ago. "Fifteen more glocks. It's the least you can do, in my opinion."

Bolillo. White bread. Mason works hard not to let the slur throw him off his game. After all, he knows a thing or two about slurs.

"Well, you know what they say about opinions," he responds. Like any creature raised to kill and maim, Mason lacks a certain finesse.

"You sure about that, man?" Razo asks, his voice pleasant as the cheerful picket fences surrounding the perimeter of each house in the cul-de-sac. He casually rests his cigarette hand on the butt of the piece sticking out of his waistband. The gun is even more ostentatious than his tattoos: gold plated with a pearl grip, featuring a huge honking silver cross. Pretty as a girl, but lethal beneath the sexy exterior. A clear message to Mason that Razo doesn't give a flying fuck what anyone says about opinions, and if Mason knew what was good for him, he'll give Razo what he wants.

Mason suppresses a smile. He almost has to give the guy some respect. Razo's balls are a thousand times bigger than most of the two-bit dipshits Mason usually deals with. And he clearly knows how to read a situation.

See, Mason always does these secret side deals alone. To protect the fragile egos of the Kool-Aid drinkers among the ranks of the SFK who might take issue with the fact that some of the funds in their "race war" hope chest come from selling guns to non-white clientele.

Razo, like Mason, had clearly run his own diagnostic: Mason was one guy to Razo's four (and that didn't include his men on the porch, or any other gang bangers he might have hidden throughout the cul-de-sac). So as far as he was concerned, Mason would either give him what he wanted to get out alive, or Razo and his boys would take out a major player in one of the nation's top white supremacist organizations. Either way, it would give the little cholo something to brag about over tacos at the next gang banger potluck.

It would actually be a pretty solid plan *if* Razo was dealing with anyone other than Mason Fairgood. So even as Mason grudgingly gives the gang leader his due, he's working out exactly how to eliminate this motherfucker in the best way possible. Point blank? Too fast. Maybe snatch that pretty gun Razo was so casually threatening him with and use it to shoot the three beaners lined up behind him. Then use Razo as a human shield to stave off any fire that came from the houses. Yeah, that sounds like a plan—

KABLOOM!!!

The echo of a projectile hitting the conversion van he drove here in reverberates across the cul-de-sac. No, not a projectile...a soccer ball, he realizes, when a raggedy orb rolls past him as he runs toward his van.

What the hell!? What they do, shoot the damn thing out of a cannon? His van's still rocking from the impact.

And when he yanks open the back doors, his heart freezes at what he sees.

His baby. The sweet baby he'd brought along for the trip, lying on her side.

Imploding deal all but forgotten, he pulls his poor motorcycle out of the van and sets it carefully on the sidewalk. "You okay, baby?" he asks the lovingly restored chopper as he checks it everywhere for damage.

Only after he's sure she's okay, does he turn his attention back to the street. Was it a distraction? Maybe this is all a set-up, designed to confuse him. Bracing himself to get jumped he pulls out one of his Colt M1911s. Not nearly as fancy as Razo's piece, but it'll do the trick, he decides, scanning the darkened cul-de-sac for the motherfucker who'd dared kick a ball into his van.

"Oh, man, is that your bike?!?!""

Mason stops, his eyes narrowing when he spots a kid standing there, the same worn soccer ball that hit his van tucked under his thin arm. The boy is small and scrawny as fuck. Nine, maybe ten at the most. Darker than Razo, possibly mixed with something other than Mexican. Black maybe. Some kind of kin to Razo? Maybe a son? Nephew? Whoever he is, the kid is goggling Mason's bike so wide-eyed, he's completely failed to notice the gun Mason's aiming at him.

"What the fuck do you think you're doing out here, kid?" Mason demands.

The boy finally looks up from the bike, finally sees the gun in Mason's hand.

"I was just...I was just..." he says, taking a big, nervous step back.

"You were just what?" Mason asks, cutting off the kid's sudden case of the stutters. "Looking to get killed?"

The sound of running footsteps startles him, and Mason realizes maybe this is all a set-up, designed to distract him so the beaners could get the jump on him from behind.

Mason aims, preparing to shoot first and ask questions later. But then his vision is completely filled with the figure of a girl.

But not a little girl. Not with those curves. This is a young woman, he realizes, his finger freezing on the trigger.

She's darker than the boy, with a wider nose—a black woman. Which is strange, because he usually don't see blacks, like at all, on these runs. But aside from the color of her skin, she looks exactly as you'd expect a girl living in a cholo neighborhood to look: tight white tank top that barely contains her large breasts, and a pair of fringed denim shorts that cover her thick hips, but leave the bottom of her ass exposed. She's even wearing an L.A. Dodgers cap over her long straight black hair. All she's missing is the chola teardrop tattoo next to her eye...

Definitely beaner girlfriend material. Maybe even Razo's woman. She looks like someone he'd want. Arresting and different.

She's parked herself in front of Mason's gun, and doesn't seem to be thinking about moving, even though her eyes are wide and terrified beneath the wide blue brim of her Dodgers cap.

And she stays put as the kid behind her says, "Sir, sir...please put away the gun. She didn't do nothing to you."

Mason Fairgood doesn't take orders from anybody, especially colored kids.

But he re-holsters his gun, even as he spits out, "That ghetto monkey of yours just kicked his fucking soccer ball into my bike."

His eyes flicker over to his baby, and then back to the girl. She visibly swallows, but still says nothing.

"You hear what I'm saying?" he asks.

No answer. Just more standing there like she don't exactly trust him to keep his gun out of sight.

"You retarded?" he finally asks.

"No, sir, she ain't retarded. She just don't talk much," the boy answers from behind her. His young voice is perfectly friendly as he asks, "Did I hurt your bike? Because if I did, I apologize. But if I didn't..."

Mason squints at the kid. "You still need to apologize. Do you know how much work went into that bike? Me and my cousin built it from the ground up. That's a 50K custom job right there. Bike's worth three of you—"

The woman startles the shit out of him with a sudden movement. She turns her head, and shakes it at the boy over her shoulder.

"She don't agree with you about that bike being worth more than my life," the kid translates, before asking, "Did you really build it yourself? How long did it take?"

What the hell is this kid's damage? Still no apology, and now he has the nerve to ask questions. But despite himself, Mason answers, "Few months. Hammered out all the body panels, mixed the paint. Even skinned and tanned one of our old cows to make the seat."

"Whoa!" the boy says, stepping around the woman, and moving toward the bike as if drawn by a magnet.

More sudden movement from the girl. This time, she grabs the kid by the back of his shirt, drawing him to his original position behind her.

"It's okay, June. I just want to look—"

"Why you two out here?" Razo's voice cuts him off.

The woman goes completely still, like prey scenting a predator in the wild. And the night seems to tick with a new tension as she urgently motions the boy back towards a house that's parallel with the passenger side of his van.

But the kid just laughs, like he's run into an old friend on the street. "Hey, Razo!" he calls out. "I didn't know there was anybody out here. I was just kickin' a few balls before June left out..."

Mason's now wondering if the kid, not the girl, is the retarded one.

The girl—June—is obviously terrified. He can see the whites of her eyes, reminding him of a deer he shot last season, just before he pulled the trigger. The woman starts pushing the kid towards the house. When he doesn't budge, she squats down to his eye level and they have some kind of argument, made up mostly of head shakes and pointing. One she apparently wins.

Under the orange light of the street lamps, Mason can see the shadow that falls over the boy's face. One so familiar, it feels like he's staring into a dark mirror. The kid gives up, and without another word, skulks away. Back to the house the girl was pointing at.

At least that's where Mason figures he's headed. The boy disappears from his view, but Mason's eyes stay on the woman.

That's when he realizes he actually can't stop staring at her. Because even when the boy moves away, Mason's eyes remain where they've been since she stepped in front of his gun. Stuck on her, and only her. *What. The. Fucking. Hell?*

There's no reason for him to react like this to her. No reason he should stand in the street, not caring that he's surrounded by gang bangers who could turn on him at any second.

She's...not beautiful. A black girl can't be beautiful. He wasn't raised to think like that.

But she *is* mesmerizing. So mesmerizing, it feels like it's just him and her standing out here in this roach-infested cul-de-sac. And for some reason, his dick—which is supposed to be deaf, dumb, and blind to her kind—is thrumming like an engine revving inside his pants.

Mason doesn't understand. Cannot reconcile it. This girl ain't white. She ain't even one of them darkie spics who won't let you call them black, far as he can tell.

So why can't he stop looking at her—?

He's released from her spell abruptly. Because suddenly Razo's standing between them, grabbing her by the throat. "What I tell you about him and that fucking soccer ball, huh, *puta*? What I say you about staying out the way when I'm working?"

It's not exactly fair. Mason prefers to keep his business meetings on par with the most fucked up of cable guys. He provides a vague window of days during which he might stop in with the goods, and usually shows up around dinner time on the first day when he knows they'll least expect him. Ain't no way this woman or that boy had any way of knowing who he was, or why he was here, when they left the house.

But the girl doesn't try to argue with Razo or make excuses. Her body just stiffens, her eyes rolling to the side of her face that's the farthest from Razo, in a way Mason recognizes more than he cares to admit. June knows she's about to get hit but doesn't want to see it coming.

And she's right.

Razo gives her a short, vicious punch. He's obviously had a lot of practice. It's just enough to deliver a painful blow without damaging her face. The woman's head lulls, but she doesn't throw up her hands, doesn't try to protect herself. It's as if she's flipped on a zombie switch. Figured out a way to disappear while her boyfriend's doing this to her. At least Mason assumes Razo's her boyfriend.

June's lack of fight seems to diffuse the tension and stop Razo from hitting her again. Instead, he shoves her, sending her stumbling backwards onto her butt. "Get back to the house, bitch," he spits at her. "I'll deal with you later."

Get back to the house. Familiar language you'd only use with someone you were intimate with. *Definitely Razo's girlfriend*, Mason thinks. His to command. His to hit. His to do with as he pleases.

But for some reason, Razo's command to go back to the house brings the girl out of zombie mode. She starts pointing toward something at the end of the cul-de-sac.

"You think I'm gonna let you take the bus to go see that fag now?" Razo answers, voice nearly screeching with anger. "After this!? You out your mind, *puta*!"

He grabs her by the arm, yanking her to feet—but not out of any sense of chivalry. No, this assist is only given so he can really get up in her face. Bare his teeth at her as he....

Mason doesn't see it coming. If he had, he would have turned away. But the next thing he knows, he's watching Razo push the orange end of his cigarette into the woman's chest, pressing so hard, it collapses like a small, white accordion against her dark skin.

Again she doesn't make a sound. There's only a grimace, quick as a flash, like her face has become a valve for releasing pain in silence.

But for Mason, it's too late. His heart stops, seizing up as his brain's engine reverses hard into memory.

It's an old, old male Fairgood tradition, dating back almost to when Winstons first hit the shelves back in the fifties. Fairgood men put their cigarettes out on their boys. It wasn't considered cruel. It was training. Training the boys up to be men who knew how to endure, so they wouldn't become too soft, so they could handle pain...

"Now get in the house like I told you!" Razo calls out in the distance.

But in Mason's mind, his father, Fred Fairgood, is telling him to get back to his room, while he "deals" with Mason's mother.

She said something wrong again.

Did something wrong.

Maybe asked the wrong question.

Or looked at Fred the wrong way.

Got too fucked up on the drugs Fred plied her with.

There are a million things that could set his parents off. So many, it's almost not a surprise when a hot cigarette burns against the back of Mason's neck and he's told to go, *now*.

And Mason does, just like that half-darkie boy. Wanting to stay, but knowing from experience he'd only make it worse. That any action or word he could possibly think of would prolong his mother's suffering rather than end it.

He goes, but the fighting follows him down the hallway. The sound of his father's low menacing voice growling at his mother. And, depending on how high she is, his mother shrieking right on back at him, telling him he's washed up, that both him and his brother are disappointments to the SFK board. That he's lucky to have her. How she knows he's sleeping with [insert name of latest SFK groupie here]. How if it wasn't for Mason, she'd have left his ass the first time he laid hands on her. How he'd better not ever sleep too deep, because one night she'd cut his dick off—

And so it goes, a verbal release before the beating. The more creative his mother gets, the longer she staves off the inevitable. His father almost seems to enjoy listening to her. To Mason, her shrill voice sounds like the equivalent of squeezing hard on the throttle. Of someone getting a motorcycle nice and angry, so it'd make the biggest amount of noise as it speeds down the road.

By the time Mason reached the soccer ball kid's age, he'd learned to climb out his bedroom window during this part. To be anywhere but there while his mother was still shrieking.

But when he was little...

When he was little, all he could do was cower behind the bedroom door. Listen to the shrill screams and the low-pitched yells until the noise of the beating ended all the talk.

Then it was just the hard, dull slaps of fists raining down on skin. The kind of sound that doesn't remotely resemble what you hear on TV or in movies. This would go on for a surprisingly short time. Five...ten minutes, tops. Then the aftermath. The weird quiet after the beating. Also not what you see on TV. In real life, there ain't no sobbing after your father's done beating on your mother. Not if he's done it right. Not if he's a Fairgood. After a Fairgood beatdown, the only sound anybody's going to hear is *him*...his breath, panting from the exertion of putting his old lady in her place. The soundtrack of him standing over her, waiting to see if she dares get up. Or say so much as another word.

And then he stops breathing hard. And there's nothing left but the quiet. And if you're a Fairgood boy who hasn't learned to climb out the window yet, you just have to wait and see what happens next. Because maybe your father will leave out, go have a few more drinks at the clubhouse. Maybe he'll head to his room and pass out from drink the way your mom has passed out from her beating. Or maybe he'll come after you. Finish releasing the rest of his anger, finish what the cigarette burn started—

When Mason returns to reality, everything has changed. The woman is gone. And Razo and his original three-guy crew are in front of him. Exchanging unsettled looks with each other in a silent conversation Mason can easily translate as, *What the fuck is up with this loco gringo*?

Bad things happen when he's triggered. Most often people get hurt. Sometimes they get dead. Are they looking at him that way because he snapped?

But no...he looks around the cul-de-sac. No blood, no dead bodies, and the porches are empty now—but in a smart, disappearing act way, not in an aftermath sort of way. He knows aftermath. Really well. And this ain't it.

Mason lets himself breathe again, somehow knowing she's inside one of those graffiti-covered houses. Maybe the same one as the boy. Safe. At least for now.

"Hey, you alright, man?"

His eyes flicker back to the cholos.

"You was just standing there," Razo tells him. "Breathing real weird. Like you fixing to explode or something."

The other three snicker at their boss's observation.

Only to stop short when Mason hits them with a look. The one he usually saves for right before he pulls out the bowie knife his uncle, D's dad, gave him for his twelfth birthday. *"You can use it on any animal gives you trouble. Don't matter if it's on four legs or two."*

At Mason's look, Razo actually shrinks back, but then manages to regain his poise and find some courage inside his small chest. "We doing this or what?" he asks, lowering his voice a few octaves and tapping both hands against his HIJOS DE LA MUERTES tattoo.

Mason blinks, a deliberate motion that serves to reset his face into business mode.

Yeah, crazy shit happens when he's triggered. Take, for example, right now when he opens his mouth and unleashes words. Three of them, directed at Razo. "That your girl?"

Razo's brow furrows, his confusion at Mason's unexpected question written clearly across his face. "Yeah, and don't worry, homes. I'm going to make her pay for what happened with your bike. As soon as we get our fifteen extra, you know."

It's both a promise and a threat. The original request for fifteen extra guns hangs over the conversation like a storm cloud, warning of shit to come.

But Mason ignores the cloud and asks, "You sick of fucking her yet?"

A thoughtful beat. Then as if just now realizing it himself, Razo answers, "Gettin' there. I mean she fine, but that kid and—"

Razo cuts off, the obvious question suddenly occurring to him, "Hey, why you askin' about her?"

Crazy, crazy, shit, Mason thinks. But he asks the next question anyway.

"How much you want for her?"

C'mon, you've GOT to find out how this one ends!
go to theodorataylor.com to finish HIS TO OWN

ALSO BY THEODORA TAYLOR

Her Russian Beast

Her Russian Brute

ALPHA KINGS

Her Viking Wolf

Wolf and Punishment

Wolf and Prejudice

Wolf and Soul

Her Viking Wolves

ALPHA FUTURE

Her Dragon Everlasting

NAGO: Her Forever Wolf

KNUD: Her Big Bad Wolf

RAFES: Her Fated Wolf

Her Dragon Captor

Her Dragon King

ALIEN OVERLORDS (as Taylor Vaughn)

His to Claim

His to Steal

His to Keep

THE SCOTTISH WOLVES

Her Scottish Wolf

Her Scottish King

Her Scottish Hero

HOT HARLEQUINS WITH HEART

Vegas Baby

Love's Gamble

ABOUT THE AUTHOR

Theodora Taylor writes hot books with heart. When not reading, writing, or reviewing, she enjoys spending time with her amazing family, going on date nights with her wonderful husband, and attending parties thrown by others. She LOVES to hear from readers. So....

Join TT's Patreon
https://www.patreon.com/theodorataylor

Follow TT on TikTok
https://www.tiktok.com/@theodorataylor100

Follow TT on Instagram
https://www.instagram.com/taylor.theodora/

Sign for up for TT's Newsletter
http://theodorataylor.com/sign-up/

Made in the USA
Middletown, DE
24 April 2023

29433259R00170